EVERY SECRET THING

EVERY SECRET THING

ACTS OF VALOR, BOOK TWO

REBECCA HARTT

RISE UP
PUBLICATIONS

Book and cover design by eBook Prep
www.ebookprep.com

June, 2020
ISBN: 978-1-947833-91-3

ePublishing Works!
644 Shrewsbury Commons Ave
Ste 249
Shrewsbury PA 17361
United States of America

www.epublishingworks.com
Phone: 866-846-5123

ACKNOWLEDGMENTS

Good things come in threes, and that is certainly the case for me. Over the course of writing this book, I was blessed to have not just one amazing editor, but three of them! My utmost gratitude goes to Sydney Baily, Penny Doyle, and Julee Schwarzburg for giving your time and talent to this project. I could not have been more blessed!

To every Navy SEAL who has died in the line of duty. You are the good guardians of the sheep. May God honor your sacrifice.

GLOSSARY OF MILITARY ACRONYMS

CO – Commanding Officer
XO – Executive Officer
NCO- Non-Commissioned Officer
NVGs – Night Vision Goggles
NCIS – Naval Criminal Investigative Service
BUDs – Basic Underwater and Demolition/SEAL Training
NWU – Navy Working Uniform
PTSD – Post-Traumatic Stress Disorder

FROM THE AUTHOR

Dear Reader,

If you are reading this story without first reading
RETURNING TO EDEN, you'll be fine. The first chapter is
packed with information from Book One. I know it's a lot to
take in, but press on, and you'll soon be turning pages, unable to
put this book down. In other words, it's okay to read my stories
out of order. Each book stands alone.
Enjoy!

Rebecca

PROLOGUE

The droning of a fly roused Charlotte Patterson from an unnaturally deep sleep. Fighting the unwanted drug that fouled her system, she forced herself to sit up. Her sluggish respiration quickened as she failed to recognize the antique bed in which she lay, on sheets damp with sweat.

Her gaze rose to high papered walls. More details came into focus as she blinked—a window with plantation shutters currently propped open at the bottom, an adjacent bathroom with old-timey fixtures, and a tray on a table by the door with food that had been delivered, she assumed, while she'd been sleeping.

Where am I?

The only sound besides the buzzing fly was that of a downpour outside the window. She recalled waking up once previously, long enough to sense the pitching motion of a boat. But that feeling was gone. Clearly, she was back on land.

Compelled by her full bladder, Charlotte swung her feet to the floor. The drug that had caused her to sleep so deeply also made the walls shift closer and the floor jump up, as if at an amusement park funhouse. As it hit her bare soles, she wondered when and where she'd lost her shoes.

Nausea roiled up suddenly as the memories rushed back.

She'd been driving up Rt. 301 in Virginia en route to the headquarters of the Defense Intelligence Agency outside of Washington, DC. Although midday on Labor Day, she remembered being one of merely a handful of people on the road. The black SUV surging toward her in her rearview mirror had come out of nowhere.

As Charlotte swore and increased her speed, the female in the passenger seat stuck her head out of her window. A pistol flashed in the sunlight—Charlotte's only warning before her Mustang's rear tire blew with a pop.

The steering wheel jerked in Charlotte's grasp. In that same instant, she realized her attempt to get time-critical information to the DIA was being thwarted.

"No!" she remembered raging. She'd been so certain no one had seen or followed her.

In her fury, Charlotte jammed on the brakes by way of reprisal. The SUV plowed into the back end of her car with a terrific crash.

Her Mustang was still moving when she opened her door and leaped out of it, sparing a thought for the iPad she'd hidden under her seat. It was supposed to be in the DIA's possession within the hour, but saving her own life took precedence at that moment.

Running toward trees that edged the highway, she spared a fearful, backward glance, revealing a man in hot pursuit. Even as fit as she was, he overcame her within seconds, threw his arms around her, and tackled her into tall grass, all without hurting her.

The same could not be said for him. As she flailed and scratched and bit him, he overcame her struggles with difficulty, then pulled a syringe from his back pocket. Using his teeth, he freed the needle and jabbed it into her thigh, injecting her with something that blurred her vision instantly.

Charlotte's head lolled. Looking back at the two cars, she watched the woman duck inside of the Mustang. It wouldn't take her long to find the iPad containing critical evidence hidden under the driver's seat.

The last thing Charlotte could recall was being lifted like a ragdoll off the ground and carried to the man's SUV. She'd figured she was going to be killed, just like her supervisor had been, for knowing too much about corrupt Navy SEAL Commander Daniel Dwyer.

Only she wasn't dead—not yet, anyway.

Instead of killing her, someone—possibly the man who'd tackled her--had gotten rid of her, apparently by putting her on a boat and sending her . . . *where?*

Charlotte forced herself to rise on legs that jittered. She had to hold her head with both hands to keep the room from shifting. Crossing in a wobbly line to the bathroom, she used the toilet, then stared at her ghastly reflection as she splashed water on her face.

Revived by the water, she headed straight for the bedroom door and found it locked from the other side. As she'd suspected, she was a prisoner, albeit a well-fed one, given the sumptuous fare left out for her. Remembering the drugs that had kept her unconscious, she cautiously helped herself to the glass of fruit juice, slaking her thirst as she gulped it down. Picking up a strip of chicken cooked in pineapple, she chewed it carefully. Detecting no strange taste, she wolfed down another piece.

How long was I sleeping? She didn't know. *Perhaps days?*

Abandoning the food, Charlotte approached the screen-covered window. The partially open shutter admitted a humid breeze. She realized she was standing on the second story of what appeared to be a plantation home. Rain spattered the lush lawn below her. Vegetation quilted the landscape in a tapestry of lilies, fronds, and blooming bougainvillea.

Ducking to see under the raised shutter, Charlotte discerned, farther afield, a walkway leading from the home's main entrance to a massive moon gate. Through the window of the adjacent gatehouse, she spotted two mulatto men smoking cigarettes.

The gate was appended to a stucco wall that appeared to encompass the entire estate. Peering past the wall, through the fronds of palm trees sloping downhill, she gasped—first with appreciation, then with dismay—at the aquamarine body of water so vibrant that even the rain failed to diminish its clarity.

Given the architecture of the home, the striking hue of the water, and the dark-skinned guards, she determined there was only one place in the world where she could be—in the Caribbean.

Despite the warmth and humidity, Charlotte lowered her heels to the floor and shivered. The Caribbean Sea covered more than a million square miles and consisted of more than seven thousand islands. Considering the bizarre events that had brought her here, no one was about to find her.

She might as well have fallen off the edge of the earth.

CHAPTER 1

Four US Navy SEALs sat around a stone table on the veranda at the Shifting Sands Club on Dam Neck Naval Air Station in Virginia Beach. The late-summer storm that sparked lightning out at sea had driven all but the SEALs indoors. Sounds of laughter and the tinkle of chinaware emanated from the brightly lit windows of the restaurant behind them. The window's reflection shone in troop leader Lucas Strong's gray eyes as he brought up the situation that had drawn them together.

"We are not going to stand for this," he assured each of his teammates.

Chief Saul Wade, codenamed Reaper for the number of terrorists he'd eliminated, scowled back at him while tugging on his goatee. "It's a freaking cover-up," Saul pronounced.

Cover-up was exactly right. Ten days ago, Charlotte Patterson, an intern at the Naval Criminal Investigation Service, had assured them her contact in the DIA was going to arrest their corrupt commander. Instead, NCIS had arrested the wrong man—not Commander Dwyer, but their former troop leader, Lieutenant Jonah Mills, called Jaguar by his team.

At Jaguar's Article 32 hearing just that morning, the staff judge advocate had determined there was sufficient evidence to go forward with a trial. Jaguar was arrested and now faced general court-martial for an Article 128 violation of the Code of Uniformed Military Justice, namely for assaulting a superior officer while not in the line of duty.

"I don't get it." Bambino, an Italian American and the youngest member in the troop—the youngest, in fact, in all of SEAL Team Six—looked to Lucas for an explanation. "Why is Jaguar in the brig, when Dwyer admitted right to his face that he's a part of The Entity?"

The Entity was the name given to a vigilante group that had nabbed weapons before the SEALs could find and destroy them. Apparently, their own commander, Daniel Dwyer, was a member of the illegal organization.

"Because no one believes Jaguar's version of the story," Lucas replied. "Dwyer's the commander of Blue Squadron, and Jaguar's just a lieutenant on medical leave."

Saul propped his tattooed arms on the table-top. "But I was there at the skeet-and-trap range when it all went down," he reminded them in his western drawl. "Dwyer shot at Jaguar first. He discharged seven bullets to Jaguar's one. If I hadn't covered Jaguar's retreat, Dwyer would've killed him. I told the investigator what happened and he seemed to believe me."

Lucas shrugged. "I can't explain that. Someone in NCIS must be covering up for Dwyer, which means Jaguar needs all the help he can get. It's not like he hasn't been through enough already." The beleaguered lieutenant had just escaped from a year of captivity, believed to be dead until his sudden reappearance about a month earlier. "Getting mad isn't going to help him, though. We need to set a course of action."

"What can we do?" Theo, who'd been sitting in the shadow, camouflaged by his black skin, sat forward suddenly. Light from the window fell upon his earnest expression. "We can't prove what the CO admitted to Jaguar. We don't know where he's stockpiling the weapons he stole."

"It's Jaguar's word against Dwyer's," Saul grimly agreed, "and so far no one's listening to me."

"Jaguar's psychiatrist says he'll testify on his behalf," Lucas reminded them.

"We're still screwed," Theo stated, shaking his closely shaved head. "Apart from Dr. Branson, anyone who could have helped Jaguar is dead or missing." He proceeded to tick them off on his fingers. "First there was Special Agent Elwood, who investigated Jaguar's disappearance and found out someone in the squadron was responsible. Next thing you know, Elwood's dead."

Lucas grimaced. The NCIS agent had been killed in a hit-and-run, his office promptly dismantled, and his hard drive stripped from his computer. Again, someone higher up the food chain had been looking out for Dwyer.

"Then there was Elwood's intern, Charlotte Patterson," Theo continued, with an edge to his deep voice.

Lucas lifted a hand to rub his aching eyes. Patterson had located Elwood's iPad containing copies of the same files that had been ripped from his hard drive. On her way to passing off the iPad to a promising contact in the Defense Intelligence Agency, the woman had disappeared. Vanished. No more iPad, no more evidence.

The whites of Theo's eyes flashed with indignation as he held up a third finger. "And let's not forget Dwyer's executive officer, Jimmy Lowery, who killed himself out of guilt for working for the CO."

"Or did he?" Saul's tone conveyed cynicism. "Dwyer probably killed Lowery to keep him quiet."

Theo's hand hit the table with a thump. "That's my point. Dwyer's been covering up his sins, killing off people left and right. Now there's no one alive who can prove Dwyer is a member of The Entity, and no one is taking Jaguar's allegations seriously."

"'Course not." Saul sat back and crossed his arms. "You think the base commander wants a scandal? Jaguar's being incarcerated so he can't talk to anyone."

"So, what do we do?" Bambino inquired.

All three men looked to Lucas for an answer; after all, he was their troop leader and the only officer present.

"Well," he said, wishing he could give them something more tangible than hope, "I'm thinking the FBI might be able to help us. I've asked Master Chief to reach out to them."

As if on cue, Master Chief Rivera came jogging up the veranda's back stairs.

"Evening, Master Chief," the men chorused, as he came into view.

With the faintest hint of a Puerto Rican accent, Rivera returned their greeting and dropped into the empty chair next to Bambino. "I have news," he said.

Thank goodness, Lucas thought.

"I've been on the phone with an FBI agent named Casey Fitzpatrick."

"He's going to help us?" Bambino guessed.

"Better than that." Rivera's dark eyes glinted with excitement. "He's located Charlotte Patterson, and he wants our help retrieving her. He told me if we bring her back, he'll do something for us."

All four men perked up, ready to do whatever it took.

"Where is she?" Lucas asked.

Rivera shrugged. "He wouldn't say, not over the phone. He wanted to meet me tomorrow at 1600 hours at his office in Norfolk, but I can't make it then."

"Saul and I will go," Lucas volunteered, glancing at Saul and getting a nod of agreement. "Why can't you make it, Master Chief?"

"My presence is strongly requested at the senior officer's golf tournament," Rivera said with a distasteful smile.

Lucas raised his eyebrows. "You're going to that? You don't even play golf."

Rivera shrugged. "Vice Admiral Holland's orders. Apparently, tongues would wag if Dwyer's senior NCO failed to make an appearance."

Lucas murmured his condolences. None of them could stand to look at Dwyer these days, let alone attend his social functions. Luckily, they were about to get two weeks of leave, having been deployed the whole summer. After tomorrow, only Rivera, Blue Squadron's most senior NCO, had to report to HQ.

Rivera handed Lucas a memo. "Here's Fitzpatrick's contact information."

Lucas looked at Saul while sliding the memo into his pocket. "We'll leave for Norfolk right after work tomorrow."

"Hooyah," Saul said, a battle cry that both affirmed Lucas's statement and showed enthusiasm for their upcoming leave. "I was thinking," Saul added, "if we could prove Lowery was actually killed that might help Jaguar somehow."

Everyone considered the long-haired sniper's proposition.

"How do we do that?" Lucas asked. The thing he loved most about being a SEAL was the collaboration that took place. Every operator's input was taken into consideration. They truly operated as a team— with the exception of their former leader, who'd turned out to be a rogue narcissist. "NCIS already ruled Lowery's death a suicide."

"That's because NCIS is protecting Dwyer. But if the evidence speaks for itself, we could hire a civilian expert to prove Lowery was murdered. That would open a whole new can of worms in which Dwyer might become a suspect. At the very least, that could take some of the heat off Jaguar and put it on Dwyer, where it belongs."

Master Chief made a thoughtful sound in his throat. "Problem is, to get into Lowery's apartment, we'd have to break in. The military police have cordoned it off."

"Then we break in," Saul suggested, like that was child's play. "I can tell from the stains if he blew his own brains out or if someone else did it."

As a sniper with sixteen kills under his belt, Saul understood the physics of bullets better than most, and Lucas would trust his conclusion. If Saul believed Lowery had been murdered, Lucas would pay for a forensic expert of their own to say as much.

"I'll break in," Master Chief volunteered. "I'm too senior to have my rank stripped from me if I'm caught—not so for the rest of you. I'll bring the reconnaissance camera and take pictures. Can you tell enough from those?" he asked Saul.

"If you take plenty of pictures," Saul affirmed.

"Hey," Theo interrupted, "do we know who Jaguar's defense counsel is gonna be?"

Lucas hesitated, revealing his disappointment. "He hoped to get the premier JAG, Captain O'Rourke, but, as you can guess, O'Rourke was already detailed to the prosecution. Jaguar's got a young JAG named Carew, who was top in her class in law school."

"Why doesn't he hire a civilian lawyer?" Theo demanded.

Lucas shrugged. "Jaguar says this one's smart as a whip, and he trusts her."

"But she's inexperienced," Saul protested.

"Which means she's eager to prove herself," Lucas pointed out. "That's Jaguar's decision, and he's already made it." He reached for his glass and lifted it high. "I'd like to propose a toast."

The others followed his example, snatching up their half-empty beverages.

"To Jaguar," he stated. "May justice prevail for him."

"Here, here."

With gusto, the men clinked their tumblers.

Lucas's toast was, in fact, his most fervent prayer. Unlike Master Chief, who was good at praying out loud, Lucas wasn't. But without God's help, Lucas feared his role model, the man who'd taught him everything he knew about being a good troop leader, was about to suffer the gravest punishment any SEAL could imagine—dishonorable discharge.

After tossing back the rest of his drink, Lucas set his glass on the table and pushed to his full six feet, six inches. "I need to call it a night, guys," he apologized, towering over the table. "It's been a long week."

"Good night, sir."

Reading compassion in the faces looking back at him, Lucas turned away and took the quickest exit off the veranda, jogging down a flight of stairs that conveyed him to the parking lot.

The rain began to fall just as he jumped into his Ford F250, black with an extended cab. With the windshield wipers slapping a fervent tempo, he drove to his modest condominium in a newly constructed neighborhood, not far from the main gate.

No sprawling mansion for Lucas, not anymore. He'd given up his privileged lifestyle when he'd promised to live the rest of his life for God. Being rich and worldly hadn't given him any satisfaction. Living humbly and in tune with his Maker felt much better.

Pulling up to his house, Lucas eyed the dark windows with a pang. No one was waiting for him, but—hey—that was fine. Since he'd broken off his engagement with Monica, he no longer had to worry about his fiancée cheating on him. None of his teammates had ever dared to point it out, but Lucas could see for himself how much she flirted with other men. Her ultimate betrayal was stealing critical evidence from Master Chief's desk at Dwyer's behest. He had confronted her the same day he'd heard about it, but she'd admitted to nothing and stormed out.

Dashing through a light rain, Lucas let himself in, snapping on the lights and averting his gaze from the empty living room and dining room. Just a few weeks earlier, he and Monica had picked out all new furniture in anticipation of their spring wedding. Apparently, though he'd paid for it, she'd felt entitled to keep it for herself. All that remained in the wake of their breakup was the dinette set in his kitchen, a sectional sofa too heavy or too large for her to tote away, and his 48-inch screen TV.

Let it go, he advised himself as he stowed his combat boots in the coat closet. Heading up the stairs to his bedroom, he stripped off his uniform as he went.

His thoughts returned to Jaguar and the unfair charge that had been *preferred* on him, as that action was called in the military—like anyone would prefer facing charges. At least Lucas had something to think about other than how the woman he'd been planning to marry— the woman who'd managed to capture his affections while pulling the wool over his eyes—had chosen loyalty to Commander Dwyer over loyalty to him.

With a shake of his head and with his pride still stinging, Lucas headed straight for his shower. While soaping away traces of his grueling day at work, he asked himself what part of his carefully crafted marriage plan had gone awry. Obviously, it was falling for the wrong woman.

Monica was beautiful, well educated, and raised in a two-parent home, meeting all of Lucas's criteria. She'd attended church with him and alleged to be a true Christian—a crucial quality in his book. Clearly, she had hidden who she really was, until it was almost too late. At least, she'd hidden it from him, if not from his teammates who had seemed relieved to see her go. So what, exactly, had he overlooked that had nearly cost him everything?

Perhaps, her career had meant too much to her. Yes, that had to be it. She'd enjoyed a prestigious position as a civilian secretary for the most elite strike force in the world—SEAL Team Six, also known as DEVGRU. But when it came to choosing between stealing at the behest of Commander Dwyer or doing the right thing and not stealing, she had made the morally wrong choice, ensuring she kept her job.

Amazingly, Dwyer had given her an alibi, even though Master Chief had practically caught her red-handed. Dwyer claimed Monica had gone to Spec Ops on Labor Day to shut down his computer. Dwyer had then transferred her to a different office within DEVGRU. At least Lucas didn't have to look at her every time he went to work.

Next time, if there is a next time, he told himself, *I won't choose a woman whose career matters more than her relationship. I'll pick a sweet, uncomplicated woman who puts God and family before everything else.*

With that new plan in place, Lucas turned off the shower feeling better about himself and his future.

❧

FBI Special Agent Casey Fitzpatrick was as Irish looking as his name suggested. His auburn hair was the first thing Lucas noticed as he and Saul entered the man's office to greet him, then his colorful attire and spry frame. He had left his sky-blue suit jacket hanging on the back of the chair and rolled up the sleeves of his button-up shirt—white with blue-and-pink stripes.

"Call me Fitz," the agent said as they all introduced themselves.

With bright green eyes and lines of experience etched into his freckled face, Fitz reminded Lucas of a fox, a man who'd been around the block a time or two.

"Have a seat," he added, waving them toward the leather armchairs facing his polished oak desk.

The chairs creaked in protest as Saul and Lucas dropped into them. Lucas's gaze went straight to the certificates, diplomas, and awards festooning the opposite wall. Fitz had been recognized by the New York City Police Department for meritorious service. He had graduated with a bachelor's degree from one prestigious university and a master's degree from another. On top of that, he'd received an award given by the FBI. The odds of finding Charlotte Patterson and possibly proving Jaguar's innocence seemed suddenly less bleak.

Returning to his high-backed chair, Fitz took closer stock of his visitors while rubbing a medallion that hung from a sturdy chain around his neck.

"I used to watch you play football, didn't I?" he asked, focusing on Lucas first. "You're Jonathan Strong, aren't you?"

"Yes, sir. But I go by Lucas now."

Fitz's eyes glinted with interest. "What caused you to change your career?"

"I made a promise to God," Lucas said. People either wanted to know more, or they changed the subject.

Fitz fell into the latter category, looking over at Saul. "Native American ancestry?" he guessed, noting Saul's mahogany ponytail and the gold hoop adorning his left ear.

"Yes, sir, my grandfather was Creek."

"Where are you from?"

"Oklahoma, sir. Broken Arrow, Oklahoma."

"Well, you're an impressive pair," the special agent said, sitting back and glancing down at the notes in front of him. "I understand from speaking with your master chief that a colleague of yours is in a pickle. You all believe your commander, Daniel Dwyer, has been stealing weapons in advance of other SEAL teams. Unfortunately, proof of Dwyer's thefts went missing along with NCIS intern Charlotte Patterson as she was delivering it into the hands of the DIA. You still require that proof since your colleague, one Lieutenant Jonah Mills—aka Jaguar—is being prosecuted for assaulting his commander with a weapon while not on duty. Did I get all that right?"

"Yes, sir," Lucas said, impressed with the man's grasp of the situation. His hopes rose in anticipation of the news Rivera had passed on —that Patterson had been located.

"I think we can help you," Fitz admitted. "But first you'll need to do something for me."

"Bring Patterson back?" he guessed.

"That's not all," Fitz warned. He leveled them with a look that commanded Lucas's full attention. "I'm about to tell you something that stays within these walls," he added quietly.

Lucas glanced at Saul, then sent Fitz a silent nod. "Agreed."

"We are aware that your commander has been stealing weapons."

Relief welled up in Lucas only to freeze at Fitz's next words.

"For the time being, however, we can't let Dwyer know that he's been made. We want the man he works for. Dwyer doesn't call the shots with The Entity, as this group has been called. Someone else is in charge, but we don't have enough proof to arrest him. We're getting there."

Lucas exchanged a charged look with Saul.

Fitz elaborated. "The Entity is comprised of a handful of powerful men, military and civilian, most of whom have top-secret clearance and access to classified information. As such, they are influential and highly organized. They have allied themselves around a common goal

—stockpiling weapons that would otherwise find their way into the hands of our enemies. As such, they view themselves as peacekeepers. After all, you SEALs seize weapons for the same purpose, but you destroy them; you don't horde them. These men were neither elected nor chosen to protect our country. Their actions are illegal, and they must be stopped."

"Commander Dwyer is no peacekeeper, sir," Lucas assured the agent. "We've come up with at least three people he's killed or tried to kill. We assumed he had killed Charlotte Patterson, too."

"She's not dead," Fitz assured them, pulling his keyboard closer. "Let me tell you how we found her."

Intrigued, Lucas watched as the special agent opened a document on his computer and scanned it.

"The first thing to turn up was her vehicle, a brand-new Ford Mustang, left on the side of the road in the wake of an apparent hit-and-run. We found her purse and identification in the vehicle but nothing else—certainly not the iPad she was taking to the DIA."

Fitz pulled his desk drawer open, withdrew a badge on a lanyard, and slid it across his desk toward Lucas. "This is what she looks like."

Lucas realized he was holding Charlotte Patterson's NCIS badge, identifying her as an intern. She had short auburn hair and cherry-brown eyes that shone with intelligence and daring.

"Patterson herself had disappeared," Fitz continued. "We were stymied for days, until the Coast Guard came to us with footage of a man carrying a woman matching Patterson's description aboard a yacht. Using taped satellite imagery and marine radio communications, we managed to trace the yacht's route to a small island in the Bahamas, privately owned and purchased by Roger Holden in 1997."

"Who is Holden?" Saul growled, surprised by his own feeling of outrage on behalf of the woman whose photo he was looking at.

The FBI agent smiled thinly. "A Texas oilman turned senator. When his radical right-wing platform caused him to lose his seat in Congress, he left the country, stopped paying taxes, and forfeited his

US citizenship. Interestingly, his plantation home is walled and protected by twenty or so armed men."

"You think he's a member of The Entity," Lucas guessed. "What if they stash the stolen weapons on Holden's island?"

"We intend to find out," Fitz assured him. "But the island is out of our jurisdiction. That's why I need you to recon the island for me, grab Patterson, and bring her home. I'll supply everything you need logistically, but our collaboration has to be completely off the records. The Entity has eyes and ears everywhere, even in the Department of Justice. I can't risk exposing what I know. Do you agree to my terms?"

Lucas considered the logistics. Planning operations—planning anything, really—was his forte. Apart from his failed marriage plans, which somehow had been firmly in a blind spot he hadn't even known he had, he was recognized for considering every contingency, every conceivable outcome.

"How many men are needed?" he inquired.

"The fewer the better. The whole operation shouldn't take more than two men or last more than twenty-four hours. Apart from his security guards, Holden's property is fairly penetrable. I have all the intel you need to plan your approach."

Lucas turned and met Saul's glinting eyes. The Reaper couldn't resist a challenge involving stealth under a time constraint.

"I'll need to look at the intel." Lucas wouldn't make promises he couldn't keep.

Fitz pointed a remote control at the large monitor hanging on the wall next to them. "Can't say I blame you," he said, powering it on and simultaneously switching off the lights.

For the next twenty minutes, Lucas and Saul examined photos of Holden's island. Satellite images showed a sheltered bay for boats, which was the only way to access the island as it wasn't big enough for a runway. Other images appeared to have been taken from a boat, using a long-range lens.

"Look right here." Using a laser pointer, the agent pointed to a second-story window in the photo they were perusing.

Lucas spied a pale face peeking out from under a raised shutter. As blurry as the image was, the shock of red hair identified her.

"That's Patterson," he said, comparing the image with the photo in his hands.

"We think so, too," Fitz agreed.

The slide show abruptly ended, and Fitz turned on the lights. "These images, plus everything else you need to know, is on this thumb drive." He dipped a hand into his suit pocket and passed it off to Lucas, while gesturing for the badge back.

"I'll keep that for now. Time is of the essence, gentlemen." He eyed the SEALs expectantly. "Can you help or not?"

Lucas looked over at Saul, who sent him a minimal nod of assent.

"We can," Lucas agreed. He looked at his watch. "Today's Thursday. We can leave by tomorrow night."

"That will work. Meet me Friday at 8 p.m. at the private airfield next to Norfolk International. A friend of mine owns a jet. He'll fly you to his second home in the Bahamas and brief you on the way down. From there, you'll take his boat as close to the island as he can get you. You can go the rest of the way by dingy. Bring your wetsuits and your personal weapons."

Lucas nodded. Something Fitz had said earlier prompted him to ask, "You said there was more we had to do than just rescue the target."

"Ah, yes." The agent slid his hands into his front pockets. "I'll need you to protect Patterson until The Entity is rounded up. You see, she has a photographic memory, which means anything that was on Elwood's iPad might also be in her head, at least for a short while longer. After three weeks or so, the memories fade and she's less of a threat."

"Is that why she wasn't killed, just kidnapped?"

Fitz narrowed his eyes. "I can't answer that question," he answered inscrutably.

Can't or won't? Lucas wondered. "You're asking us to protect her until her memories have faded," he reiterated.

"Until I tell you she's safe," Fitz amended. "It won't be for long."

"Why can't you put her in a safe house?" Saul asked.

Fitz gave a short laugh. "The Entity would know it in a heartbeat. They're too well connected. They would also realize she's been talking to the FBI, and the leader would pull the plug. I can't have him leaving the country where I can't get to him."

The words inflamed Lucas's imagination. Just how big and far-reaching was The Entity? And who was their leader?

"I guess it makes sense for us to protect her," he reasoned, "since she promised she could help Jaguar. Maybe she still can."

Fitz put a finger up. "About that. You realize any mention of The Entity would compromise my investigation."

Lucas regarded him, thunderstruck. "How are we going to prove Lieutenant Mills's innocence without bringing up Dwyer's connection to The Entity?"

Fitz grimaced apologetically. "You may not be able to. But here's my offer. In exchange for protecting Patterson, I promise if Jonah Mills is convicted, his conviction will be overturned after I make my arrests."

Lucas's expectations wavered. "I'm sure that would be appreciated, sir, but in the meantime, Mills is being kept in the brig away from his family. He could be dishonorably discharged."

Fitz shook his head. "I'm sorry. I really am. Maybe you can cast Dwyer's testimony into doubt some other way. But, as I said, you are forbidden from mentioning The Entity, whatever you do."

Squelching his disappointment, Lucas pondered all the conceivable ways to make Dwyer look bad. Maybe there was more than one way to skin a cat.

"All right." Jaguar had too much at stake for them to turn Fitz down. "We'll agree to your terms on one condition."

"What's that?"

"We want Lieutenant Mills restored to active duty once Dwyer is gone. Aside from a few missing memories, there's nothing wrong with him. Any one of us would follow him into an assault."

Fitz rubbed his medallion as he contemplated the request. "That's not something I can do myself, but I might be able to nudge the right people."

Lucas glanced at Saul and got another slight nod. "All right," he agreed. "We have a deal. We'll retrieve Patterson and protect her for as long as you need us to."

"Deal," Fitz confirmed. "Have a look at the files on the drive and contact me with any questions." Plucking two business cards from a tray on his desk, he handed one to each of them.

Lucas and Saul stood up, pocketing the cards.

"Unless I hear from you otherwise, I'll see you at the airfield at 8 p.m. tomorrow." Fitz put a hand out.

Returning the agent's firm grip, Lucas hoped Fitz was an honorable man. He'd certainly done commendable work, given the plaques on his wall. But was he guided, like Lucas was, by higher principles? Or were his actions dictated solely by the laws of men?

Foxes were sly and cunning, but were they really trustworthy? Lucas figured he would find out in the end.

CHAPTER 2

Charlotte lurched from the clutches of a too-familiar dream. Sitting up in the bed she'd come to abhor, in the room that had been her prison for nearly a week, she found herself clammy, her heart racing. If she lay down again, she would fall right back into her recurring nightmare.

She couldn't understand why she dreamed she was in the plane with her parents when it crashed. The accident that had taken their lives three years earlier haunted her still, even though the longest, loneliest years of her life had occurred since then. With shaky fingers, she brushed the hair from her damp face and looked around.

Moonlight melted through the slats of her shuttered window, informing her of the lateness of the hour. Over the roar of waves outside, Charlotte heard a noise that pushed her unpleasant dream aside and brought her more widely awake.

There were footsteps in the hallway.

Holding her breath to listen, she recognized the plodding footfalls of her host. The day she'd regained consciousness, he'd dropped by to chat, introducing himself as Roger Holden. Middle-aged with a face and body that betrayed a sedentary lifestyle, he hadn't struck her as particularly threatening.

"Why am I here?" she'd demanded immediately.

"I'm protecting you until it's safe for you to go home." The gold watch at his wrist paired with his quality clothing screamed of wealth. He spoke with urbanity and a touch of condescension, as if she ought to be grateful for his putting a roof over her head.

She had gathered from Holden's words that he was somehow connected to Dwyer, or perhaps The Entity itself for whom Dwyer acquired weapons. She'd also concluded that The Entity knew about her photographic memory. Having seized her supervisor's iPad, all the evidence of Dwyer's activities was now gone, except for what she might possibly reconstruct by reviewing the files stored temporarily in her head. But why not just kill her as they'd killed her supervisor, Lloyd Elwood? It made no sense why they would keep her alive until her memories faded—and then what? Just let her go?

Either way, unless Holden gave her paper and a pen with which to record what she remembered, Elwood's findings would fade from her mind in just a few more days.

"I'd like some items to help me pass the time," she'd told Holden. *"Could I have some books, plus a pen and paper? I'd also like a pair of shoes."*

Holden had returned the following day, bringing books and a change of clothing.

"What about a pen and paper and a pair of shoes?" she'd reminded him.

"You won't need those for a while. Go ahead and sulk," he'd told her when she had glowered at him. *You'll thank me for protecting you one day.*

Not likely, she'd thought.

Nor was it likely he was bringing her what she'd requested at this time of night. Whatever his intentions, they could not be honorable.

As was his custom, he knocked first. Regardless of her silence, the lock gave way with his electronic key, and the door swung open. Lighting in the hall cast his portly silhouette into relief, including the pistol he wore holstered under his left arm.

She'd contemplated how she was going to relieve him of that pistol when the time came, but not until she had a pair of shoes to wear. She might be impulsive, but she wasn't stupid. Escaping wouldn't be easy, given the shift rotations of the guards, made more obvious by the motion-activated spotlights placed throughout the yard.

Like those spotlights, her lamp came on suddenly, revealing a bottle of wine and two glasses clasped in Holden's pudgy hands.

"Are you all right?" he asked with seeming concern. "I thought I heard you scream."

She might have cried out in her nightmare without realizing. "I'm fine."

"Still sulking?" With a tolerant smile, he stepped into the room, and the door locked automatically behind him. When he left, he would fish the electronic key from his breast pocket and let himself out again. She'd been watching.

The slight slurring of his speech paired with the half-empty bottle of wine set off an alarm in Charlotte's head.

He's drunk, she thought with wariness. Then she realized what an edge that gave her.

He's drunk!

Despite his advantage in size, inebriation was bound to slow him down. He didn't look like a man who worked out often. She, on the other hand, was going to CIA training camp as soon as her brother landed a job out of college. Having known since adolescence what she wanted to do with her life, she had studied martial arts from a very early age. She could easily debilitate Holden, grab the gun, let herself out and…then what? She had yet to plan an exit strategy that wouldn't get her caught.

Her heart pounded as he approached her. Glancing at his shoes, she gauged whether his Ferragamo slip-ons might just fit her. Not unless her feet grew several sizes, she surmised.

"Thought you might like to have a drink with me," he stated. "Get to know me better."

She considered the offer, deciding she might as well see what happened. "All right."

Looking pleased, he promptly poured them both a glass and put the bottle on her table.

"To your future," he said, handing her the second goblet.

She refused to toast to that but lifted the glass to her lips and pretended to sip.

The mattress dipped as Roger sat next to her, close enough that she was assaulted by his overpowering cologne. He proceeded to talk about himself—how he'd been a Texas senator once, how many famous friends he had. As he talked, Charlotte asked herself if she should seize the opportunity presented or wait until she had a plan.

Flying by the seat of her pants was her usual *modus operandi*.

"Who sent me here?" If she made it home again, she wanted to know who to thank.

Roger frowned at the question. "Tha's not up for discushin," he retorted. Standing up, he turned his back on her to pour himself another glass.

His condescending tone helped Charlotte make her mind up. She was escaping tonight.

Now, in fact.

Springing off the bed, she snatched the pistol from its holster. Startled by her actions, Roger dropped his goblet as he spun around. It shattered as it hit the wooden floor, spraying wine and scattering shards of glass in all directions.

She released the pistol's safety as she backed up. The familiar weight of the gun lent her courage as she aimed it at his heart. She'd trained herself to be an excellent marksman.

"Don't move," she growled.

His surprise faded, giving way to a strange smile. "Do you really think that's loaded?" he taunted, sounding alarmingly sober.

Roger's lack of fear suggested he was telling the truth. He stepped closer, bits of glass crunching under the soles of his shoes.

"Is this any way to treat your host?" he chided. She got the impression he was enjoying himself.

"Let me leave," she demanded, backing up, "and I won't hurt you."

His only response was to chuckle. All at once, he lunged at her. Charlotte squeezed the trigger automatically. The hollow-sounding *click* that reached her ears had her throwing the useless weapon at him. He flinched but kept on coming.

Charlotte met his attack with a block, driving her knee simultaneously into his belly.

Her thrust doubled him over. She followed it with a spinning roundhouse kick that sent him sprawling across the wine-stained floor. His head struck the wall with an ugly thud, yet he didn't lose consciousness.

Charlotte kicked again while he was still on his back, but he grabbed her ankle and jerked, causing her to topple backward. She landed on her elbows. Bits of glass sank into her forearms, yet she scarcely felt their sting, too angry at herself for her rookie mistake.

As Holden rolled, coming up and over her, Charlotte reacted quickly, wrapping her long legs around his head and under his left armpit, putting him promptly into a figure-four stranglehold. Hooking her right foot under her straight left leg, she squeezed hard, cutting off his oxygen.

With mixed repugnance and fascination, she watched his eyes widen at the extent of her training. He thrashed and struck her with his free hand but could not get away. As his eyes began to bulge, he groped for the jagged stem of his wine glass, thankfully just out of reach of his straining fingers.

Timing was everything. Charlotte had no intention of killing him. Feeling his chest convulse with the need for air, it took everything in her not to free him. Once he lost consciousness, she would let him breathe again. Her thighs began to burn as she continued squeezing.

Finally, when it seemed he would never go under, his lids sank shut and he slumped, completely limp.

Charlotte relaxed her muscles slowly, ready to tense them again should he be faking. When he didn't move, she let go and squirmed out from under him.

Now what?

Take his key and run, Charlotte.

The advice was uttered by such a familiar and audible voice she looked around, half-expecting to see her mother standing behind her.

Disconcerted by her hallucination but all too willing to comply, Charlotte dipped her fingers into Holden's breast pocket and nabbed the flat key. Then she pushed to her feet and, skirting the broken glass, let herself out of the room, cutting out the lights as she went and locking the door behind her.

She found herself in a hall she couldn't remember ever seeing before. Electric wall sconces lit several other doors just like hers. She supposed they housed the unending stream of guests she'd seen coming and going in the week she'd been lucid.

At the top of the stairs, she stifled a gasp and shrank back at the sight of two armed guards climbing the steps in her direction. Spinning away before they noticed her, she sprinted down the hall in search of another exit. A fearful backward glance showed the tops of the guards' heads about to crest the landing. Using the key she still clasped, she unlocked the closest door and slipped through, finding herself, miraculously, in a servants' stairwell.

The old wooden treads creaked beneath her feet as she raced down them. The room below appeared to be a pantry with countertops for plating food. She crossed to the only door, lifted the latch, and cracked it open. To her amazement, she had found an unguarded exit.

Easing into a dark, humid yard, Charlotte's gaze went straight to a light shining in what had to be an outdoor kitchen. The buzzing of insects masked her footfalls as she raced toward it, searching for the outer wall enclosing Holden's compound.

Over the pounding of her heart came the sound of running water and the clanking of pans. Hugging sandstone, Charlotte rounded the building, and there loomed the outer wall, fifty yards or so away. Palm fronds draped over it, preventing her from guessing how high it was or whether she could even climb over.

All at once, the cry she'd been dreading came from her second-story window at the front of the house. "Guards! Find my *guest* and get me out of here. She's getting away!"

A commotion at the gatehouse meant the guards were scrambling to block her escape.

It's now or never, Charlotte realized. Bolting from her hiding spot, she sprinted for the wall, flinching as her movements triggered motion-detecting spotlights. Several more blinked on, revealing her mad dash.

"There she is!" a man shouted some distance away. "Stop!"

Ignoring the order, Charlotte ran full tilt at the wall. Leaping up, all she managed to grab hold of was a slippery frond. The top of the enclosure stood well beyond her grasp.

Bullets peppered the wall next to her—a deterrent, she realized, quelling her panic. They weren't trying to kill her. Guessing she still had time, Charlotte seized the frond like a rope. She would use it to climb higher. She pulled with her arms, scrabbling with her toes to assist her ascent.

By then, the guard was almost on top of her. Any second, he would grab her and pull her down.

Suddenly, a shadow blocked the moonlight. Something closed around her wrist—a huge hand, she realized—and it hauled her upward. In the same instant, a silenced weapon discharged with a hiss, and she heard the guard below her spill onto the grass with a grunt of surprise.

Charlotte found herself sitting atop the wall, gaping at two dark figures crouched on either side of her. Black faces, slick caps, and clothing resembling diving suits made them nearly invisible. In the blink of an eye, one of them disappeared, springing silently to the ground.

"Charlotte Patterson?" whispered the one still gripping her.

"Yes, who are—?"

But he was lowering her into the arms of the first man before she'd finished. Then he joined them. One minute, Charlotte was gaping up at him, the next she was hanging over his shoulder in a fireman's hold. She squawked in protest.

"Quiet," the commando ordered before breaking into a run.

His shoulder pummeled her abdomen painfully.

"I-can-run-on-my-own," she protested, trying to draw breath.

"Not without shoes you can't." He was moving fast, and she had to appreciate that fact because Roger Holden was now bellowing out of the window, waking everyone on his property with his demands to recapture her.

To keep from swinging like a ragdoll, Charlotte grabbed her rescuer's webbed belt and hung on tightly. In the forest of palm trees, she could see nothing, but he apparently could.

With lightning speed and the grace of a superior athlete, he headed straight toward the water. Suddenly, a beam of light strafed the tree-tops. Perhaps a beacon for ships, it was being used to hunt her.

But she wasn't afraid. The man beneath her moved with absolute confidence. There were several weapons, a pistol and a Gerber blade strapped to his belt. He and his companion knew what they were doing. Already they had reached the surf and were jogging parallel to the water, covering ground fast.

From her upside-down perspective, Charlotte noted the moonlight dancing on the waves. Craning her neck, she spied a sickle-shaped beach. They weaved through an outcropping of rocks before her rescuer abruptly stopped and tipped her into warm, ankle-deep water.

As the blood drained from her head, his companion pushed a rigid inflatable boat into the water and held it for them.

She was picked up like a baby this time and dumped in the middle of the boat, on the rubbery floor.

"Sit here," her hero instructed, before climbing in to sit at the prow. His partner rolled in behind them, started the motor, and shot them out of the cove and into deeper water. Charlotte grabbed the closest straps and held on for dear life. Warm seawater sprayed her face as she watched the big searchlight swing in their direction.

Their small, speedy boat veered away from it. Up and over dark waves they flew, soaring and falling. Marveling at her miraculous escape and the timeliness of the men who'd saved her, Charlotte's fear of being caught subsided.

I did it! she marveled. *I actually got away.* The memory of her mother's voice raised goosebumps on her wet skin.

The island was a wavering light in the distance when the motor of their boat died without warning. They slid across the swells to a standstill where, aside from water sloshing the rubber sides, all was quiet until her rescuer flipped a switch on a transmitter. As he spouted code-speak to request a pickup, Charlotte guessed the men were with the US military.

The reply they got was distinctly civilian in nature, however. "Sorry, I didn't think you'd be done so soon. I'm fishin' for giant snappers 'bout twenty minutes away. Be there as soon as I can."

With an impatient, "Out," her rescuer put the radio away.

Charlotte pried her fingers from the straps to which she'd been clinging. "Th-thank you," she said, shuddering with belated shock.

The commando slipped from his seat and joined her on the floor. The boat bounced with his movements.

"Are you hurt?" Large but gentle hands swept over her wet clothing.

She winced where the glass from Holden's goblet had cut her forearms. "Nothing serious." Her teeth began to chatter.

"Saul, toss me a blanket," her hero requested, and his partner tossed him a rolled object. He shook it open and draped it over her shoulders. Grateful, Charlotte gathered the crinkly material closer.

Light-colored eyes pierced the darkness. "What happened back there?" he asked.

Detecting some level of annoyance in the question, Charlotte stiffened. "Um…I was trying to escape."

"Did you have help?" This time he sounded suspicious.

"No."

"You got that far on your own?" He sounded dubious.

"Yes."

"How'd you get out of the room they were holding you in?"

"I put my captor into a figure-four stranglehold."

A suggestion of respect had crept into his voice. "You rendered him unconscious?"

"Yes." She felt a sense of pride in her own resourcefulness.

"And you didn't know we were on the wall preparing to spring you out of there?"

"Of course not," she said, envisioning them trying to rescue her.

The warrior chuckled with amusement. "Wow. Talk about divine intervention." His teeth flashed, a sliver of white against the backdrop of his painted face. "God is the master planner," he murmured to himself.

"I'm sorry, but who are you exactly?" Charlotte asked.

"Oh, sorry." He put a conciliatory hand on her knee. "I'm Lieutenant Lucas Strong. Just call me Lucas. And that's Chief Wade. You can call him Saul. We're Navy SEALs."

She had guessed as much. "From SEAL Team Six, Lieutenant Mills's Blue Squadron?"

"Yes," Lucas affirmed.

"I was trying to help him," Charlotte told them. "I was taking evidence on an iPad to the DIA for him."

"We know."

She should not have reminded herself. Memories of her capture, then her captivity, panned through her head, driving the breath from her lungs. Charlotte closed her eyes and hugged herself to quell her shivering.

It's over, she assured herself. *Don't cry about it.* All the same, a sound like a sob escaped her.

The lieutenant's hand slid up and down her back. "You're okay. You're safe now," he soothed. "We're going to look after you."

Her shuddering compelled him to slide closer. He put his arm around her and, suddenly, all was well with the world.

Even through his neoprene wetsuit, Charlotte could feel his heat, not to mention the awesome proportions of his body. For the first time in a decade, she knew what it felt like to feel petite and protected.

Tears of relief brimmed her eyes and tracked down her grubby face. A sniffle prompted her rescuer to tighten his hold, absorbing her occasional shudders. The thud of the SEAL's heart and the rocking motion of the boat soothed her until her shivering subsided.

"Patrol's coming," Saul announced, interrupting the lull.

Releasing her, the lieutenant flashed a penlight and hailed the approaching craft. With no lights and with a motor that was practically silent, the larger vessel seemingly appeared out of nowhere to glide up alongside them.

Lucas grabbed hold of the ladder and, keeping the dingy steady, assisted Charlotte's ascent with sure and professional hands.

After they'd hoisted the smaller boat onto the back of the bigger one, they took off at a good clip.

Seated in a dark wheelhouse, Charlotte asked Lucas, "Where are we going?"

"For now, a house on a nearby island," he said, hovering close to her. "Tomorrow, we fly back to the States. Why don't you come into the galley, ma'am, and out of the wind? It's a long boat ride."

Leaving Saul to assist the skipper in steering the boat through inky darkness, Lucas led Charlotte by the elbow down a short run of steps into a dark enclosed space. Faint blue lights illumined a galley that made Charlotte realize the boat was probably just someone's private, midsized yacht.

"I have a lot of questions," she admitted, as she dropped onto a cushioned bench.

"I'm sure you do," he said with patience "But you can ask them in the morning. Right now, you should rest," he said, handing her a pillow and a throw. "I'll be right here, sleeping across from you."

It occurred to Charlotte as she reclined on the cushion and watched Lucas Strong squirm onto the small bench across from her, that luck alone wouldn't have gotten her this far. Her rescuer was quick to credit God, though Charlotte doubted God would have bothered Himself on her account.

Her mother, on the other hand, had addressed her from the grave. *Take the key and run.*

If not for the key, the guards would have caught her frozen like a rabbit in the hallway. She would never have found the back staircase leading her to the unguarded exit.

Some heavenly being had been looking out for her—that much Charlotte could admit.

CHAPTER 3

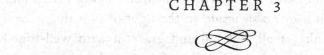

*L*ucas quit knocking at the door to the room where Charlotte lay sleeping and put his ear to the wood to listen. Could she have gotten up and left her room already?

Eric, Fitz's friend, had brought them back to his house at 0400 hundred hours. Given Charlotte's exhaustion, Lucas had expected her to sleep the day away, but since Eric was flying them back to CONUS —the continental US—in a matter of hours, Lucas thought he'd better wake her up.

The silence answering his knock had him spinning toward the living room, somewhat concerned. With relief, he spied Charlotte and Saul on the other side of a wall of windows, seated on the terrace by a pool overlooking the Caribbean Sea.

The scene looked like something straight out of a vacation magazine, complete with a red umbrella and brightly colored chairs. Eric was living the good life, and he was kind enough to share his resources with the FBI.

Heading outside, Lucas marveled at Charlotte's transformation. Last night, with her hair plastered to her head, she'd resembled a wet Irish setter. Her limbs were long and lanky. She'd looked so worn out, with dark circles under her eyes, he'd thought he was going to have to strip off her clothes and tuck her into bed himself when they got to Eric's house. Instead, she'd said good night and shut the door firmly in his face.

In just a few hours, she had morphed into a cover model. Eric must have given her a sundress from his wife's wardrobe, along with a pair of sandals. *Too bad it wasn't a swimsuit!* In the light of morning, Charlotte didn't look lanky at all, but tall and graceful with well-toned arms. The dress's peach color suited her fair complexion, and the morning sun turned her short hair into flame.

As she looked over to mark his approach, Lucas had to concentrate so as not to trip over his own two feet, which had suddenly grown unwieldy.

Her cherry-brown eyes, fringed by dark lashes, took frank appraisal of him. Even with a dusting of freckles across her nose, her skin was flawless. She had winging, russet eyebrows, a trim but strong nose, and lips that were wide and pink, even without lipstick.

As their gazes locked, awareness spurred Lucas's heart rate, a circumstance that thoroughly annoyed him. He didn't want to be attracted to Charlotte Patterson. It was unprofessional for one thing. For another, he doubted she was the sweet, uncomplicated female he was looking for. But here he was, stuck with her, at least until Fitz declared her safe from The Entity.

"Good morning," she intoned.

Even her voice, a honeyed alto, pleased his senses.

"Ma'am." He nodded rather stiffly.

Ever the enlisted officer, Saul had jumped to his feet. "Have a seat, sir," he said, sounding in awfully good spirits as he gestured to one of the chairs at their table.

"Thanks." Lucas folded himself into the brightly cushioned chair and looked back at Charlotte, who was clearly trying to reconcile him with the dark, camouflaged being she'd seen the night before.

"I'll get us drinks," Saul said into the silence. He promptly disappeared, leaving Lucas alone with a woman he'd held in his arms having no idea how gorgeous she was.

"So, how do you feel?" he asked, determined to ignore her effect on him. His gaze fell to the red marks on her forearms.

"Good," she reassured him. "I had to pick some glass out with tweezers, but I think I got it all."

"What happened?" he asked, curious to hear her story.

As she described how her captor had come to her room drunk, Lucas could only imagine how fearful she must have felt.

"Roger Holden?" he asked.

"Yes. You know his name? He pretends to be a pushover, but he's actually more clever than he acts, and a fair fighter, too." She described how she'd fought to overcome him long enough to slip away.

Lucas's respect for her quick thinking rose.

Slipping a hand into a pocket on the side of her dress, she produced what looked like a hotel room key, only thicker. "I wonder if he's still locked in," she said with irony. "I think this is the master key. I used it to find a servants' stairwell, which led to the exit near the kitchen."

Glancing from the key to her wry smile, he marveled at her bravery.

"Sorry if I botched your plan by breaking out early," Charlotte added kindly.

He felt bad for having grilled her on the dinghy. "No, I should apologize for being rude. You're safely away from there, and that's all that matters."

"Thank you," she said, conveying sincere gratitude. "If you hadn't been there, right where you were, I doubt I'd have made it over the wall."

"Don't thank me. That was all God," he said, repeating basically what he'd said the previous night.

"You think?" Her dubious tone told him right away she wasn't a believer. All the same, he had to tear his gaze off her as Saul reappeared, bearing three glasses of vividly colored juice.

"Blend of papaya, pineapple, and orange," the chief explained as he put them on the table.

Lucas and Charlotte both reached for a glass and their fingers brushed.

For Lucas, the contact felt like an electric shock. Draining his glass, he concealed her effect on his senses. Just last night, he'd comforted her as he would have comforted one of his sisters. Today, she possessed a quality that tickled his awareness.

The sweet juice sluiced over his tongue, bright and complex, rather like Charlotte. He fought not to look at her.

"We have a lot of catching up to do," she said, giving him an excuse to regard her again.

"Yes, we do," he agreed, sobering at the reminder.

"How's Lieutenant Mills?" she asked, looking suddenly concerned.

Reminded of his teammate's predicament, Lucas set his glass down with a thud.

"Unfortunately," he replied, loathing the circumstance that had brought him and Charlotte together, "he's been arrested."

~

The ten-seater Hawker 800XP taking her home was just like the plane in which her parents had perished.

Gripping the arms of her seat, Charlotte peered out the window, determined to fight the fear that kept her stomach churning. She would never be successful in the CIA if she didn't overcome her fear of flying.

Lucas, who was seated across the small aisle, with a long leg stretched into the aisle, had reclined his seat and was sleeping like a baby, while Saul did the same thing in the seat in front of him. Despite her exhaustion, and knowing she could never relax enough to sleep, Charlotte resigned herself to enduring the four-hour flight in fearful silence. In any case, she had plenty to think about after what Lucas had shared with her that morning.

What Commander Dwyer had done to Lieutenant Mills, turning the tables on him, made her shake her head in disbelief. More unbelievable, still, was the news that Dwyer wouldn't be made to answer for his crimes—not yet, anyway. The FBI was building a case against not only him, but The Entity as a whole.

It was precisely as Lloyd Elwood, her supervisor, had begun to suspect before he'd been murdered—Dwyer wasn't stealing and hoarding weapons on his own. A whole group of men with similar political leanings had banded together to safeguard the country. Or so they believed. Their leader was apparently so powerful and influential, the FBI needed hard and fast evidence before indicting him.

Questions chased through Charlotte's mind like a dog chasing its own tail. Lucas had explained how the FBI had found her, but who had kidnapped her in the first place? She had assumed it was Dwyer. But Dwyer didn't know about her photographic memory. Only NCIS, with whom she was interning, knew from her personnel file that she could remember stuff she'd seen and read, in detail, up to three weeks. Whoever it was, they'd intended Holden to "protect" her until she no longer posed a threat.

Sudden turbulence brought a panicked gasp out of Charlotte, waking up the warrior at her side.

"You okay?" he asked, clearing his throat and raising his seatback.

Charlotte fought to keep the fear from showing on her face. "Sorry. I didn't mean to wake you."

He rubbed sleep out of his dove-gray eyes, then regarded her more closely. Charlotte looked self-consciously back at him. His all-American features, paired with his light-brown hair and amazing physique, made her think of Captain America.

"There's nothing to worry about," he assured her, shooting a look out his window and then hers. "Trust me, I have my pilot's license, and these are optimal flying conditions. Low winds and almost no precipitation."

Charlotte eyed him in surprise. "You have a pilot's license?" The knowledge made her feel instantly more secure. "Do you have a plane, too?"

He shook his head. "Used to, back when I had more free time on my hands. Flying is fun," he added. "Why don't you like it?"

She looked away briefly. "My parents died in a plane crash three years ago," she admitted.

"I'm so sorry." The sincerity in his voice, coupled by his reaching across the aisle and squeezing her hand, brought tears to Charlotte's eyes, appalling her. She never let herself cry in front of strangers, and she'd done it in front of him. Twice!

"That must have come as such a shock."

His offering of comfort was similar to the way he'd held her on the dinghy the night before, only now she was supremely conscious of the large, warm hand cradling hers.

She mustered up a smile. "It did. I thought I'd have another thirty years with them, at least. Instead, I was just finishing college and about to go to The Farm for training."

"The Farm?" He pulled his hand back and angled himself in his seat to regard her with astonishment.

"CIA training camp."

"I know what it is. You'd been accepted into the CIA right out of college?"

"Well, yeah. Some might think I had an obvious advantage. My father was the Deputy Director of Talent. But I'd have got myself accepted no matter what," she added, in case he concluded she'd been given special treatment. "It was always my goal."

Studying his confounded expression, she could see him processing everything she said. The man was an open book.

"So, you didn't go the CIA-route," he deduced.

"Not then." She shook her head with lament. "My parents' death changed everything."

"I'm so sorry," he said again.

Grief threatened to resurface, so she made herself talk. "I have a younger brother named Calvin. He's the spitting image of my father, while I look like my mom. He had just started college when my parents died. He's going to school in Norfolk."

"Old Dominion University?"

"Correct. They'd offered him a full scholarship, but because he was only sixteen—"

"Sixteen and going to college?"

"He's brilliant, also like my dad," Charlotte explained with a fond smile. "At the time, he was so vulnerable. I didn't feel like I could just disappear on him by going off to training. Plus, the CIA would have sent me overseas the minute I graduated. So, instead, I moved to Norfolk to share an apartment with Calvin. I applied to be an intern with NCIS while earning a master's degree at night. NCIS isn't the CIA, by any means, but I figured the experience couldn't hurt me."

Lucas studied her face with interest. "You're still going to the CIA, then?"

"Absolutely," she said, ignoring a twinge of uncertainty as she recalled her fear of flying. "I can't be an intern forever. When my brother graduates, I'll put in my resignation."

"In another year?"

"This December, actually. Calvin's graduating early."

"Wow." Wonder shone in Lucas's gray eyes. "You're pretty amazing, both you and your brother. Not every sister would stick around like you have."

His praise warmed her to the core. "Do you have siblings?" she asked, tired of being the center of attention.

"I have two older sisters," he admitted, smiling at the thought of them. "They tormented me when I was growing up. In fact, SEAL training was nothing compared to the hell they put me through."

She laughed at what was obviously an exaggeration. "What did they do to you?"

He peered around the seat in front of him at his recumbent teammate, leaned across the aisle toward her, and whispered, "They used to dress me up and put makeup on me." He launched into an elaborate tale of how Liberty and Justice—and, yes, those were their names—

wrote a script for a play and made him take the role of the femme fatale.

"They curled my hair for that," he added on a horrified note. "Why do you think I cut it so short now?"

Charlotte burst out laughing. "You're pulling my leg," she guessed, though his expression was the very picture of earnest suffering.

He sat back and sighed. "I wish I were."

For the next half hour, he recounted still more stories of his sisters and their manipulative and humiliating shenanigans. Charlotte laughed until her stomach hurt.

"Oh, my goodness," she exclaimed, wiping a tear of mirth from the corner of her eye. "You have to be making this up."

He shook his head. "I can't tell a lie."

Maybe he really is Captain America, Charlotte thought.

"Speaking of honesty, there's something I haven't told you yet. Not that I've been lying. I just don't like saying it because it seems to give me an unfair advantage."

He looked at her with interest. "Go ahead."

"My contact in the DIA, the one I was delivering the iPad to, he's my Uncle Larry. Well, he's not technically my uncle; he's actually my godfather. He and my dad joined the CIA together, back in the eighties. My father stayed in, and Uncle Larry transferred to the DIA right after 9-11. He's the director now."

Lucas blinked several times. "Your godfather is *the* Larry Martin, Director of the DIA?"

She smiled ruefully. "That's why he said he would arrest Commander Dwyer as soon as he saw the evidence. If only I'd gotten it to him, Lieutenant Mills wouldn't be facing general court-martial for something he didn't do."

"Don't beat yourself up," Lucas said, eyeing her thoughtfully. "Maybe there's something you remember in the evidence that could help him."

She dropped her head against the back of her seat thinking. "I can still remember most of the details in the files on Lloyd's iPad, but my memories don't replace the evidence. For example, there was a video of Dwyer meeting with a bunch of men in a cabin in the middle of the night—all Entity members, no doubt—but that's gone. There was also an audio file of him chewing out Lowery for not killing Jonah Mills when he had the chance. Either one of those would've gotten Dwyer in big trouble."

"What about the document files? Can you remember any information in his documents that we could use, even if it's just a starting point for Jaguar's defense?"

Charlotte searched mental databanks. "I don't know. I'd have to picture each file individually and kind of reread them, so to speak. I kept asking Holden for a pen and paper because the memories are fading already, but, of course, he wouldn't give me either."

"I've got a pen and paper with me under my seat," he offered half-jokingly.

She shook her head. "I'm sorry. I can't concentrate on a plane."

"Understandable," he assured her, then added, "No pressure, but if you remember anything that proves Dwyer is a liar and a thief, that would be a big help to us."

"No pressure," she repeated with irony. "I'll give it my best shot once we're back on the ground."

"Actually, I forgot to tell you this," Lucas added. "Even if Jaguar gets convicted, the FBI special agent who coordinated your rescue promised to get Jaguar's conviction overturned once The Entity is rounded up. So, really, there is no pressure."

Charlotte realized Jaguar was Lieutenant Mills's code name. "I'd rather spare Jaguar the humiliation of a dishonorable discharge than wait for Fitz to undo everything that's done to him."

"Me, too."

"And wouldn't it be nice to expose Dwyer publicly?"

Lucas sent her a hard smile. "Yes, it would."

"Then I need to remember something useful." All at once she did. "Wait. Lieutenant Mills showed me a journal that described how

Dwyer's executive officer was sending classified emails to unauthorized recipients."

"Lowery's dead now, too," Lucas informed her. "Did you know that?"

"Lowery was the XO?"

"Correct," Lucas affirmed. "Supposedly he shot himself in the head."

"How awful," she breathed.

"Exactly. Anyway, you were saying you saw Blake LeMere's journal. When was that?"

"Lieutenant Mills—Jaguar—invited me over to look at it right after Lloyd was killed. I took pictures and emailed them to my godfather. He probably still has them in his inbox."

"Well, that would give us something, anyway," Lucas agreed, "since we don't have the original anymore."

Charlotte frowned. "Yeah, I heard it was stolen out of Master Chief's desk by Dwyer's secretary."

Lucas's jaw muscle jumped. "That's correct."

"Too bad," she commented, noting the sudden tension in him.

"I sure wish Agent Elwood was still alive," Lucas commented.

A shaft of sorrow pierced Charlotte's heart. "Me, too." Lloyd had been more like a father to her than a supervisor.

"Ever since his death, NCIS has been on Dwyer's side," Lucas continued, his tone resentful. "They ignored Saul's statement completely, even though he was there at the skeet-and-trap range and even saved Jaguar's life."

"Someone in NCIS must be a member of The Entity," Charlotte concluded.

"Exactly."

"Makes perfect sense," she agreed. "On a Thursday, I got the news that Lloyd was killed. The next day, men in suits came in and cleared our office, yanking the hard drive from his computer. And I was told to take a vacation!"

"Yeah, you went to the Bahamas, right?"

She made a face at his tasteless joke. "Ha ha. Yes, I did. But first, I went and found Lloyd's body at the medical examiner's office way out on the Northern Neck."

"Where is that?"

"Couple of hours north of Virginia Beach, between the Potomac and Rappahannock Rivers."

"Did he have family there?"

"No, his family is in Illinois. Lloyd was there on vacation, supposedly. Even so, I knew he never went anywhere without his iPad and, sure enough, he had it in his jacket when the accident happened. It was still there when I went to the morgue and identified his body."

"That's when you called your godfather, who promised to arrest Dwyer based on the evidence you described in the iPad."

"Exactly." Charlotte glanced out the window and was pleased to see the Virginia Beach oceanfront practically underneath them. Lucas had taken her mind completely off the fact that they were flying. "We're almost there," she marveled, as they sailed over the boardwalk and the roofs of the tall hotels, bound for the airfield not too far ahead.

Suspecting he'd distracted her on purpose, she looked back at him and experienced the same tug of attraction she'd felt upon first seeing him without paint on his face.

"Thank you," she told him, touched by his thoughtfulness. "Are you sure you're not Captain America?"

His shout of laughter awakened Saul, who sat straight up, reaching for the weapon he wasn't wearing because he'd stowed it in the front of the plane.

"No one's ever called me that before," Lucas said, looking highly amused.

"I don't know why not," Charlotte drawled.

Not only did Lucas look and act like an all-American hero, but he had kindness and integrity to match. Good thing she had plans of her own that left no leeway for falling in love. Otherwise, she might already have a crush on him.

CHAPTER 4

Escorted by the two SEALs, Charlotte crossed a hot, windy tarmac at Norfolk airport, headed for the small terminal for private plane owners. Awaiting to debrief her was the FBI special agent who'd coordinated her rescue. Saul held the door open, and Lucas gestured for Charlotte to precede him. The aroma of freshly brewed coffee greeted her as she stepped into the cool interior. The small terminal came with a coffee shop, which was empty save for two employees and a gentleman seated at a table.

Meeting his gaze, Charlotte faltered to a halt. Lucas, who was close behind, bumped into her, propelling her forward another few steps. His hands flashed out, keeping her on her feet.

Whirling to face him, she whispered urgently, "He's the man who cleared out Lloyd's office. He took his hard drive and all of his paperwork!"

"Easy," he said, steadying her with a look and a firm hold. "That doesn't make him the enemy."

Charlotte drew a calming breath and nodded. But maybe she'd been wrong in assuming someone in NCIS was responsible for

45

clearing out Lloyd's office. Maybe it had been the FBI who hadn't wanted Lloyd's findings falling into the wrong hands.

Concealing her suspicion behind a bland mask, Charlotte faced forward again and continued her approach.

Pushing back his chair, Casey Fitzpatrick stood with a polite yet ironic smile on his freckled face. Wearing a pale-yellow jacket and white slacks, he scarcely resembled the man in an austere black suit who had raided Lloyd's office, but his auburn hair and green eyes gave him away. The word *leprechaun* sprang to mind as he came around the table to greet her.

"Miss Patterson. It appears you recognize me. Special Agent Casey Fitzpatrick, but everyone calls me Fitz. Welcome home," he said, thrusting out a hand.

Returning his firm grasp, Charlotte murmured her thanks to him for enlisting the SEALs to rescue her. Then they all sat down, with Charlotte on Fitz's right side where he'd pulled out a chair for her, and Saul and Lucas dropping into the other empty seats. One of the employees came over to take their order.

While surveying the menu, Charlotte was aware of the agent's scrutiny.

"I'll have an iced tea and a croissant, please," she requested.

"You're looking good," he said, once the waitress disappeared, "despite your ordeal."

She found herself wondering if he was the mastermind behind her disappearance. After all, if he was that eager to seize Lloyd's hard drive, perhaps he'd seized the iPad, as well, if only to keep it out of the DIA's hands. Arranging her rescue would have been a piece of cake if he knew exactly where he'd stashed her.

"Thank you. I didn't like being drugged or stuck in a room, but at least I wasn't starved."

"Can you tell me anything about Roger Holden?"

More than you already know? She was tempted to ask. "He said he was from Texas and he used to be a senator."

Fitz nodded at Lucas and Saul. "I asked these two to recon Holden's island for me. They found no evidence of a warehouse, though we have to assume Holden's a member of The Entity. Did he say what he does now?"

Charlotte thought back to the conversation she'd had with her host right before she strangled him. "He said he was a businessman. He seemed to host a lot of parties."

Fitz nodded thoughtfully. "Did you see any of his guests?"

"I saw people come and go through my window—mostly men—but I didn't recognize anyone," she answered. "He probably put up his guests in the other bedrooms." Remembering the key still in the pocket of the dress loaned to her, she pulled it out. "This key might actually open their doors. I took it off Holden."

Fitz's eyes lit up. "May I have it?"

Suffering slight misgivings, she handed it across the table to him and watched him pocket it neatly.

The conversation halted as the waitress returned with their orders, placed drinks and pastries in an efficient manner before them, then withdrew again.

As Charlotte dumped three packets of sugar into her tea, Fitz pulled a photograph from the pocket inside his jacket and passed it to her. "Do you recognize this couple?"

Adrenaline flooded her bloodstream as she studied the photograph.

"They're the ones who took me," she affirmed, before handing the photo to Lucas. "Do *you* know who they are?" she asked Fitz, who would certainly know if he'd hired them himself.

"He's a former SEAL," Fitz affirmed, sparking Saul and Lucas's interest. "Jason Dunn."

Peering at the photo, both SEALs claimed the man looked familiar.

"And the woman is his wife, Laura," Fitz added.

"How'd you figure out they took me?" Charlotte quizzed.

Fitz's mouth quirked. "Facial-recognition software. A security camera caught the man carrying you onto Holden's yacht.

"What happened to my car?" she demanded as Lucas handed the photo back to the agent.

"It was towed to Quantico and gone over with a fine-tooth comb. You can have it back once it's safe for you to return to life as normal."

Life as normal? She stared at him hard. "I don't suppose you found an iPad under the driver's seat."

His expression betrayed disappointment. "We did not. We did, however, recover some of your personal effects." Reaching under his chair, he produced a plastic bag and gave it to her.

"My badge from work," she exclaimed. "And my purse!" she added, pulling it from the bag and digging into it, relieved to find her wallet, driver's license and credit cards all intact.

"Obviously, they weren't thieves," she commented, looking back into the bag for her cell phone. To her disappointment, it wasn't there. "They took my cell phone, though. Shoot, how am I going to call anybody?" she muttered to herself.

"There's something else in the bag for you," Fitz prompted.

With a quizzical glance at him she pulled out both a box and a manila envelope, then set them on the table. Opening the envelope first, she found a credit card inside it and some kind of form to fill out.

"What's this about?" she asked him.

The agent leaned closer and pitched his voice low. "Listen carefully." His green-as-grass eyes bored into hers. "The Entity will have heard by now that you escaped Holden's island, but they don't know if you're back in the States. I'd like to keep it that way. I need you to alter your appearance."

Charlotte squelched the urge to laugh.

"They'll be looking for you," Fitz added ominously. "The gift card has five hundred dollars on it. Use the funds to alter your appearance. Don't touch your own credit cards. Once you've changed the way you look, take a passport-style photo of yourself, pick a pseudonym, and fill out the paperwork enclosed. Mail everything in the envelope provided and you'll get a new ID in two days. Carry on under your alias, and don't contact anyone you know."

Intrigued by the idea of disguising herself, Charlotte cracked open the box and found an android cell phone and a charger inside. "What's the phone for?" she asked, doubting it was meant to replace her stolen one.

"I need to be able to reach you at a moment's notice," he explained. "Keep it charged and carry it with you at all times."

"Can I call my brother?" she asked, though she had already called him from Eric's home in the Bahamas.

"You've already called him," Fitz said, proving himself aware of that fact. "Now that you're stateside, you can't do it again."

She balked at his restrictions. "Why not?"

The agent smiled thinly. "Because The Entity expects it. They want to find you, and they want to keep you quiet until you're no longer a threat."

"How long will that be?" she demanded.

He shrugged one shoulder. "That depends on you. You're only a threat to them as long as you remember something that could set off a renewed investigation. In the meantime, indulge me," he requested on a hard note. "And don't contact anyone."

Charlotte thought of the photos she'd taken of LeMere's journal, the one stolen by Dwyer's secretary. She had emailed the photos to her godfather. "Not even the director of the DIA?" she pressed, thinking Jaguar could use LeMere's written testimony to make Dwyer look bad.

Fitz sent her a tight smile. "Not even him. Trust me, The Entity is fully aware of your relationship with Larry Martin. They're hoping you'll reach out to him. If and when you do, they'll know you're alive. They'll know where you are. And they will pick you up as they did before and keep you somewhere until your memories aren't a threat anymore."

"Maybe at a resort in Switzerland next time," she proposed sarcastically.

Draining his coffee, Fitz forbore to comment. "Not to rush off, but I have a very busy schedule today. Keep your seats," he added, as the SEALs started to stand. "Miss Patterson." He put out a hand for her to shake. "Be careful."

Is that a threat or a warning? she wondered, returning his firm grip.

"I'll be in touch," he promised. Looking at both SEALs, he said, "Don't let her out of your sight. Not even for a second."

"Yes, sir," they answered in unison.

With a final nod, Fitz headed for the exit and promptly disappeared.

Charlotte looked back at Lucas and found him frowning at her. "What?" she asked him.

"You could have been a little more grateful," he stated with bemusement.

"Was I rude?" She looked to Saul for confirmation and got a nod. "Well...," she trailed off and crossed her arms, pondering her intuition. "Maybe I don't trust him. I feel like he has an agenda."

"Clearly he does," Lucas agreed. "Keeping you safe while tearing down a syndicate."

Charlotte inspected the phone Fitz had given her plus the envelope with the gift card in it. "Okay," she agreed. "I'll trust him if you trust him." Picking up her croissant, she eyed it hungrily. "Can we eat now? I'm starving."

"I'll say grace," Lucas offered.

Charlotte set her pastry down while heaving an inward sigh.

Lucas groaned aloud as he and Charlotte pushed through the glass doors at MacArthur Center mall in Norfolk and found the place packed. Eyeing the crush of humanity in the food court, he put a hand on the small of Charlotte's back and propelled her toward the nearest locator map.

"Where do you need to go?" he asked her.

His terse tone earned him a quizzical glance. "Aren't you going to take off your sunglasses?"

"No," he said, using the dark lenses to conceal his roaming eyes. "Why couldn't we have gone to a thrift shop or somewhere else? This place is way too busy."

"I already told you," she said, studying the mall's layout. "The mall is the only place I can get everything I need." She lifted a finger to the map. "Here's where we are now." Consulting the legend several times, she traced their route.

"We're going here to the wig store, here to get glasses, then down to Nordstrom for makeup and for clothing."

"Let's do it," he agreed, catching up her hand in his, just in case he needed to pull her to safety.

The self-conscious glance she cast him made him wonder if having her hand held bothered her. It felt perfectly natural to him. Maybe he was just used to having a girlfriend—though, come to think of it, Monica hadn't liked holding his hand in public. And this was different anyway. He was keeping Charlotte Patterson safe. Touching her was part of the job, but he ought to get permission first.

"You okay with me holding your hand?"

"Of course," she said on a breezy note.

Good. Then he didn't have to let go. Besides, Fitz's words about The Entity picking her up and whisking her away again still echoed in his head. Keeping a sharp eye out, he marched her briskly from the food court toward the first stop on their shopping spree.

"Why are people staring at us?" Charlotte murmured as they neared their destination.

The question let him know for sure she had no idea who he'd been before becoming a SEAL. "Probably because you're so pretty," he replied.

"Smooth," she said, shooting him a grin. "But I think it's because you look conspicuous wearing sunglasses indoors." She arched her eyebrows at him.

"They're not coming off," he informed her.

She rolled her eyes and tugged him into the wig shop.

Releasing her to find a wig, Lucas guarded the entrance and left it to Charlotte to make her own selection.

Within minutes and with convincing pathos, she had made the store attendant believe she was going to lose her lovely red hair due to chemo. Together, they selected a chocolate-brown wig that was too dark, in Lucas's opinion, for her complexion. Charlotte paid for it with Fitz's credit card, thanked the lady, and reclaimed Lucas on her way out.

Her small smile informed him she was enjoying herself.

"Where is Saul?" she asked, peering around her as they headed toward an ocular shop.

"Don't bother looking," Lucas told her. "You're not going to see him unless he wants you to."

"He's a sniper, isn't he?" she guessed, glancing up at him for corroboration.

"Yes. And he excels in the art of camouflage."

"What about you?" she asked. "What's your specialty?"

"Little bit of everything," he replied. "Last year, I took Jaguar's place as troop leader."

"When he disappeared?"

"Yes. I'd like to be the operations officer one day, though," he admitted. "I like planning missions."

"I bet you've planned out your whole life, haven't you?" she asked with a sidelong glance. Her eyes immediately widened. "You have!" she guessed. "I can tell by the look on your face. Gosh, you have got to work on that."

He steered her around the slow couple blocking their path. "Work on what?"

"Your poker face," she explained. "You are utterly transparent. I can see everything you're thinking."

He did not like the sound of that.

"It's okay," she assured him. "I'd rather you were transparent than inscrutable, like Special Agent Fitz."

Her mention of the agent reminded Lucas to pay more attention to their surroundings. He'd noticed several people watching them already, though most likely they just recognized him from television. He couldn't just assume that, though. If anyone recognized Charlotte, word might get around that she was back in the area. According to Fitz, the hunt for her would be on.

"Here we are," she said, leaving him at the door of the ocular shop while she headed inside for a pair of glasses.

The store was so busy it took her almost thirty minutes just to get plastic-framed glasses with prescription-free lenses. Lucas leaned against the wall, waiting. At last, she approached him, wearing them as if she'd had them on all along.

"What do you think?" she inquired, angling her face up at him.

She looked so much like a sexy librarian that he could think of nothing else for several seconds.

"They look good," he said, rather abruptly. "Come on. This is taking too long."

Grabbing her hand, he towed her toward the escalator that would take them to the lower level.

They were descending the escalator amidst the crush of other people when the kid behind them tapped Lucas on the shoulder. He realized, looking back at him, that the youth was wearing a Cowboy's jersey.

Oh, crap.

"Aren't you Jonathan Strong?" Blue eyes searched his face with awe.

"No, sorry," Lucas lied. "I just look like him."

Given the disbelieving look he got, the kid wasn't convinced. With a pricking of his conscience, Lucas turned his back on him. Usually, he liked talking to young people, telling his story and encouraging them to give their lives to God. But the last thing he wanted was for this kid to snap a photo of him and publish it on Snapchat or Instagram, especially if Charlotte was also in the picture.

As they stepped off the escalator, he hustled her toward Nordstrom, a department store located at the far end of the mall. Watching for the teen's reflection in the glass storefronts, he was conscious of Charlotte's sidelong glances.

"That's why you're wearing sunglasses," she finally guessed. "You're famous and you don't want people recognizing you! I should have guessed," she muttered to herself.

"Guessed what?" he asked, wondering what she'd concluded.

"You're a movie star, aren't you? You *played* the part of Captain America."

He could tell she was teasing, but he laughed at her obsession with the superhero.

"Haven't you ever watched football?" he asked incredulously. "I'm Jonathan Strong. I was a tight end for the Dallas Cowboys. Now I go by my middle name."

"You are *not* a Texan," she declared, jerking him to a stop.

"What do you mean? I was born and raised in Texas."

"If you were a Texan, you would talk like Roger Holden or like Saul, with all your vowels drawn out."

Lucas grinned and urged her to keep walking. "Saul wasn't raised by my mother, who's an English teacher. We had to have perfect grammar and no vernacular."

"And no cussing, either," Charlotte guessed.

"Well, that's more of a personal endeavor."

"Because of your religion," she guessed.

He shot her a startled look. "I'm not overly religious," he protested.

"What are you then?" Her tone was more curious than ridiculing.

"A child of God," he said simply, "same as the rest of us. I know God loves me, and I try to show His love to others."

Charlotte fell thoughtfully silent.

"What about you?" Lucas prompted.

"I used to think God loved me."

Her short reply conveyed pain and disillusionment.

Remorse tore through Lucas for not considering how her parents' deaths must have affected her.

"That would have shaken my faith, too," he admitted, squeezing her hand.

Averting her face so he couldn't see her tear-bright eyes, she gestured at the department store in front of them. "We're here."

Lucas glanced at his watch. "Think you can get everything you need in less than an hour?"

She looked up at him wryly. "You don't like shopping, do you?"

"Actually, Saul has to pick up his dog from the sitter's by 1700 hours. He didn't leave enough food."

Her eyes widened. "You should have told me that earlier. Step on it." She pulled him toward the women's wear. "If I only have an hour, then you're going to have to help."

"I said less than an hour," he reminded her, but let her drag him into the section of colorful clothing.

She homed in on a rack of blouses.

"You see this?" she asked, snatching up a hideous leopard-print blouse. "This is the look I'm going for. I call it desperate divorcée with bad taste. Garish, over the top, in a size eight. Find me five blouses that fit that description—earth tones preferably. I'm going to look for slacks and undergarments. Then I'll need shoes because I can't just keep wearing these sandals. Gosh, I hope Fitz gave me enough money," she added under her breath as she spun away from him.

"Charlotte."

She stopped and looked back at him, one eyebrow raised above the other. The look almost made him laugh.

"Don't leave my sight, please," he requested.

She sent him a smile that melted his insides. "Thank you for saying please."

Whirling, she strode away like a woman on a mission. He watched her for a minute, enjoying the athletic yet graceful way she moved, then applied himself to the task she'd given him.

Having had two older sisters and an ex-fiancée, all of whom loved to gossip about women's fashion, he had a fair idea of what Charlotte was looking for. Within ten minutes and channeling the Kardashian sisters, he'd picked out five blouses in varying colors and styles.

Carrying them to Charlotte for her approval, he realized she had already selected several pairs of slacks and was picking out lingerie.

"How do these look?" he asked, averting his gaze from the lace bra dangling in her right hand.

She cast a critical gaze at the blouses he'd selected. "Hideous. They're perfect."

"Do you need to try them on?" To avoid looking at the bra, he fixed his gaze on her face while suspecting, by her tiny smile, that she was enjoying giving him an awkward moment.

"There's no time for that," she declared. "I'll keep the tags on and return anything that doesn't fit. Hold this?" She dumped the slacks in his arms and turned her attention to picking out panties. "I still have to find shoes after this."

"I'll take these to the register," he volunteered, distancing himself quickly.

On his way to the check-out counter, Lucas found himself wondering if God was testing his commitment to his new plan. He'd just promised himself his next relationship wouldn't be with a career-oriented woman. He wanted a wife who put God and family first. A woman who doubted God's existence and was bound for the CIA was obviously not the woman for him. He just wished he didn't find her so attractive.

Leaving the articles with the helpful cashier, his gaze alighted on the jewelry counter near the cash register. A dainty silver crucifix immediately caught his eye, reminding him that Charlotte would need jewelry to complete her disguise. A cross glinting at the base of her throat ought to remind him to remain professional.

He picked up the box it was in, then selected two silver studs to match. Seeing Charlotte trying on shoes in the next department, he carried the jewelry over to her to see if she liked it. As he neared her, she stood up hefting two boxes.

"You're done already?"

"Almost. I still have to get makeup." Her forehead furrowed with concern. "I don't know if Fitz's gift card is going to cover everything."

"No worries. I'll pay for the rest," he assured her.

Her chin went up. "Only if you let me pay you back."

"That's up to you," he said, squelching inappropriate thoughts about how she could do that. "Here, I'll take the shoes to the register. What do you think about this jewelry?" he asked, handing off the smaller items in exchange for the shoe boxes.

She looked at the cross, then up at him. "Is this supposed to be a talisman?"

He considered his reason for picking it out. "Sort of. But every woman wears jewelry. Your disguise wouldn't be complete without it."

"Good point," she acknowledged. "Now I'm *sure* Fitz's credit card won't cover everything."

"Like I said, I'll pay the rest."

"Thank you," she replied, handing him back the jewelry to add to her mounting pile. "I still need to get makeup." She tipped her head in the direction of the makeup counter.

"Go for it." With his hands full, Lucas watched her stride away.

Fifteen minutes later, they left Nordstrom laden with her purchases. The sum total proved to be quite a bit more than Fitz had supplied with the gift card. Charlotte reiterated her promise to pay him back.

"Look, I have money to spare," he finally told her, "and I'm not trying to be a sugar daddy either," he added, earning a startled glance. "I just want your disguise to be complete. That way my job is easier. Understand?"

She considered his words for several seconds, then nodded. "Okay, but I'm still going to pay you back. It's time to put on my disguise and take my picture," she added.

They struck out toward a photo kiosk they had located earlier, not far from the public restrooms.

As Charlotte disappeared into the women's room to change, Lucas held the remainder of her purchases and waited.

A man bending over the water fountain straightened and bumped forcibly into him.

"Sorry, partner," he said with a western drawl.

Lucas realized he was looking at Saul, who'd stuffed his hair into a ball cap and changed his shirt. "Seen anyone suspicious?" Lucas asked him.

"Just the kid who took your picture when you weren't looking."

"He did?" Lucas searched the crowded corridor for the culprit.

"Don't worry," Saul assured him. "I kindly asked him to delete it."

"Oh, boy." Lucas pictured the conversation they must have had.

"Scared the crap out of him," Saul admitted. "But I watched him delete it. Charlotte's face won't be on Instagram tonight."

"Who is Charlotte?" asked a husky female voice with a southern drawl.

Both men pivoted toward the woman who'd just stepped out of the restroom. It took Lucas a full second to realize he wasn't looking at a stranger.

"Wow," he breathed. She'd altered her appearance so drastically she could have walked right by him without him knowing it was her.

Wavy brown hair paired with black-framed glasses and an entirely different complexion was the secret. Her wardrobe—leopard-print top, black slacks and pointy-toed black heels—screamed *Check me out, boys!* Picturing the undergarment she had to be wearing, Lucas focused intently on the cross shimmering above her plunging neckline.

His and Saul's astounded expressions brought a smile of amusement to her mauve lips.

"Picture time," she declared. From her purse, she produced the envelope Fitz had given her. "I need a name."

"Jezebel," Saul drawled.

"A *serious* name," Charlotte said, taking no offense. "I like Justice, your sister's name," she said, looking at Lucas for his permission. "Justice Strong. I wouldn't want to endanger her, though," she qualified.

Lucas took in Charlotte's stance, the way she held her chin high with her head defiantly tilted. "Justice suits you, and her last name's Adams now, anyway, so why not? If anyone asks who you are, I'll say you're my sister visiting from Texas."

"Perfect," Charlotte replied. Stuffing the sundress she'd been wearing into one of the bags Lucas held, she crossed to the nearby photo booth and disappeared behind the curtain, only to poke her head out seconds later.

"I need a credit card," she stated with chagrin.

By the time they left the mall with her photo taken, it was late afternoon. Lucas, who was driving, swung by a post office, and Saul jumped out to mail off Charlotte's new photo and the ID form in the envelope Fitz had given her. Saul had suggested she use his address.

With that task checked off, Lucas put a lead foot on the accelerator, only to become mired in rush-hour traffic.

"Aww, c'mon," Saul muttered, glancing at his watch.

When Charlotte kept quiet in the backseat, Lucas glanced over his shoulder at her, not surprised to see her head lolling on the headrest, her eyes closed. Considering all she'd been through, she had to be exhausted. A protective compulsion seized him, causing him to depress the brake pedal more gently.

Sleep in peace, brave girl, he caught himself thinking. *I won't let anyone harm you.*

~

Eyes glued shut from sheer exhaustion, Charlotte willed herself to take a nap, but the quiet conversation coming from the front seats piqued her interest.

"You realize we can't split up," Lucas said to Saul, "so where are we keeping her, your place or mine?"

"You've got the security system," Saul pointed out.

"And you've got a dog. I don't have any furniture downstairs," Lucas added.

Saul swore under his breath. "Monica had no right to take your furniture, brother. It's bad enough she took the ring if she ain't going to marry you."

Lucas hushed him. "I don't care about the furniture or the ring," he retorted.

Lucas's words, spoken in a terse tone she hadn't heard from him before, brought Charlotte more fully awake. She kept her eyes closed, however, processing what she'd heard. Lucas had been recently engaged to a woman named Monica! And, apparently, she'd taken his furniture, not to mention her engagement ring, when they broke up.

Peculiar feelings sluiced through Charlotte. On the one hand, she was pleased to hear that Lucas was single—not that she considered herself a candidate for a relationship with him. On the other hand, it panged her to hear that such a great guy had been treated badly. He'd shown her nothing but patience and consideration all day long. A guy like him deserved a woman every bit as kind as he was.

"My place is fine," Saul relented. At the same time, a chime sounded up front, and Charlotte peered through her lashes to see Saul frowning at his cell phone.

"Master Chief says he's breaking into Lowery's apartment tonight," Saul conveyed.

Lowery, Charlotte recalled, was the XO who'd committed suicide. Why would Master Chief Rivera be breaking into his apartment?

"You really think you can tell from the photos if Lowery shot himself?" Lucas asked.

Ah, that was why. They wanted to know if Lowery might have been murdered.

"Should be able to," Saul replied. "Wish he'd have let me go with him to see for myself. Be safer with a buddy."

"God won't let him fall," Lucas said, with absolute certainty.

Fall? Charlotte couldn't imagine how Master Chief was breaking in. Surely, he wasn't climbing the face of the building.

Saul just grunted. Charlotte could tell by the cynical sound that Saul wasn't as naïve as Lucas was. God didn't protect everyone who loved Him. If He did, her mother would still be alive today.

CHAPTER 5

Charlotte rolled onto her back and sighed. She couldn't sleep any better here in Saul's house guarded by two SEALs than she had as Holden's captive.

It wasn't the bed's fault. Saul's guest bed, with a thick mattress and a handcrafted headboard he'd carved from butternut, was plenty comfortable. Tucked under the eaves of a 1930s bungalow-style cottage, his spare bedroom was quaint and cozy. The rest of the white-washed home touted a front porch, a big backyard, and a chocolate Labrador retriever named Duke. Charlotte ought to be sleeping like a baby. God knew she was tired enough.

But how was she supposed to sleep knowing Dwyer had gotten away with killing Lloyd, and an innocent man was sitting in jail awaiting court-martial? There had to be something she could remember from her boss's files that would help the SEALs prove Jaguar's innocence and implicate Dwyer at the same time. Though she had spent hours prior to sleeping copying documents she could still picture in her head, nothing of any use to Jaguar had presented itself.

Determined to remember something that would help him, Charlotte mentally opened some of the remaining files on the iPad she had

61

yet to think about. Lloyd had documented so much it was hard to see the forest for the trees. Envisioning one file at a time, Charlotte searched for something—anything—that Jaguar might use in his defense.

By the third document, the mental exercise had nearly drained her ability to concentrate. Names of places Dwyer had been and the people he'd contacted all began to run together. However, one name in particular jumped out at her—Sabena, Virginia. According to Lloyd's notes, Dwyer had gotten a long-distance call on his home's landline phone from Sabena.

Charlotte's eyes sprang open. *Sabena, Virginia?* She had written down that name earlier while recording her memories on paper. Sabena was the historical town on the Northern Neck, where Lloyd had said he was going to take a vacation—a vacation from which he'd never returned.

With the feeling that she'd stumbled onto something important, Charlotte tossed back the covers and jumped out of bed. She knew she would find Lucas in the kitchen, keeping watch until Saul took over at two in the morning.

Wearing an oversized Hard Rock Cafe T-shirt Saul had loaned her in lieu of the pajamas she'd forgotten to buy, Charlotte descended the narrow staircase to the first floor and entered the kitchen, a large room added to the back of the house.

Lucas had pulled the blinds so no one could see in from the dark backyard. Seated at a rustic table, he had the components of a submachine gun spread out on a towel in front of him, illuminated by the antler candelabra hanging over the table. At her approach, his gray eyes flickered toward her bare thighs, sparking awareness in her like a flare.

"Join me," he invited. "I promised myself a Sudoku puzzle if I clean my weapon first."

"The carrot and the stick," she commented, taking a seat across from him. "Is this a Heckler and Koch?"

He eyed her with astonishment. "How do you know that?"

Bittersweet memories flickered. "My father used to take me to the shooting range."

"You're probably an expert marksman—markswoman," he corrected quickly.

"I'm okay," she acknowledged with a humble shrug.

His eyes shone with admiration. "Is there anything you can't do?"

Charlotte sighed and slumped in the chair. "I can't sleep," she admitted.

He rubbed a component of his gun with an oiled cloth. "A lot of SEALs have the same problem."

"I bet *you* don't."

His eyebrow quirked upward. "What makes you say that?"

She shrugged again. "Just a guess. What does Saul use for his sniping?" she asked, returning to the previous topic.

"A Remington 700 with bolt action. The drug lords down south call him *El Segador*, which means The Reaper. They're scared to death of him."

The chilling words made Charlotte think about her own chosen career. Shooting to kill wasn't something she professed to being comfortable with, not even in defense of her country. She would have to get over that, along with her fear of flying.

"Did Saul use the Remington to defend Jaguar at the skeet range?" she inquired.

Lucas paused to think. "No. He used his hunting rifle, a Weatherby, which happened to be in the back of his car."

"Isn't that a violation of Article 134, carrying a concealed weapon onto a military installation? Or did he have permission pursuant to the DoD's 2016 directive?"

Her question earned another look of amazement. "Honestly, I don't know. There's sort of a 'don't ask, don't tell' policy regarding personal weapons on military bases right now. I mean, I've never known an MP who's going to ask a SEAL if he's carrying a personal weapon in his vehicle. It's kind of a given."

"Hmph." Charlotte propped her elbow on the table and her chin on her hand. "Then I guess it's safe for Saul to testify about what happened at the skeet-and-trap range."

Lucas nodded. "He's planning on it. Saul is Jaguar's main witness."

"Do you know if Jaguar's going to take the stand?"

"Not a good idea, according to his lawyer," Lucas said with a shake of his head. "A prosecutor like O'Rourke could pick apart his testimony, find flaw in it, and bury him."

Charlotte sighed at the prospect. "I'd like to help with Jaguar's defense," she offered. "Can I meet his lawyer? I know a bit about military law from my internship."

Lucas oiled another component. "I don't see why not. There's a pretrial proceeding tomorrow for Jaguar's lawyer to meet with his witnesses. Since we can't let you out of our sight, I guess you're coming, too."

"In my disguise? How will I get on base without an ID?"

Her question caused his forehead to furrow. "I guess you'll have to get on base as yourself, using your NCIS badge. Then you can put your disguise on before we enter the building."

"I'll be your sister, visiting from Texas." Charlotte opened her eyes wide and grinned at him.

"Right." His gaze went straight to the cross at her neck.

"What about when you have to go to work?" she asked him.

He looked back at his weapon. "Luckily, we don't have to for a while. Alpha Troop is on leave for the next two weeks."

Charlotte was pleased to hear it. "Great, then we can concentrate on Jaguar's defense. I've been scanning Lloyd's files in my mind, and something cropped up that I'd written down earlier. I think it's a clue."

He looked up at her hopefully. "What?"

"It's a place name—Sabena, Virginia. Dwyer got a long-distance call from there. It happens to be the same place Lloyd was taking his so-called vacation, right before he was killed. I don't think that's a coincidence."

"Where is Sabena, Virginia?" Lucas asked with a frown.

"On the Northern Neck where I found Lloyd's iPad. What if he was investigating something in Sabena and not taking a vacation? What if he found something Dwyer didn't want him to find, and he was run off the road because of it?"

Lucas regarded her thoughtfully. "We should definitely look into that."

"Yes, we should," she agreed. "If we could prove Dwyer is a murderer, Jaguar would certainly be found innocent."

Putting down his rag, Lucas sat back and crossed his arms. The muscles bunching beneath the thin cotton of his T-shirt and bursting out of his short sleeves riveted Charlotte's gaze.

"No tattoos?" she asked, covering up her reason for staring. "No girlfriends' names inked into your arm, crossed out and rewritten? Isn't that what Navy guys do?"

He sent her a patronizing look. "Regular Navy, maybe. SEALs have more class than that."

"What happened with you and Monica?"

Her question caught them both by surprise.

His eyebrows had shot to his hairline. "You certainly keep your ears open." Reaching for the frame of his submachine gun, he started to assemble it.

"Sorry," she muttered, beyond embarrassed. "You don't have to answer that. I'm so tired I don't know what I'm saying."

"That's okay." He found several pieces, slid and clicked them into place. "She put her career before her loyalty to me. That's what happened." *Slap. Click. Snap. Slap.*

"Sorry to hear that," Charlotte murmured, wondering what that meant.

Lucas glanced at her. "On Dwyer's orders, she entered our office building on Labor Day and took LeMere's journal from Master's Chief's locked desk."

Charlotte gasped. "*She* was the secretary who took the journal?"

"One and the same," Lucas affirmed. "She betrayed my teammate; therefore, she betrayed me."

Ouch, Charlotte thought. "Maybe she didn't have a choice," she suggested. "You just said Commander Dwyer ordered her."

Lucas's expression turned incredulous. "You seriously think that justifies her actions? She could have refused him on the basis that stealing is immoral."

"But she might have lost her job for refusing him."

His eyes flashed with anger. "That's exactly the excuse she gave me," he retorted. "Keeping her job mattered more than doing the right thing, and now Jaguar's in jail with less evidence to defend him from Dwyer's false charges."

Charlotte told herself not to say another word, but she couldn't help making one more observation. "Maybe she doesn't realize how corrupt Dwyer really is."

Lucas's expression hardened. "I don't care if she knows or not. What she did was wrong. End of story."

Charlotte gave up trying to prove a point. She'd put Lucas's back against the wall, and now the tension in the room made lighthearted conversation too much of a struggle. She rose from the table, and Lucas just looked at her.

"Guess I'd better try and sleep," she said.

When he didn't say anything else, she hung her head and retreated. She had one foot on the stairs before he called on a forgiving note, "Good night, Charlotte."

"Good night."

On the landing, she ran straight into Saul, who appeared out of nowhere wearing boxers and a Harley Davidson T-shirt. With his long hair swirling around his shoulders, he resembled a wild man.

Charlotte reared back, clapping a hand to her heart.

"Sorry," he said, edging around her.

"Did we wake you up?"

"No. My turn to keep watch," he said, letting her know how late it was. "Back to bed with you." He pointed toward his guestroom. "And take the dog with you," he suggested.

They both looked at Duke who sat at the top of the stairs issuing a mighty yawn.

"His snores are the best tranquilizer on the market," Saul insisted.

Desperate for sleep, Charlotte would try anything. "C'mon, Duke," she called, returning to her bedroom with the dog dutifully following.

Approaching the checkpoint at Naval Air Station Oceana, Lucas slowed behind the cars in front of him and studied the guard with misgivings.

"Shoot," he said, watching the MP take the ID from the car at the front of the line and point a laser at it. "They're scanning IDs today."

He and Saul both turned their heads to assess Charlotte in the backseat. Though dressed in a new outfit and heavily made-up with foundation that covered her freckles, she'd kept her wig and glasses off so she could still pass for herself while using her NCIS badge.

"What happens if they scan my badge?"

Saul and Lucas shared a worried look.

"It means your name will go into a database," Lucas answered. "If The Entity is keeping an eye on it, they'll know you were here."

"We gotta turn around," Saul stated.

Glancing at the truck's digital clock, Lucas swallowed a curse. Jaguar's pretrial hearing was taking place in a half hour.

"But I want to be at the hearing," Charlotte protested. "Plus, you promised Fitz you'd keep an eye on me. How are you going to do that if you leave me and go on base by yourselves?"

"I'll stay with her, sir," Saul volunteered. "You can go to the meeting alone."

Lucas shook his head. "No, you're Jaguar's key witness. I'll stay with her."

"Oh, for heaven's sake," Charlotte protested from the backseat. "Just leave me somewhere with a pistol. I can defend myself."

Making up his mind to turn around, Lucas turned his truck into the nearest cross street and sped them away from the gate.

"Where are you taking me?" Charlotte asked a minute later.

Lucas had sifted through his options and made a reluctant decision. "My place. Between my security system and the Glock I'm going to give you, you should be okay for an hour. Also, it's close by."

"I'll be fine," Charlotte assured him, sounding slightly less put out, perhaps even curious about where he lived. He glanced back at her expression, but her face was averted.

Twenty minutes later, Lucas approached the gate again with only Saul in the car. It felt anticlimactic not to bring in Charlotte after going to such lengths to rescue her, but her anonymity came first. Like Fitz had said, The Entity had eyes and ears everywhere. Bringing her through the gate might have tipped them off she was back.

Lucas and Saul, both dressed in their Naval Working Uniforms, checked their phones in at security and reported to a stuffy conference room on the second floor. At their entrance, Master Chief, who was the only one who'd beat them there, saluted Lucas and made his way toward them.

"Sir," he said, producing the reconnaissance camera.

"You found something," Lucas guessed.

"Have a look." Stepping between the younger men, Rivera held the camera in such a way so they could all see the digital display.

"This is the lock to the balcony door," he said.

Lucas regarded the photo with confusion.

"It's been cut," Saul observed.

"Yes. Brace yourself," Rivera warned, forwarding to the next image and the next and the next.

Lucas and Saul studied the remaining pictures with repugnance.

"So, what do you think?" Master Chief asked Saul after they'd seen the last one.

"He didn't shoot himself," Saul declared, confirming Lucas's private conclusion. Using hand motions, Saul explained how the distance a bullet covered before hitting its target determined the diameter of the exit matter out the back of the cranium.

"If he'd held the gun up to his own head, that spatter would have been bigger."

Lucas nodded. "I'm going to find a forensic expert who agrees with you."

"Then you'll need this," Rivera said, putting the camera into Lucas's hands.

"Don't get your hopes up," Lucas said to both men. "As far as evidence for Jaguar's trial, I'm pretty sure this won't be admissible since it's not related to the charges he's facing. But if he's found guilty, we'll go after Dwyer with both barrels."

"Hooyah," Saul and Rivera both replied.

Just then, a couple edged into the room—Jaguar's wife in the company of a pudgy, older man who had to be Jaguar's psychiatrist. Lucas pocketed the camera and hurried over to them.

"Eden," he said, embracing the blond fitness instructor.

Blinking back tears, she accepted his comfort, then received hugs from Saul and Master Chief.

The latter kept an arm around her shoulders. "Don't worry, ma'am. We're going to get Jonah out of the brig soon."

Eden made introductions. "Everyone, this is Dr. Branson, Jonah's psychiatrist. Doctor, these are Jonah's teammates, Master Chief Rivera, Lieutenant Strong, and Chief Wade."

Branson shook hands with each of them while peering sincerely into their eyes.

Any conversation they might have had was cut short by the stomping of feet. As two military policemen escorted Jaguar into the room, Eden hurried over to him. Jaguar, grim and pale-faced, held her gaze as the MPs divested him of his handcuffs. The second he was free, he hauled her into his arms and held her tightly. Once the guards retreated to stand outside the door, Eden's composure crumbled. Over her head, Jonah acknowledged his doctor, Lucas, Saul, and Master Chief with a nod.

Seconds later, the JAG arrived, shutting the door behind her.

Lucas took one look at the young woman with her fraying bun and big blue eyes, and his optimism wavered. Meeting Saul's cynical expression, he read his thoughts.

Like I said, inexperienced.

"I'm Lieutenant Commander Carew." The young woman introduced herself before gesturing for them to take seats at the table. "Shall we get started?"

Once seated, she asked all present to introduce themselves.

"Thank you for coming," she began. Opening the dossier she'd brought with her, she withdrew a notepad and a pen. "Lieutenant Mills and I have spoken at length about the event that resulted in his charge of assaulting a senior officer. He requested this meeting so that I could review the evidence and meet his witnesses. At least one of you can corroborate his story."

Her gaze rose briefly to Saul, then jerked away as if his fierce demeanor frightened her.

"Others of you may have ideas as to how to discredit Commander Dwyer's testimony or to call his character into question." She nodded at Dr. Branson. "However, as some of you already know, the FBI has requested we not mention Dwyer's association with The Entity. I had no idea what The Entity was until I looked it up," she admitted, drawing in a quick breath.

Lucas peeked at Saul, who very nearly rolled his eyes.

"On the flip side, FBI Special Agent Fitzpatrick assures me that Dwyer will be brought to justice and any sentence handed down to Lieutenant Mills will eventually be overturned."

"Oh, thank God," Eden Mills exclaimed, her tense expression yielding to relief.

"But Dwyer's trial could be months in the making," Carew warned, causing Eden to stiffen again and glance at her husband. "In the meantime, since my client is being unfairly incarcerated," Carew continued, "and since Dwyer is eager to retire, we are both motivated to get this trial done swiftly. All the same, we need to do it right."

She distributed a long sheet of paper to each one of them. "First things first. These are the panel members—the jury, basically—hand-picked by Vice Admiral Holland. All of them are senior officers. My concern is that some may be friends of Dwyer or even members of The Entity itself. We have one opportunity to get Dwyer-sympathizers off the panel, and that's it."

Master Chief knew three of the panel members already and heartily embraced them.

"That leaves these two to research."

Rivera raised a hand. "I'll do that," he volunteered. "I can reach out to their NCOs and get an honest opinion."

Carew accepted his offer with relief. "Thank you. Now we need to list all witnesses to the event and any evidence that might prove Lieutenant Mills's innocence." She glanced at her watch. "We have fifty-six minutes left."

"Let's do this," Lucas agreed, giving his full attention to the task at hand.

CHAPTER 6

harlotte walked from one room to the next in Lucas's open-concept condominium, intrigued at what she found. The newly constructed building had every amenity one could possibly desire—hardwood floors, a gas fireplace in the living room, granite countertops in the kitchen, and a gas-burning stove. It wasn't very big, but devoid of furniture, the rooms seemed immense, and her footsteps echoed loudly, emphasizing her solitude.

Poor Lucas. He had to feel robbed. The only furniture apart from a dinette in the kitchen was a cream-colored sectional sofa and a television. Thank God for the built-in shelving throughout. Without all those shelves, Lucas's books and personal effects would be lying on the floor.

Scanning the shelves in the living room, Charlotte noted with a droll smile how Lucas had categorized his books as either fiction or nonfiction, then shelved them from smallest to biggest. He had a predilection for international thrillers by Tom Clancy and DeMille. Multiple versions of the Holy Bible attested to his faith. But the most revealing artifacts were the framed photos of the people closest to him.

Examining them with interest, she identified the two women hugging him as Justice and Liberty, his sisters. Their eyes and lips betrayed their blood relationship.

Given their friendly faces, Charlotte decided she would like them if she met them in person—not that that was ever likely to happen.

Other frames included photos of Lucas posing with either SEAL team buddies or football buddies. It was hard to tell the difference when they weren't wearing uniforms. She recognized Saul in one picture, hefting his Remington 700, and Lieutenant Mills in another.

Standing up a small frame that had tipped over, Charlotte realized she was looking at the infamous Monica, posing with Lucas in a portrait that been taken the previous Christmas, given the year printed at the bottom. The petite brunette barely came to the middle of Lucas's chest. Her turquoise eyes sparkled with happiness, but it was Lucas's smile of contentment that made Charlotte murmur, "Now there's a man in love."

Keeping her job mattered more than doing the right thing.

Recalling Lucas's words made Charlotte frown. Didn't he realize Monica was as much a victim in this situation as Jaguar was? She would have lost her job if she'd refused to steal the journal as Dwyer had ordered her to.

With a huff of disapproval, Charlotte left the frame standing up so Lucas could see it and reconsider his judgment, even though she now realized it hadn't tipped over but had been set on its face.

Touring the lower level one more time, Charlotte realized she would have to empty her parents' townhouse soon and dispose of the furniture somehow. She'd been putting off the unpleasant task because it was nice to have a familiar place to return to. But Calvin was graduating soon, and her own career in the CIA was about to start. Keeping the historical townhome was impractical. Nor was it right to leave such a lovely home unused.

The sound of a car door shutting wrenched Charlotte's attention outside where the sight of a seafoam-green SUV parked in the driveway jumpstarted her adrenaline. The pretty brunette walking briskly toward the door was none other than the woman in the photo.

Oh, dear. Did Monica still have a key?

With her wig in the kitchen and no time to put it on properly, Charlotte nonetheless backed in that direction as a key slid into the lock.

Yes, apparently, she did.

Heart pounding, Charlotte slipped out of view just as the door swung open and then closed.

"Lucas?" called a voice from the entryway.

Calling out was just a precaution, Charlotte realized. Monica was confident she was utterly alone. The sound of her heels clicking across the dining room confirmed as much. Frozen next to the refrigerator, Charlotte asked herself what she should do.

Just in case, she picked up the pistol Lucas had left with her. Sudden inspiration had her pulling the cell phone Fitz had given her from her purse. She'd refused to charge it like he'd requested so the phone was dead, but only she knew that.

A plan formed in her head as she peeked through the opening at the woman searching the shelves. Monica had paired a navy skirt with a flattering floral blouse and smart navy pumps. Charlotte liked her sense of style. Finding what she was looking for, Monica issued a groan of annoyance.

"You would put it way up there," she groused. All at once, she turned her head, presumably to look for something to stand on, and her gaze collided with Charlotte's.

Shrieking in surprise, she did a tap dance of fear.

Gripping the pistol casually and affecting a Texan drawl, Charlotte approached her. "Can I help you find something, darlin'?"

Monica's eyes widened to the size of saucers. "Who...who are you?" she demanded.

"No one important," Charlotte replied, realizing she couldn't say Justice Strong because Monica had seen pictures of Lucas's sister on the shelf, maybe even met her in person. "The real question is, does

Lucas know you were planning to come over?" She raised an imperious eyebrow.

"Um, no, not really," Monica admitted. "But I only wanted to get one thing I forgot to take with me." Her gaze darted to the vase on the highest shelf. "I'll leave the key when I go," she offered with a nervous glance at the pistol.

Charlotte sent her a hard smile. "Nope. I don't think that's how this is gonna work," she declared. "Unless you want me calling 911 right now to report a break-in," she threatened, holding up the useless phone in her left hand as if about to dial, "then you'll need to surrender that key right now."

The suggestion paralyzed Monica momentarily. "Okay," she agreed. Producing an enormous collection of keys, she riffled through them with fingers that shook.

Charlotte glimpsed a diamond solitaire on Monica's perfectly manicured left hand and realized, with a sense of shock, that his ex-fiancée still wore the engagement ring she'd taken with her when they'd broken up.

Anger prompted her to add, "How 'bout you take that rock off your ring finger while you're at it?" she demanded in a no-nonsense voice.

Monica raised a stricken face and blinked at her. "But he gave it to me."

"Before you betrayed him," Charlotte pointed out.

"Betrayed him how?" the woman shot back, unsettling Charlotte, who secretly sympathized with her. "By doing what my boss told me to do? I have a career, just the same as Lucas. If Dwyer gave him a direct order, he would certainly have followed through or suffered the consequences. How is my situation any different?"

Fortunately, the impassioned question was rhetorical because Charlotte wondered the same thing. Nor was Monica done venting.

Her jewel-like eyes flashed. "Did he tell you I cheated on him or something? Just because I work in an all-male field, that doesn't make me unfaithful. I can't help it if other men try to make moves on me. I'm not about to quit my job because Lucas doesn't trust me. *I'm* not the one who betrayed our relationship. That was *all* him, so I'm keeping the ring!" she added, stamping a small foot.

Charlotte could totally see her point. Nonetheless, she brought up Lucas's objection. "Following orders doesn't justify stealing."

Monica threw her hands into the air. "I didn't know I was stealing! He told me Master Chief forgot to give him something."

"So you broke into Master Chief's office and unlocked his desk to get it back?"

Monica's face hardened, but then her eyes narrowed. "Wait a minute. How do you know so much?"

Instead of answering, Charlotte gestured to the shelves with the gun. "Put the house key on a shelf," she said, retaining the upper hand.

Monica slapped the key down with finality. At the same time, her gaze flickered toward the top shelf.

"What's so special about that vase?" Charlotte demanded, keeping her Texan accent in place while belatedly realizing that since Lucas didn't have one, the real Justice probably didn't either.

"I bought it, and I want it back," Monica answered a tad too quickly.

Charlotte stared at her, waiting for more. Her father had taught her silence was an interrogator's most valuable tool. Most people couldn't stand the tension it created.

Monica was no exception. "If you must know, the vase was a gift from Commander Dwyer for a job well done, and I want it back for that reason." A self-conscious blush suffused Monica's face.

Intrigued, and wishing she could read Monica's thoughts, Charlotte approached the shelf, stood on tiptoe, and managed to snag the vase without the aid of a chair. Monica watched with mistrust as Charlotte inspected the frosted green vase with a trained eye.

Turning it upside down, she pried a plastic covering off the bottom and stared in astonishment at what lay beneath.

She showed the hardware to Monica. "You know what this is?"

The woman shook her head.

"It's a bug. Dwyer asked you to bug your fiancé's house. Were you aware of that?"

Blood actually drained from Monica's lovely face. It was clear to Charlotte she'd had no idea.

"He's probably listening to this conversation right now," Charlotte realized, unsettled by the possibility. Hopefully, he would not connect her to being the recovered Charlotte Patterson.

Without another word, she smashed the butt of her pistol into the device, hopefully hard enough to disable it. Sadly, in the process, the vase cracked down the side and fell into two pieces.

"Please let me go," Monica pleaded, frightened by Charlotte's sudden ferocity.

Looking at her, Charlotte considered her options. She could keep Monica there until Lucas got back and let him deal with her, or she could deal with the situation herself. Considering the bug, that choice seemed to make the most sense.

"Tell you what," she said. "You find yourself a piece of paper and a pen. Write down what you just told me about Dwyer ordering you to break into Master Chief's office and about him giving you this vase. Then I'll let you leave with the ring." Lucas had said he didn't care about it anyway, she reminded herself. And the vase would be evidence.

Monica slid a possessive glance at the rock on her left hand. "Okay," she finally agreed, in a voice strained with emotion. "But what if Dwyer fires me? I'll never get another job in Spec Ops."

"That's not going to happen," Charlotte assured her. "Dwyer is the one who's going to lose his credibility. Believe me, you don't want to go down with him."

Eyeing her with consternation, Monica thought for a moment. Then, fishing in her oversized purse, she produced a pen and notepad.

Five minutes later, Charlotte held a handwritten statement of what Dwyer had requested of his secretary and what he'd given her to put in her fiancé's home. Escorting Monica to the door, she suffered a twinge of her conscience for not allowing Lucas to handle the matter of his ex's intrusion himself.

As she watched Monica slip into her SUV, Charlotte could see why Lucas had been drawn to the woman. She was delicate and beautiful, the kind of woman who summoned a man's protective instincts, the kind a man wanted to cherish. Moreover, in Charlotte's opinion, she deserved to be forgiven for her sins. That was the Christian thing to do, wasn't it?

Perhaps once Lucas saw Monica's handwritten confession, he would find it in himself to forgive her. Then the two would get back together again, just in time for another holiday season.

Struck by her sudden solitude, Charlotte considered the vase she was still clutching. A chill enveloped her as she realized she had quite possibly revealed her whereabouts to The Entity. If Dwyer had been listening in—or would listen at some later point to a recorded conversation—he would certainly want to know why a woman in Lucas's house knew so much about what had happened in Spec Ops. If he asked Monica what the woman looked like, wouldn't he immediately guess she was Charlotte Patterson, wanted by The Entity? After all, how many six-foot-tall, redheaded women were there in Virginia Beach?

Swallowing a whimper of uncertainty, Charlotte turned toward Lucas's kitchen and found a plastic garbage bag in which she placed the vase. To be extra certain, she put it in the refrigerator so, even if the bug still worked, it wouldn't pick up the next conversation she had with Lucas.

"I got a bad feeling," Saul muttered, as they approached Lucas's condo.

Lucas shot him a startled look as he turned into his driveway. "We were gone for an hour. What could go wrong?"

If anything, the day was off to a great start. Lucas had left the pre-trial hearing feeling more optimistic than before about Jaguar's odds of proving their commander was a liar. Between Saul's promised testimony and that of Jaguar's psychiatrist, Dwyer didn't stand a chance of substantiating his fabrication that Jaguar had tried to kill him.

Nonetheless, heedful of Saul's premonition, Lucas parked his truck swiftly and chased Saul to his front door. Before he could unlock it, the door popped open and there stood Charlotte, not wearing her wig.

"Was someone here?" Saul demanded as Lucas shooed her back inside and shut the door behind them.

"Yes." Surprising Lucas, she thrust a piece of paper at him.

"What's this?" Dismay pegged Lucas as he recognized Monica's perfect cursive.

"Read it," she invited both of them. Saul leaned in, and they both read the note in silence.

"Holy crap," Saul swore, looking up at Charlotte in amazement.

Lucas said nothing. Conflicting emotions kept him tongue-tied as he pictured Charlotte and Monica conversing in his house.

"She saw you with your wig off," he realized, glancing at Saul, whose incredulous look turned suddenly wary.

"I didn't have time to put it on," Charlotte told him. "She surprised me, zipping in here after using the key she still had, which I got back for you, by the way."

Withdrawing it from her pocket, she thrust it into this hand. "You can thank me later," she added, spinning away and stalking into the dining room.

"Wait," Lucas called, chasing after her. Both Charlotte's prickly behavior and the fact that Monica had seen her without her wig unsettled him. "Where's the vase she came for?"

"Right here." Spinning away, Charlotte collected the bag of shattered hardware and brought it back to them. "Here's what's left of it."

"What the—?" he began but Charlotte held up a finger to her lips and opened the bag so he could see the vase that used to be on the top shelf. It was clearly damaged. He recalled Monica bringing it home from work one evening, full of summer lilies. She'd set it on the table as a centerpiece for the get-together he was planning with his teammates.

Drawing it out carefully, though it was cracked down the middle, Charlotte turned it over and showed them the underside. "Check it out," she whispered.

It took Lucas several seconds to realize what he was looking at. Surprise vied with betrayal as he took it out of Charlotte's hands to inspect it more closely. Monica had brought a bug into his house!

"I think I've disabled it, but you should check before you say anything more," she told them softly.

He examined it and nodded, satisfied that it was dead.

"It's a high-end VOX, or voice-operated transmitter," Charlotte added, though he already knew what it was. "It probably uses a UHF band, which can broadcast several miles. Like Monica said in the note, Dwyer gave it to her," she added grimly.

The ramifications were clear. Lucas handed the vase to Saul. "It was on the table the night Jaguar talked about his disappearance."

Saul's hazel eyes narrowed. "Then Dwyer heard everything he said that night."

"What did he say?" Charlotte asked.

Lucas raked a hand through his hair and thought back. "Jaguar told us he believed Lowery had turned on him in Carenero and left him for dead. We thought it was crazy talk, but it turned out he was right. Jaguar must have confronted Lowery about the unauthorized emails because Lowery struck him in the face with the butt of his rifle, cuffed him, and left him in a building The Entity was about to blow up."

They all regarded the mangled transmitter with horror.

"So Dwyer overheard Jaguar's suspicions," Charlotte surmised slowly. "And soon after that, Lowery supposedly killed himself?"

"Right," Saul said.

Lucas contemplated Monica's role in the subterfuge they'd uncovered. "I can't believe she helped Dwyer spy on us," he grated. Any lingering affection he felt for Monica vanished.

"Dwyer gave it to her as a *gift*," Charlotte insisted, "apparently to commend her for her hard work. She said she didn't know about the VOX, and from the look on her face, I believe her."

"Hard work?" Saul snorted.

Charlotte rounded on him with a look of indignation. "What are you implying? Just because she's a secretary that doesn't mean she doesn't work hard."

Saul set his jaw and kept quiet.

"None of that matters now," Lucas interrupted, then held up the confession Monica had written. "This is what matters. We want to impugn Dwyer's reputation—this ought to do it. Not only did he ask her to steal, but he used her to put a bug in my house. And here it is," he added, gesturing to the vase Saul still held. "We need to get this to Jaguar's lawyer ASAP. She's got to call Monica and prepare her."

"I'll take this evidence to Carew after lunch," Saul offered.

"She never promised to testify," Charlotte pointed out, "but I'm sure she will if you ask her, Lucas. At the very least, she'll need to be deposed."

Lucas wasn't about to call Monica and have a heart-to-heart chat. "I'll text her," he relented.

He would not, under any circumstances, give her an opportunity to use her charm on him. "Right now, we need to get Charlotte out of here. Grab your bag and put your wig on. We're leaving. You can tell me in the truck what Dwyer might have overheard before you smashed that bug."

CHAPTER 7

*A*nother sleepless night! Again, Charlotte stared up at the ceiling from the bed in Saul's guest bedroom unable to lose consciousness. As the wind sighed through the screen of her open window, the limbs of the huge oak in the yard stirred, casting mesmerizing shadows above her. She had hoped to fall asleep while watching them, but thoughts zipped through her mind like cars on a busy interstate, keeping her alert.

Kicking off the sheet, she rolled out of bed and headed down the stairs as she had the night before in search of Lucas. He was sitting on the sofa in Saul's living room, working on his laptop by the light of a dim lamp. The blinds had been lowered, the curtains pulled. At her approach, his gaze jumped up, turning instantly wary.

"Can't sleep?" he guessed, looking back at his screen.

Charlotte flopped down on the couch next to him. "What do *you* think?"

"I think you have a right to be worried." He tapped the down arrow while clearly searching for something on the spreadsheet in front of him. "If Monica bugged my house for Dwyer, who's to say she didn't go back for the vase because he asked her to."

Charlotte rolled her eyes. "I already told you, Lucas, she had no idea there was a bug in the bottom of the vase, and I believe her."

"Why did she want it back today?" he retorted, still staring at his laptop.

"Because it was given to her for a job well done. She wanted to be reminded of that."

He finally looked at her. "You seriously believe that?"

Charlotte queried her intuition. When it came to people and their motives, she was usually right on target.

"Yes," she insisted. "She's not the villain you've made her out to be. She took LeMere's journal from Master Chief's desk because Dwyer told her to. You'd have done the same thing."

Lucas shook his head while smiling bitterly. "Five minutes in her company and you think you know her," he commented.

"It was more like twenty minutes," Charlotte retorted.

Sighing heavily, Lucas finally met her gaze. "Look, I don't blame you for defending her." A suggestion of warmth crept back into his voice. "Monica can seem entirely innocent when it suits her. She pulled the wool over my eyes," he admitted ruefully. "I'm not going to blame you for not seeing what I couldn't see."

Charlotte decided she would let it go, but not without one last push. "I just think there's a misunderstanding between you two. If you want to work things out, all you have to do is respect her career and trust her integrity. She still wears your ring, you know."

"So I've heard," he clipped.

"She obviously still loves you."

Lucas's eyes narrowed until he was looking at her through his lashes. "Thank you for your advice, Charlotte," he said pointedly, "but it isn't wanted. I don't need a wife whose career comes first."

Stung by his last sentence and chastised by his tone, Charlotte focused on what he was doing. "Looking for the unauthorized emails?" she guessed

He sucked in a breath and looked back at his laptop. "Yes. I finally got access to the server, and I've gone through hundreds of emails from the time Lowery was sending them, but there aren't any here with blind-copied recipients. Someone must have logged in before me and deleted them."

"Dwyer?" she guessed.

"He would have access," Lucas agreed.

"So what's next? What else can we accomplish?"

He sat back and thought. "Well, I've hired a forensic expert, and I've sent him the pictures from Lowery's apartment to look at, but those aren't going to impact Jaguar's trial, I don't think. Jaguar's motion hearing is on Friday. That's when Captain Englert, whom Holland picked to preside over the hearing, decides what evidence will be admissible. Monica's letter and her testimony ought to impugn Dwyer, but I wish there was something more we could use that would demonstrate how he's up to no good. That's not easy without mentioning The Entity. Lowery would have made a great witness, but he's dead. Same thing with Lloyd Elwood."

Charlotte thought for a second. "Why don't we go to Sabena, then," she suggested, "and try to figure out what Lloyd was doing there? He must have found something Dwyer didn't want him to see, or he wouldn't have been killed."

"You said it was a hit-and-run?" Lucas asked.

"Yes, right outside of town."

"Was the other driver ever identified?"

"I don't know. I was about to look into it when I was kidnapped."

Lucas logged out of the email server and did a Google search.

Sliding closer to him, Charlotte enjoyed the scent of sportsman's soap and dryer sheets clinging to him. It was all she could do not to put her nose to his shoulder and inhale deeply.

"Here we go. This was written over a week ago but there's nothing newer." He clicked an article, and they both scanned it in silence.

Police Chief James Blanchard reports no additional leads regarding the identity of the hit-and-run driver who killed Illinois native Lloyd Elwood, a guest staying at Magnolia Manor. Elwood was driving on Highway 227 when he was apparently driven off the road and struck a tree. Police are looking for a white car. Faulty air bags are believed to have contributed to Elwood's death.

"Faulty air bags," Charlotte scoffed, sitting back. "Lloyd drove a two-year-old Taurus in mint condition. I want to know more about this James Blanchard. Did he even look to see if someone tampered with the air bags?"

Researching James Blanchard, Lucas came up with a dozen results, including a picture of the police chief, who was middle aged with a dark mop of hair and a big bushy mustache.

"That mustache looks like Dwyer's," Charlotte commented.

Lucas looked sharply over at her. "You've met Dwyer in person?"

"Yep. Lloyd took me with him when we interviewed Dwyer about Lieutenant Mills's disappearance."

Lucas made a thoughtful sound in his throat and started a new search.

She watched him type "Daniel Dwyer" and "James Blanchard" into the same search bar and hit the ENTER key.

To Charlotte's surprise, a result came up. "What's that?" She leaned on Lucas's arm to peer at the screen.

"It's a wedding announcement from the same newspaper." Opening the link, Lucas read out loud. "*Police Chief James Blanchard marries Anna Dwyer.* Whoa. This was dated two years ago. Is the bride related to the CO? Oh, yes, she is." He read a line farther down the article. "*The bride is the daughter of the late Marshall and Dotty Dwyer. Her older brother, Commander Daniel Dwyer, United States Navy, gave the bride away.* Gotcha, you sneaky crook!"

Charlotte tore her gaze off the article. "Not exactly," she corrected Lucas. "All we have is information linking Dwyer to Sabena, not to mention to the police there. Oh, no!" She clapped a hand to her forehead picturing what might have happened to Lloyd.

"All Dwyer had to do to get rid of Lloyd was to tell his brother-in-law to get rid of him while he was up there. The police chief could have gone after him in his police car. Lloyd would have seen the lights and started to pull over—" Her throat closed as she envisioned the police car ramming into Lloyd's Taurus and sending it off the road into the trees. Grief had her covering her eyes, chagrined to cry in front of Lucas yet again.

He set aside his laptop and promptly put an arm around her.

Leaning into the wall of his body, Charlotte marveled at how right it felt, and how comforting. Maybe because he'd rescued her, she associated him with safety. All she knew was listening to the thud of his heart, inhaling his clean scent, absorbing his heat—he felt like home. Only her father's hugs had ever felt so perfect, but in an entirely different way.

But then she pictured Monica, who'd just been doing her job when Lucas condemned her. With a sharp sniff, Charlotte straightened and scooted away.

At the same moment, Lucas's cell phone vibrated on the end of the couch, and he released her to pick it up.

"It's Fitz," he relayed, shooting her a glance before answering. "Yes, sir?"

Charlotte could just make out the tinny voice on the other end. "Sorry to bother you so late, Lieutenant, but I'm a night owl when I'm working on a case. I've been trying to reach Charlotte all day but her phone doesn't even go to voicemail."

As Lucas looked over at her, Charlotte indicated with very clear gestures that she didn't want to talk to the special agent.

"I'm sorry, sir. She's sleeping," Lucas said, frowning at her for forcing him to lie, "and I'd hate to wake her up."

"Of course. Tell her that her new ID is due to arrive at Chief Wade's address tomorrow morning. FedEx is overnighting it. I need to know if someone will be there."

"Yes, sir. Saul will get it," Lucas stated, forbearing to add that they were all staying at Saul's for the time being.

"Excellent. Make sure she carries the ID at all times. I saw the picture and I'm impressed," he added. "Looks nothing like her."

"I'll tell her, sir."

"Everything going okay?" queried Fitz. "Has the motion hearing been set yet?"

"Yes, sir. Friday morning."

"Good. Good. You'll keep from mentioning The Entity," he reminded Lucas.

"There won't be any need, sir," Lucas assured him.

"I'm glad to hear that. I'm close to making arrests, and I don't need my target forewarned in any way. Do you understand?"

"Loud and clear, sir."

"Good night, then. Thanks again for your help with the girl," he added, hanging up.

"The *girl*? I'm a girl to him? Ugh!" Charlotte threw herself against the back of the couch.

"Why haven't you charged that cell phone he gave you?" Lucas asked, ignoring her fit.

Charlotte folded her arms across her chest and scowled. "I don't trust him."

Lucas cocked his head at her. "Why not?"

"I feel like he knows way more than he's telling us. He acts like he's doing us a favor when all he's done is tie our hands. Sometimes I wonder if he didn't take Lloyd's iPad from me himself."

Lucas looked at her like she was crazy. "Are you suggesting he arranged for your disappearance? Why would he do that?"

"To keep me from getting the iPad to my godfather. He didn't want the DIA involved in *his* investigation."

"He could have just requisitioned the iPad from you," Lucas pointed out. "He didn't need to make you disappear."

"True," she acknowledged. "But then there's the phone he gave me. I feel like he's using it to track my location. If he wanted to talk to me, he could always call you, like he just did." She gestured at Lucas's cell phone.

Her suspicions appeared to amuse Lucas, who was trying not to smile.

"You think I'm delusional," she realized. Dropping her arms, she pushed to her feet and stood a moment, stretching out her back. "Maybe I'm so tired I don't know what to think."

Lucas tore his gaze off her bare thighs. "Try to sleep," he urged, setting his laptop back on his knees.

She heaved a hopeless sigh. "Fine," she agreed, turning away.

Climbing the stairs quietly so as not to awaken Saul, she used the restroom first, then returned to the guestroom. She was heading for the bed when a shadow shifted in the tree outside her window. Freezing to a halt, Charlotte stared into the tree's dark branches. It had to be her tired brain imagining someone out there looking in at her.

The headlights of a passing car strafed the yard and briefly lit up the tree. What Charlotte saw—a man balanced on one of the oak's sturdy branches and regarding her through a pair of night-vision goggles—brought a shriek to her throat. With a loud thud, she dropped to the floor out of his line of sight.

A flurry of footfalls heralded the arrival of a wild-eyed Saul at her door, pistol in hand.

"What happened?" he demanded.

"There was someone in the tree outside," she squeaked.

Saul slid toward her window and used the tip of his pistol to lift one end of the gauzy curtain.

Charlotte remained on the floor, her heart thumping at the realization that Dwyer must have heard her conversation with Monica and wanted to see for himself who she was.

"I see him," Saul said with a growl. "Stay here," he added. "Stay low."

In a flash, he was gone, leaving his dog sitting in Charlotte's doorway regarding her sleepily. Charlotte scooted toward the dog and grabbed his collar.

Straining her ears, she overheard Saul's terse exchange with Lucas. Lucas suggested Saul go out the front while he went out the back. She heard the rear door thud shut, then all was quiet. They'd left her alone in the house, unarmed.

Charlotte regarded the dog she was hugging. "You'll defend me, right?"

Duke's only answer was to yawn.

The open window filled Charlotte with a sense of terrible vulnerability. *I need a weapon.*

Releasing the useless canine, she scooted out of the room and down the stairs on her bottom, paced by Duke, who decided to accompany her.

In Saul's big kitchen, all but one of the blinds were pulled. Keeping her head low, Charlotte crawled on hands and knees toward the butcher block with Duke snuffling her ear inquisitively. She had to stand up to reach the biggest blade.

She had just grabbed hold of it when the back door flew open. Charlotte straightened and whirled as a giant ducked inside. Widening her stance, she envisioned Jason Dunn and drew her hand back, preparing to launch herself at him.

The light flicked on and Lucas reared back, uttering a rare swear word.

Charlotte lowered her weapon and sagged against the counter as the strength drained out of her. "What did you find?" she demanded.

Instead of answering, Lucas approached her with caution and gently pried the knife from her grasp, then slid it back into the butcher block. "You're okay," he said.

She didn't realize she was trembling until he put both arms around her and pulled her tightly to him.

"Whoever it was, he disappeared," he told her. "We saw a car pull away, and Saul ran after it hoping to get the make and model, if not the plates."

"I think it was Jason Dunn," Charlotte said with certainty. "I saw him fairly clearly when a car went by."

Lucas stiffened. "You think Dwyer sent him here because he overheard your conversation with Monica?"

"I think so. We need to leave the area," she added, trying not to panic. "Before Dwyer tells the rest of The Entity where to find me."

Just then Saul appeared from the front of the house, still breathing hard, and Lucas relaxed his embrace.

"I couldn't catch up. It was a black SUV, Escalade probably. That's all I could tell."

"That's what Jason Dunn drives," Charlotte told them. "I'm telling you, that was him. We need to leave the area."

Lucas dropped his arms completely, causing her to feel suddenly bereft.

"I need to think this through." He raked a hand through his short brown hair.

Charlotte waited, confident that he would see things her way.

Saul cast her a look while pulling the refrigerator open. "You okay, ma'am?"

"Please don't call me ma'am," she retorted. "I'm younger than you are."

He sent her an evil grin as he extracted a bottle of juice. "You okay, babe?"

She pointed a warning finger at him. "Not that, either."

Lucas cut in, "We'll leave tomorrow as soon as your ID arrives, and we'll go to Sabena. Maybe we'll find out what your supervisor was up to and why he was killed."

"Magnolia Manor," Charlotte recalled from the news article they'd read earlier. "That's where he was staying."

"I'll check into it," he promised. "You go on back to bed," he added, nudging her toward the stairs.

Charlotte dragged her feet. With adrenaline still cycling through her bloodstream, she knew she wouldn't sleep a wink. "Can't I stay here with you?"

He glanced at the clock on the stove. "My watch is almost up. I'm going to crash on the couch."

Saul drained the bottle in his hand and set it on the counter. "I got it from here, sir."

Charlotte stood at the bottom of the stairs, waffling.

Lucas pointed at the ceiling. "Go to bed."

"I won't sleep," she told him. "Couldn't you...?" She had to swallow her chagrin to get the rest of the words out. "Couldn't you lie down next to me? Please?" she added when he just stared at her.

Saul snickered as he pulled a chair out.

Lucas shot him a glare and looked back at Charlotte. "Will it help you sleep?"

His dubious tone brought Charlotte's hands to her hips. "Yes."

His broad shoulders rose and fell. "All right, then," he agreed, and gestured for her to precede him.

Seconds later, the sturdy bedframe creaked as Lucas shucked his shoes and joined her on the double bed. Charlotte wriggled closer to the wall to give him space. Still, their shoulders touched. Avoiding looking at the window, she heaved a huge sigh of relief and closed her eyes.

"Do you have enough room?" he asked. His voice was like the rumbling of a lion.

"Mm-hmm." The warmth of his body and the security of being tucked so close to him lulled her at once.

"Sweet dreams," he added, squeezing her hand.

That was the last thing she remembered as she fell into a deep, sound sleep.

CHAPTER 8

*I*t was already 10 a.m., and Charlotte's ID had not yet arrived.

In preparation for their departure, Lucas helped Saul guide his midnight-blue Camaro through the gate at the side of his house and into the backyard. There, the dense foliage concealed their activities as they packed the trunk with enough supplies to last them until the motion hearing on Friday. The plan was to leave Lucas's truck in the driveway to mislead The Entity into thinking they were still in the area.

Contributing only the single suitcase Saul had loaned her, Charlotte, dressed in her disguise, chafed to leave. She stood in the kitchen watching the men pack the vehicle with weapons and bags. The likelihood that The Entity now knew of her location kept her on pins and needles, anticipating their departure.

Lucas came into the kitchen for a glass of water.

"Monica returned my text," he announced. "She's agreed to testify in person." He chugged his glass without looking at Charlotte.

"Good," she said. It couldn't be any more apparent that Monica hoped to mend bridges with Lucas. Why else would she have agreed to state in front of Dwyer, who would obviously be in attendance, that he had instructed her to steal for him? Her testimony was bound to get her fired, at least for as long as Dwyer remained the DEVGRU commander.

"Look at that. She's showing you she cares about *you* more than she cares about her job," Charlotte pointed out.

Lucas put his glass down with a thud. Wiping a droplet of water from his chin, he faced her squarely. "I think we should tell Fitz what happened last night," he said, ignoring her comment.

"No." Charlotte's response was purely instinctive. "He asked you to protect me, and no one has grabbed me yet, so I'm fine. He doesn't need to know where we're going either."

Lucas considered her opinion with a furrowed brow.

"All right," he finally agreed. "But if something goes south, he's the first person I'm reaching out to."

"Fair enough," she acceded.

As if on cue, the doorbell rang. Charlotte's heart threw itself against her ribs as Lucas snatched up his Glock and approached the door cautiously.

"It's FedEx," he said, peeking out the window at the truck idling at the curb. Jamming his gun into the waistband of his jeans, he cracked the door and smiled at the deliveryman, who requested his signature.

Seconds later, Lucas handed her an official-looking envelope. Charlotte used the scissors in the butcher block to open it. With Lucas peering over her shoulder, they inspected her new ID together.

"Looks real to me," he pronounced.

Examining her photo, Charlotte wondered if she'd be wearing similar disguises as a case officer in the CIA. To the casual eye, the woman in the photo looked nothing like her.

"Just for the record, I like your red hair better," Lucas told her.

"Thanks." Lifting her head to smile up at him, Charlotte realized he was standing close enough to kiss her if he wanted. He must have had the same thought, for his gaze dropped to her lips. The air in the kitchen seemed suddenly denser and hard to breathe.

Perhaps they shouldn't have slept in the same bed the night before, Charlotte thought. It had them both acting weirdly today.

"I'm all set to leave," she said, moving away to put her new ID into her purse.

"Yep." Lucas strode abruptly toward the door. "I'll go tell Saul."

Lucas kept his eyes peeled for a tail, as Saul, having dropped his dog off at the sitter's earlier, sped them toward the highway. Twisting in his seat at one point to peer out the back window, Lucas caught Charlotte looking at him. He quickly looked away, but not before her lips curved toward a smile that caused his own lips to twitch and his stomach to somersault.

Facing front again, he fretted over his response to her. How could he have known her for merely a few days? He felt like he'd known her for ages. The thought of The Entity pursuing her totally unsettled him. He didn't like the fact that she was forced to disguise herself. The real Charlotte was beautiful—Justice Strong not so much. Ironically, despite the present danger, he anticipated spending the next few days hunting for clues about her supervisor's death.

It took a full hour to cross the Hampton Roads Bridge Tunnel and one more hour of driving through stop-and-go traffic before Lucas could breathe easily. They zipped through the drive-through of a fast-food restaurant for lunch. Then civilization fell away, leaving nothing but fields and farmhouses and the occasional church, all basking in the dog days of summer.

"Hot damn," Saul exclaimed on a gleeful note. "We're in the hicks now!"

Lucas didn't want them letting their guard down. "Let's set a course of action."

Saul cut him a dry look, which he ignored.

"We need to know why Elwood went to Sabena in the first place. What's out here that sparked his interest?"

"How are we supposed to figure that out?" Saul asked.

"By talking to the locals," Charlotte suggested from the backseat. "Someone is bound to know something."

Concern had been gnawing at Lucas for some time. "Don't you think we're going to raise some eyebrows, the three of us going around asking questions?" He didn't bother mentioning the likelihood that someone would recognize him.

"We should split up," Saul suggested. "You and Charlotte can stay at the B&B. I'll do my own thing."

Lucas knew Saul could look after himself, but staying alone with Charlotte in the same room wasn't going to lessen his growing fixation with her.

"I shouldn't be your sister, either," she added, unsettling him further. "I don't know any brothers and sisters our age who go on vacation together. We should say we're married. Easy enough, since I took your last name."

Her solution both dismayed and intrigued Lucas. "We're not wearing wedding rings," he pointed out.

"Because we eloped," she suggested, "and now we're looking for rings in one of the antique stores. Sabena is known for its antique stores," she added persuasively.

With no more reason to protest, Lucas consigned himself to playing a married man for the next few days. *Don't fall in love with her,* he ordered himself.

"Five miles to Sabena," Saul announced, taking the next right on two tires.

They drove through a thick copse of trees, past a church and a sprawling graveyard. The road then spit them out onto a two-lane trestle bridge that hummed beneath Saul's tires.

Glancing down at the body of water beneath them, Lucas figured it looked deep enough for big boats to navigate when the bridge swung open.

"The Rappahannock River," Saul said, reading the map on his console.

A marina with a restaurant marked the edge of town. Saul slowed so they could take in Sabena's nineteenth-century stores and houses, each charmingly distinct from the next and interspersed with century-old boxwoods, oaks, and maples.

"It's so quaint," Charlotte exclaimed, poking her head between the two front seats.

Lucas glanced the map on Saul's console. "Next left coming up, Chief."

They turned into a road flanked by Victorian houses, complete with turrets and towers and porches, all trimmed in ornate lattice work. Huge oak trees blocked out the bright sun and dappled the large front yards.

The road dead-ended at the head of a driveway.

"This is it," Lucas said, reading the hand-painted plaque on one of the brick pillars. "Magnolia Manor, 1796. Wow, it really is a historical landmark."

Saul stopped the car at the head of the driveway and set the parking brake. His hazel eyes twinkled with devilment as he pushed out of the driver's seat.

"Y'all be on your best behavior, now," he ribbed them.

Lucas exited and let Charlotte out of the backseat. Watching Saul stuff his pistol into his duffel bag, he remembered that The Entity was probably already looking for them.

"Check in with me every few hours, Chief."

"Yes, sir." Sending Charlotte a wink, Saul shouldered his bag and headed back toward Main Street. He wore his hair in a ponytail, revealing the gold hoop in his left ear. There was a rip in his jeans, and the sleeves of his shirt were torn away, exposing the fearsome tattoo on one arm.

Over the top of the car, Lucas caught Charlotte grinning as she watched Saul saunter off.

"He looks exactly like a drifter," she marveled before ducking into the car.

Assuming the driver's position, Lucas had to adjust the driver's seat and mirrors to accommodate his height. Charlotte watched him all the while.

"You seem nervous," she commented.

He glanced at her sidelong. "You don't," he noted. In fact, she looked like a woman in her element—a completely different woman than the one who'd quaked with fear the night before. Armed with the new ID, she really *was* a new woman, he supposed.

"Relax," she advised. "No one knows where to find us. Plus, we have a pretty good cover, provided no one recognizes you."

"Maybe I'm the one who needs a disguise," Lucas muttered, pulling them forward down the long, shaded driveway.

Charlotte's eyes widened as the bed-and-breakfast emerged from behind the trees. The whitewashed, clapboard structure was original to the Colonial period and looked like an inn Thomas Jefferson might have frequented, complete with a wraparound porch and dormered third-story windows, all sheltered by impossibly tall pines and oaks.

Lucas parked their car in the designated area, next to two other cars.

"You made reservations, right?" Charlotte asked him.

"This morning," he affirmed.

Feeling guilty for all the expenses he was having to incur while protecting her and helping Jonah, she pushed out of the Camaro and drank in the view.

"It's so peaceful here," she remarked, hearing nothing but songbirds and the sloughing of wind through the trees. "Do you smell that?" She lifted her nose to the warm air. "We're next to the water."

"I can see it." He nodded toward the front of the house then bent to collect their luggage from the trunk. "Come on. Let's go check in. I got it," he added when Charlotte tried to take her suitcase from him.

With a shrug, she preceded him up the steps to the covered veranda. At their approach, the solid wooden door swung open.

An older woman with white hair and plump cheeks beamed at them. "Hello. You must be the Strongs," she guessed, her eyes bright with curiosity. "I'm Eleanor Digges. Welcome to Magnolia Manor." Stepping back, she beckoned them inside.

They stepped into a cool foyer comprised of old oak floors and French blue walls above white wainscoting. Charlotte's gaze went from the oil-on-canvas portrait of an unknown woman to the grandfather clock ticking loudly in the quiet. Then she glanced up the broad wooden staircase winding toward the second and third floors. There were other bed-and-breakfasts in Sabena. Why had Lloyd, who was particularly frugal, chosen this elegant and probably most expensive one to stay in?

"It says on your reservation form you're from Texas," Mrs. Digges remarked as she moved toward an antique desk. "What brings you all the way to Sabena?"

"It's our honeymoon," Charlotte said, casting Lucas a love-smitten grin.

"Oh, isn't that marvelous?" Mrs. Digges gushed. "Congratulations. Won't you sign your names in our guest book?"

"I'll do it," Charlotte offered.

With alacrity and enjoying their role-playing, she penned *Mr. and Mrs. Lucas Strong* into the book. Then remembering Lloyd, she flipped back a page and experienced a pang of sorrow as her gaze landed on his distinctive signature.

As she eyed the names written near Lloyd's to see if they rang a bell, it occurred to her this B&B was the last place he had laid his head. Grief turned her heart as heavy as an anchor. None of the other names meant anything to her.

The sound of Mrs. Digges opening a small cabinet brought her back to the present.

"I've given you the honeymoon suite, courtesy of the manor," the matron announced, taking an old-fashioned key out of the cabinet and handing it to Lucas.

"Thank you," he said, sliding it into his pocket. The tips of his ears had turned red.

He really needs to work on his poker face, Charlotte thought, highly amused.

"Let's get you settled then. Right this way, please."

Following the woman's ample hips up the staircase, they were regaled with a detailed history of the manor from its construction in 1796 to the present day. The creaking treads underscored the manor's antiquity.

As the matron paused on the second story to catch her breath, Charlotte seized her chance to mention Lloyd.

"Didn't the man who died in a hit-and-run stay here?"

The question earned her a startled look. "Well, aren't you well informed," Mrs. Digges commented.

Charlotte shrugged casually. "It was in the newspaper."

"Yes. That poor man." The innkeeper's jowls wobbled as she shook her head sadly. "He was such a pleasant guest. I hate thinking about what happened to him."

"Do you think his death was really an accident?" Charlotte pressed, ignoring the warning hand Lucas placed on the small of her back.

Pale blue eyes focused on her intently. "What do you mean, dear?"

"Well, I hear it was a hit-and-run, yet no one's been accused. I just have to wonder if he wasn't murdered."

"Heavens, no." The mere idea apparently shocked the proprietress. "We don't have crime like that out here. Don't you fret, dear. This area is as safe as they come. This way to your room."

She led them down an L-shaped hallway, lit with intermittent windows that cast bright rectangles of light on the freshly papered walls.

"I'm sure you'll love your room. The entire manor was renovated last year. All the beds have memory foam mattresses, and the bathrooms have rain showers."

Charlotte couldn't resist unsettling Lucas by leaning into him. "Oh, rain showers, honey."

The tips of his ears turned red again.

"Try your key," Mrs. Digges invited.

Inserting the old-timey key into the lock, Lucas released the catch and swung the door open. Charlotte swept in, thoroughly enchanted with what lay inside.

The proprietress backed away. "If there's anything you need, just dial zero. You can leave a message if I don't pick up. Breakfast is served from six to ten each morning. Enjoy your stay!"

"Thank you." Lucas put down their bags and closed the door quietly between them.

Charlotte was busy taking inventory of the room. A four-poster, queen-sized bed occupied the center of the large space. But there was other furniture as well, including an armoire, a vanity and a secretary desk. The walls boasted chair rails and flowered wallpaper.

"Are these real antiques?" Charlotte wondered, sliding open a drawer on the vanity to look at the dovetail grooves. "An excellent reproduction," she decided. "Don't you love this place?" she asked Lucas, who was stowing his suitcase in the large armoire.

"It's nice," he agreed. "I'll sleep in the armchair," he added, nodding at the overstuffed chair as he tucked the pistol he'd removed from his bag into his waistband.

The sight of it reminded Charlotte that they weren't on vacation.

"Don't be ridiculous," she retorted. "We can share a bed like we did last night. I promise not to take advantage of you," she quipped, keeping her tone deliberately light.

Stepping into the bathroom, she noted the white and black tiles and the electric candles in the wall sconces. "Oh, my gosh, there's a claw-foot tub! I'm so going to take a bath," she declared.

Glancing into the mirror, she was taken aback by her unfamiliar reflection. Tucking a stray red hair back under her wig, she articulated the thought that had occurred to her earlier, speaking loudly so Lucas could hear her. "I don't understand why Lloyd would have stayed in a romantic, expensive inn of all places. I know it can't be cheap, and Lloyd was definitely tight with his money."

"Maybe something to do with the view?" Lucas suggested from the other room.

Drawn by his tone of voice, she emerged to find him standing at the window where he'd drawn aside the sheer curtains.

Joining him, she looked down to see an immaculate lawn sloping toward marsh grass and the same body of water they had driven over earlier. The bluish-gray water looked about a hundred feet across. On the other side sat a pier and an old warehouse. Red and black lettering on the weathered siding read *Sabena's Crab and Oyster Company.* One old fishing boat rocked at the pier, but the pilings and the docks appeared brand new.

Something about the view didn't add up.

"I didn't smell anything fishy outside, did you?" she asked Lucas.

He turned a thoughtful gaze to her. "No."

Charlotte looked back at the warehouse. "Maybe crabs and oysters aren't lucrative anymore."

"I wonder what is," Lucas said, pulling out his phone.

"Are you texting Saul?"

"Asking him to check it out," he affirmed.

Charlotte waited for him to finish his text. "Speaking of checking things out, why don't we take a walk into town and start looking for our wedding rings?"

The guarded look he shot her made her add, "We don't have to buy them, Lucas. We're merely adding credibility to our cover."

"I know," he said, but he still struck her as uncomfortable.

"You *are* nervous," she said, repeating her earlier observation. "Because you're alone with me?"

"Of course not," he averred, but his gaze had fallen to the cross he'd given her.

She heaved a sigh. "Look, I understand that you're recently out of a relationship and, trust me, I'm not looking to complicate my life right now. Nor do I wish to take Monica's place."

Not when there's still a chance you two could get back together, she thought as he frowned down at her. "And I can behave myself," she added, "even though your hugs are the best thing on the planet."

Her compliment surprised a laugh out of him. "Really? The *best* thing?"

"You could sell them and be a millionaire," she avowed.

He laughed again, this time with irony.

Charlotte tried to reassure him. "Just think of me as one of your teammates," she advised. "We're buds, right?" she asked, playfully punching him in the shoulder.

Lucas blocked her punch, moving with lightning speed that impressed her.

Charlotte tried punching him again only to be blocked again.

Not to be foiled, she grinned and let loose a one-two tap, managing to slap Lucas lightly on the cheek.

A knock at their door startled them both. They eyed each other with momentary consternation. Then Charlotte threw herself onto the bed, rumpling the coverlet and upsetting the neatly stacked pillows.

Choking back laughter, Lucas went to answer the door, one hand near the pistol holstered out of sight against his hip. Mrs. Digges stood in the hallway with an apologetic expression on her face and a card in her hand. Her gaze shot toward Charlotte lounging on the bed.

"I'm so sorry," she apologized, looking back at Lucas. "I forgot to give you this coupon for dinner at the Marina Restaurant. You would have passed it on your way into town. Fifty percent off the second entrée."

"Thank you," he said, taking the coupon. "Sounds like a great deal."

"You'll love their seafood," the woman promised, backing away.

Closing the door on her a second time, Lucas turned and met Charlotte's gaze.

"How much do you think she heard?" he asked.

Charlotte gave a rueful shrug. "Depends on whether she was standing out there the whole time with her ear to the door."

Lucas crossed his arms and frowned. "I sure hope not."

Rolling off the bed, Charlotte went to search her bag for the other pair of shoes.

"Well, we'd better hop to it," she advised. "Gossip spreads like wildfire in a town this size. By the time dinner rolls around, the whole town might know we're here to check things out."

CHAPTER 9

Strolling hand-in-hand along Main Street, Charlotte admired the quaint storefronts and spacious Victorian homes, all displayed with pride of ownership. The streets were swept clean, the flowerbeds filled with riotous color, and the buildings trimmed in fresh paint. Everywhere she looked Rappahannock River and its estuaries provided idyllic water views. It was hard to imagine The Entity had a foothold in such a pretty place. Given the looks of suspicion she and Lucas were receiving, however, she got the impression outsiders weren't particularly welcome. Was that because the town harbored a secret it didn't want others knowing about?

When Lucas reached for her, her fear of being recognized diminished. She had just told Lucas to think of her as a buddy. Yet merely holding hands with him made her question her own ability to think the same thing. It was hard not to feel cherished, for one thing. For another, the gentle restraint in his powerful hands kept her perpetually aware of him. It was obvious they would have amazing chemistry —*if* they let themselves get involved, which they wouldn't.

She envisioned the Christmas picture in Lucas's house and how happy he'd looked with Monica for his girlfriend. Romance with a SEAL was not in Charlotte's cards, anyway. As soon as Calvin found a job out of school, she was off to the CIA and the future she'd always envisioned for herself. And nothing—not even a wonderful man like Lucas Strong—was going to get in the way of her future.

The sultry afternoon gave way to a cooling breeze as they visited one antique store after another, allegedly looking for a set of wedding bands.

Charlotte used the opportunity to feel out the locals about the mysterious hit-and-run that had killed an out-of-towner two-and-a-half weeks earlier. Several salespersons were eager to gossip but knew nothing. The proprietor of a gift shop shot them a suspicious look and refused to discuss the matter.

"I think that last guy knew something," Charlotte speculated as they made their way, finally, toward the Marina Restaurant.

"He sure clammed up when you brought up the accident," Lucas agreed.

Charlotte lifted his arm to peer at his watch. "What time is it?"

"Almost nineteen hundred."

"Can't you speak civilian anymore?" For the benefit of a couple passing them, she shoved him playfully.

Lucas teased her right back. "Anything for you, baby."

He'd seen her reaction to Saul the other night.

"You know not to call me that," she warned, digging her nails into the back of his hand.

He laughed out loud. "Yes, dear."

The sun dropped suddenly behind the rooftops, deepening the shadows cast by the buildings and prompting the streetlights to blink on.

Charlotte's gaze alighted on the lit sign across the street that read *Second Time Around*. "That must be a consignment shop. Want to check it out?"

"Sure."

They waited for a car to pass before jaywalking.

An open door admitted them into a dimly lit, musty smelling store. Antiques and collectibles abounded, shrinking the walkways and covering every wall. Spying a lit glass case full of jewelry, Charlotte drew Lucas over to it as an elderly woman emerged from a back room.

"Evenin'," she said.

Charlotte glanced up into a pair of deep-set eyes. "Hi, are you about to close?"

"Oh, not for another hour or so. Looking for anything in particular?"

"Wedding rings, actually," Charlotte stated, having used that line at the other stores. "We eloped before either of us had rings to give."

"Well, I've got a nice selection."

"I see that," Charlotte agreed, admiring one ring in particular.

"What about that one?" Lucas asked, pointing out the very ring she was looking at, a band of two metals woven into a Celtic knot.

"That's sterling silver and 18-karat gold." The old lady unlocked the case, retrieved the ring, and handed it to Charlotte.

To her astonishment, the ring slid neatly up her fourth finger, a perfect fit. "It's beautiful."

"We'll take it," Lucas declared, drawing her startled glance. "You like it, don't you, baby?" he inquired.

The forbidden endearment was meant to take her attention off the price tag, she suspected. "Of course, but..." They weren't supposed to actually *buy* rings, only look at them.

"We'll take it," he repeated, pulling out his wallet.

As she watched him pay, Charlotte reminded herself that Lucas was just playing the part. Unlike the princess-cut diamond Monica still wore, this ring didn't mean anything—not that Charlotte wanted it to. Its purpose was to mislead people into thinking they were married. She would give it back when their ruse was over. Maybe that's what he was thinking in any case.

As the older lady ran Lucas's credit card, Charlotte brought up

Lloyd's accident the same as she'd done at the other shops. "A friend of mine was here a couple of weeks ago and recommended Sabena to us. Unfortunately, he died in that hit-and-run that took place right outside of town."

The old lady looked over at her sharply. "You were a friend of his?"

"A good friend," Charlotte said. Lucas, right on cue, rubbed her back.

The woman's expression softened with empathy. "I'm so sorry for your loss."

"Thank you. Some people say it wasn't an accident," Charlotte added, as the woman handed Lucas back his credit card.

Another quick glance. "You'd have to ask the police about that." The cryptic words were uttered on a hard note. "You'll find most of 'em at the Marina Restaurant right about now."

The shopkeeper gestured in that direction with her chin. "Every Tuesday night, the chief of police treats them to dinner."

"That's awfully generous of him," Charlotte commented, sharing a quick look with Lucas.

"He's an elected official, don't you know. Reckon he's just buyin' votes," the woman added on a cynical note. "Here you go, dear." She handed Lucas the slip to sign.

Charlotte deliberated whether to ask more questions. But Lucas straightened abruptly, grabbed her arm, and pulled her toward the door.

"Thank you," Charlotte called over her shoulder on their way out.

Out on the street, they both took a closer look at the Marina Restaurant.

"She's right," Lucas stated. "Every cop in Sabena has to be there."

Charlotte counted at least five cruisers in the overflowing parking lot. Her stomach tightened at the thought of one of them running Lloyd off the road and killing him.

Lucas searched her face. "You sure you want to eat there?"

"We're not going to learn anything back at the Manor," she replied. "Let's stir up the hornet's nest and see what happens."

"Spoken like a true warrior." Reaching for her hand, he glanced at the ring he'd just bought. "Looks pretty on you."

"I'll give it back when this is over," she promised.

"No." Lucas's expression grew serious. "I want you to keep it and remember me when you're taking on the world." He sent her a crooked smile.

It dawned on Charlotte he was as drawn to her as she was to him. If not for their drastically different mindsets, they could have had a one-of-a-kind relationship.

"I will," she promised, saddened by the prospect of parting ways.

He tipped his head at the restaurant. "Shall we?"

Linking hands in a way that was becoming familiar, they headed toward the restaurant, enticed by the delicious aromas wafting inland.

As they approached the entrance, Charlotte saw Lucas adjust the Glock under his untucked shirt so that it didn't stick out so obviously above the waistband of his jeans.

"Do you have a concealed-carry permit for that?" she asked him.

"Of course." He opened the restaurant door and gestured for her to precede him.

The police would be wary of him with or without a weapon, Charlotte figured, stepping inside. The volume in the restaurant dimmed as everyone looked over at them.

Charlotte took a quick inventory. The place was packed. Despite the gaudy light fixtures and laminate tabletops, the scarcity of seating suggested there was no better place to eat for miles in any direction. Water views from the windows on three sides of the restaurant made up for the nineties' décor.

"Two please," Lucas told the hostess, who requested that they follow her to one of the only available tables.

As they passed the gathering of uniformed officers, Charlotte noted that only the cops pretended to ignore them. Everyone else was openly staring.

Lucas offered Charlotte the seat that gave her a view of the room.

"You don't want to sit here?" She had thought he would prefer having his back to the wall so he could see any possible threats coming.

"I'm good," he said glancing pointedly at the window.

Charlotte realized two things at once, and promptly sat down. First, Lucas was worried he might be recognized. Second, he could see the interior of the restaurant in the window's reflection.

"Here is our beer and wine menu," the hostess said, placing it in front of both of them. "And here's our food menu. Your waitress will be with your shortly."

Charlotte was scanning the wines when the waitress appeared and introduced herself. "What can I get you to drink?"

"Just water for me," Lucas said, surrendering the smaller menu.

Charlotte handed hers over, as well, and requested a sweet iced tea.

As the waitress moved away to fetch their drinks, she and Lucas studied the extensive food menu in silence. By the time Charlotte looked up, she was glad to note that people had lost interest in them.

"Here you go." The waitress had returned with their drinks. "Do you need more time to decide what you want to eat?"

"What's your favorite thing on the menu?" Lucas asked, while handing her the coupon.

She glanced at it briefly then tucked it into her booklet. "Honestly, everything." Her bleached-blond head bobbed with enthusiasm. "But if this is your first time, you have to try the flounder stuffed with crab. It is out of this world."

Charlotte's attention was drawn to the table of laughing policemen. The thought that one of them could have driven Lloyd off the road threatened to steal her appetite.

"I'll take that," she said, giving the waitress her menu.

"I'm going to need a second," Lucas said, still poring over the offerings.

"Of course. I'll fetch you some bread while you're thinking," the girl offered, disappearing.

The volume in the restaurant had returned to normal. People were minding their own business, all except one dark-haired officer who struck Charlotte as familiar. With a muffled gasp, she realized who he was.

Leaning over the table, she whispered to Lucas, "Blanchard has shaved off his mustache."

He looked up to search the reflection in the glass.

"He's watching us over his coffee cup," she added, her heart beating faster.

"Let's give him a show then," Lucas said, extending a hand across the table.

Craving reassurance, she took his hand willingly. The certainty of his grasp steadied her pulse. *Why does holding hands with him have to feel so good?*

Their server popped up next to them with a basket of bread. "Have you made your decision yet?"

For some reason, the question made Charlotte think of Monica, and she pulled her hand back to take a roll from the basket. Lucas ordered oysters as an appetizer and shrimp scampi for his entrée.

"Are the oysters farmed from these waters?" he asked, handing the woman his menu. "I noticed a *Crab and Oyster Company* across from Magnolia Manor."

"Oh, no, that's not used for seafood anymore. We get the oysters from a distributor in Maryland."

"Oh, too bad," he said. "What's that building used for now?"

The blonde's brow furrowed as she tipped her head to one side. "You know, I don't rightly know. I can ask Police Chief Blanchard if you like."

Charlotte kicked Lucas under the table.

"Don't bother," he told the young lady lightly. "You have enough to do. Is the restaurant always this crowded?" he added, changing topics.

"Yep. Seven days a week, three hundred and sixty-five days a year. Your food will be right up." With a friendly smile, she moved away.

Buttering her roll, Charlotte asked Lucas in a quiet voice, "Have we heard from Saul yet?"

Lucas peeked at the cell phone riding in the breast pocket of his blue button up. "Yes." He scanned the text then held out the phone so she could read it.

Place is used for shipping marine parts. Job interview tomorrow a.m.

"Impressive," Charlotte murmured, taking a bite out of her roll.

"You can always count on The Reaper," Lucas said, putting his phone away. "Saul's a game-changer. He makes things happen."

A question occurred to Charlotte. "What's your code name?"

"Little John," he replied.

She snorted at the unlikely moniker. "Oh, that's good. I love irony." She lowered her voice so only he could hear. "Plus, if you're Little John, I guess that means Dwyer is Robin Hood?"

"Makes sense," Lucas said with a crooked smile. "Only he isn't stealing from the rich to give to the poor anymore."

"Can I ask you a more personal question?" she persisted.

He sent her a heart-stopping smile. "Why stop now?"

She decided his smile was for the benefit of the couple next to them.

"You don't drink, do you?" she inquired.

He looked away to pick out a roll. "Nope."

"Can I ask why?"

"Well," he said, prying open a pat of butter. "I used to drink—a lot—when I played football. One night I drove my Porsche after drinking way too much at a party, and I got myself into a serious accident."

Her stomach lurched at the thought of Lucas coming to harm. "Were you hurt?"

"Three broken ribs, punctured lung, and a dislocated hip." His eyes clouded over at the recollection. "I flipped my car. By the time it stopped moving, it wasn't anywhere close to the highway. My legs were trapped. I was there alone for hours, in pain that got worse as I sobered up." He buttered his roll but didn't immediately eat it. "That gave me plenty of time to think about what I'd done with my life."

"What do you mean?" she pressed.

He grimaced. "I had turned my back on the values and beliefs my parents instilled in me. I was living pretty much for myself and my own pleasure. And I realized I didn't like who I was or what I'd done, but it was too late because I was going to die that night."

"You thought you were going to die?"

"Thanks to the punctured lung, it got really hard to breathe, so yes."

Pity welled up in her. "What happened?" Obviously, he hadn't died. She darted a look at their neighbors, almost certain one of them was eavesdropping.

"I prayed," he said, looking her in the eye. The pain that had clouded his eyes earlier was gone, making them look illuminated from within, but that was simply the reflection of the glinting water as the sun set outside.

"I said, 'God if You'll let me live, I'll devote the rest of my life to being selfless and following Your will for me.'"

Goosebumps scrambled up Charlotte's arms and made her scalp tingle. Lucas's promise didn't strike her as lip service. Something powerful and real had happened in his mangled car that night.

Thinking of her own lost faith, she felt suddenly adrift without it.

He studied her reaction. "Do you think of me differently now?"

She considered the question for a second. "No. I've always known you were a Christian, Lucas. It shows in you—in a good way," she added, smiling. Her smile abruptly faded.

"Actually, I think I might be jealous," she decided, acknowledging the pinch of hurt she was feeling. "You asked God for help, and He came to your rescue."

Lucas nodded. "Within an hour of my promise, someone found me. They'd seen broken reflectors on the road, so they pulled over and climbed down the hill to investigate."

The urge to cry caught Charlotte off guard. "I'm happy for you," she said. At the same time, she wondered why God had answered Lucas's prayers and yet had ignored her parents' cries for help as their plane plummeted into the ocean.

"Have you lived up to your promises?" she asked, focusing on Lucas once again.

He shrugged modestly. "I've tried to. I quit the NFL, not that I could have played for another year. Then I had to do months of rehab before I could walk again. Once I was cleared to work out, I set my sights on what I thought God wanted me to do—to serve my country —and I trained to be a SEAL."

"And obviously, you made the cut," she replied, marveling at his accomplishment.

He gave a rueful laugh. "It wasn't easy, believe me."

"I know. I've heard there's like an 80 percent attrition rate."

"Sometimes more. My graduating class had seventeen graduates, and we started out at a hundred and twelve."

"Wow. I hope my training at The Farm won't be that rigorous," she said under her breath.

He studied her frankly. "It'll be tough," he said, "but you can do it."

"Thanks," she said, taking his confidence to heart. "That means a lot."

Noticing the waitress heading toward them with their food, Charlotte flicked another glance at Blanchard and found him frowning at his phone. Her stomach cinched at the thought that he might be messaging Dwyer. But how could he possibly have connected her and Lucas to his brother-in-law?

"Looks like you're getting your meals with your appetizer," the waitress said with a slight grimace of apology. "The cook is on fire tonight."

"Fine with me," Lucas assured her.

Charlotte's mouth watered as she breathed the aromas—a blend of oysters, crab, fish, and shrimp, all cooked with butter. A portion of her appetite returned.

"Is there anything else I can get you? Tartar sauce? Ketchup?"

"I think we're good," Lucas said, encouraging her to move away.

Several minutes passed as they gave their attention to their food, pausing now and then to comment on the fare and to exchange bites off each other's plate.

By all outward appearances, Charlotte thought, *we look like a loving couple.* Glancing at the ring on her left hand, she found she loved the way it looked. More than that, she cherished the way she and Lucas were connecting.

The sight of Police Chief Blanchard heading toward their table brought her sharply back to the present. Kicking Lucas under the table a second time, she met the police chief's dark eyes as he bore down on them.

"Evening, folks," he said, drawing up next to their table. "Enjoying the food?"

Charlotte found it difficult to muster a smile.

"Yes, we are," Lucas responded with surprising ease. Dabbing his mouth with his napkin, he gazed up at the police chief enquiringly.

"Visiting from out of town?" Blanchard asked. He hadn't taken his eyes off Lucas.

"We're from Texas," Lucas replied, while Charlotte kept quiet.

"You've certainly come a long way. What brings you to Sabena?"

"We're here for our honeymoon." Lucas shot Charlotte a loving look.

"That right?" Blanchard finally deigned to look at Charlotte. "You must be stayin' at the Magnolia Manor, then. That's where all the honeymooners stay."

Really? Charlotte wanted to reply. More likely Mrs. Digges had told the chief of police all about them, including their curiosity regarding Lloyd's accident.

"You drive a Camaro, right?" the police chief asked Lucas.

Lucas stiffened slightly. "It's a friend's car. Don't tell me the registration has expired."

Blanchard waved a hand. "No, no. Nothin' like that. I check all the cars that run through town. It's good to know who's comin' and goin'. That's how I keep my town so safe. You mind showin' me some ID since I can't tell who you are by your car?"

"No problem." Lucas's tone was still light and nonconfrontational.

Charlotte wanted to protest that it wasn't legal in the state of Virginia for cops to request identification unless a law had been violated. But getting upset over a simple request wasn't worth the possible consequences. As Lucas opened his wallet, she dug into her purse for the ID that had come only that morning. The restaurant grew quiet as Charlotte and Lucas waited for the police chief's reaction.

Blanchard inspected her ID first. Fitz had assured her it would appear authentic. It apparently did, for the police chief handed it right back. It was Lucas's ID that held more interest for him.

"So, it's true," the police chief said, shooting a triumphant glance at his table full of underlings. "You used to play for the Dallas Cowboys, didn't you?"

Charlotte heaved an inward groan while awaiting Lucas's reaction.

"Yes, I did," he admitted with grace. "You caught me."

"Hah! I thought so." Smiling with more warmth, the police chief handed back Lucas's ID. "The fellas owe me ten bucks apiece," he admitted. "And I thank you very much for proving me right."

"You are very welcome." Twisting in his seat, Lucas smiled wryly at the table full of glowering patrolmen.

Blanchard inclined his head in farewell. "You two have a good night. Enjoy your stay."

"Thank you."

Charlotte and Lucas went back to eating, and the police chief returned to his table. They said nothing about the episode until the volume in the restaurant had returned to normal.

"What do you think?" Charlotte asked, taking a sip of her tea. "Has he been texting Dwyer this whole time?"

Lucas moved the noodles around on his plate. "I don't think so. I think he was looking up pictures of me and making bets with his men."

"Then we're good." Charlotte couldn't bring herself to fully believe it. "Unless Dwyer told his brother-in-law that one of his SEALs used to play for the Cowboys," she added under her breath. "I really don't want to see Jason and Laura Dunn again," she admitted to Lucas.

"We're good," he assured her, putting a hand on the table for her to take.

Playing the part of his new bride, she immediately took it. She'd have taken his hand regardless.

Lucas's eyes glimmered with a teasing light. "You having fun yet, Justice?" he inquired.

"Totally," she agreed, aiming for a note of sarcasm. Truth was, she couldn't remember the last time she had felt so content. Pretending to be married was fun, but only because Lucas was her partner. She caught herself thinking loving him would be so easy, if only he could accept her career choice.

"So, you don't want a wife who works?" she prompted, feeling him out.

He shot her a startled look. "Sure, you can work, honey. But the kids and I still need to come first."

Even knowing he was role-playing, she could tell he was serious about the kids. "Children?" she asked quietly. "How many are we having?"

"Three, at least," he said sincerely. "Not right away, of course," he added, no doubt reading the dismay she couldn't hide. "One every couple of years."

"You've planned that, too, huh?" Under the guise of needing to wipe her fingers, she withdrew her hand from his.

"I guess I have, but I'm starting to wonder if God has different plans for me."

She decided he was referring to his breakup with Monica. Obviously, his timeline would need some adjusting unless he got back together with her.

"Don't give up on her," she advised.

"Who?" Lucas asked, frowning.

"Monica, of course." Banishing her sudden disappointment with thoughts of the exciting career awaiting her, Charlotte added, "What should we do after dinner?"

He glanced casually over his shoulder. "Head back to the Manor and stay there," he decided. "I think we'd better keep a low profile for the rest of the night."

"I agree. Let's pray Blanchard doesn't get on Facebook and boast about Jonathan Strong visiting his corner of the universe," she murmured. *Jason and Laura Dunn could be after me before midnight* came the unsettling thought.

"Praying never hurts," Lucas agreed, hailing their waitress.

CHAPTER 10

Lucas tried to sleep in the overstuffed chair in their room at Magnolia Manor. The chair was comfortable enough. He had propped a pillow between the chair and the wall, giving him a headrest. Even so, sleep eluded him, which was fine. He was supposed to be keeping watch and couldn't afford to sleep too deeply, given Police Chief Blanchard's relationship to Dwyer.

Unrelated thoughts occurred to Lucas as he listened, with his eyes closed, to the eerie quiet of the old house. Every now and then a floorboard would groan in the hallway, causing him to lurch upright, fully awake. If Commander Dwyer had confirmed Charlotte's identity through the man poised in the tree outside of Saul's house, The Entity was swarming by now to locate her.

You can't have her, Lucas thought as memories of their evening together panned pleasantly through his mind. He enjoyed himself with Charlotte in a way he never had with Monica. Quick-witted and willing to take risks, she kept him on his toes, waiting to see what she would do or say next. Life with her would never get boring, he acknowledged.

For a moment in the restaurant, he had questioned his carefully planned future. What if God meant for Charlotte to be his partner in life? The possibility had electrified him, but then he'd quickly come to his senses. Her career plans were even more demanding than Monica's. Plus, Charlotte's expression when he'd mentioned having children couldn't have made it more apparent they weren't on the same page at all.

What a shame, he thought, saddened by the prospect of watching her go on her merry way.

He turned his thoughts to more practical concerns, like whether visiting Sabena had been a good idea, or not. Luckily, Blanchard had seemed more interested in who *he* was than in who Charlotte was, but that could have been a pretext. Who was to say Commander Dwyer's brother-in-law wasn't a member of The Entity himself?

"No!"

Charlotte's frightened cry brought Lucas fully awake. He turned his head to look at her.

Enough moonlight penetrated their drawn curtains that he could see her lying as rigid as a board on the four-poster bed. She had managed to kick off both the sheets and bedspread while thrashing earlier. Lucas figured she was probably cold and having bad dreams because of it.

Leaving his pistol on the arm of the chair, he got up to draw the covers over her. He was pulling them to her shoulders when she lurched with a gasp and locked her arms around his neck in a chokehold, not a loving embrace.

"Hey, hey," he croaked, impressed with her strength. "It's me," he added, before she could cut off his airway.

Her grip slackened and she reared back with a look of horror on her face. "Did I hurt you?"

"Almost," he admitted with a laugh. "I was pulling your covers up," he explained before she could ask. "Sounded like you were having a nightmare."

With a despairing groan, she pushed herself into a seated position. "Yeah. It's always the same one."

The helplessness in her voice tugged at him. "You want to talk about it? Maybe that'll help."

She regarded him a moment in the shadows, then reached over and switched on the lamp next to her. Her hair, a disheveled red halo, framed a face that struck him as haunted.

"All right," she agreed, though her voice was hesitant as if she abhorred admitting to any kind of weakness.

Lucas sat on the edge of the bed by her knees and waited.

"I dream that I'm in the plane with my parents when it's crashing," she said at last.

Dear God. He should have realized this would be about her parents' accident. He wasn't sure he could actually help her feel any better. "What happens in the dream?" he prompted.

Instead of answering right away, she told him, "My dad was the pilot. Did I ever tell you that? He had his pilot's license, just like you do, and he owned his own plane, a Cessna Citation. When I was younger, he used to take me up in it and teach me the rudiments. So, in my dream, I'm the copilot, kind of like when I was a kid. All of a sudden, the plane does this nosedive, and I realize my father has had a heart attack or something. He's passed out over the yoke, pushing it forward and causing the plane to dive. I yell for my mom and, together, we pull him out of the pilot's seat."

"Is that what happened to your father? He had a heart attack?" Lucas gently queried.

"No. The last time anyone heard from him, he was over the ocean, issuing a mayday about engine failure."

Her voice broke on the final word, and the tears hovering in her eyes slid soundlessly down her cheeks, wringing Lucas's heart.

He longed to hug her, but he feared that wasn't the best idea. She was vulnerable, and he was far, far too drawn to her to trust himself.

"In my dream," she forced herself to keep talking, even though her voice quavered with emotion, "my mom is working to resuscitate my dad, and no one is there to fly the plane but me."

Chewing her lower lip, she fought to keep her composure. "I try. I really try to remember everything my father has taught me, but it was so long ago that I can't remember what to do."

Her face crumpled suddenly, and more tears rolled down her cheeks.

Lucas changed his mind about keeping his distance. *Give me strength, Lord,* he pleaded, closing the space between them. Not comforting Charlotte would be cowardly.

Holding her, he offered whatever consolation his embrace might bring. She'd said earlier that his hugs were the best thing in the world —an exaggeration, no doubt, but they were all he had to offer at the moment.

Hiding her face against his shoulder, she sobbed in heartbreaking silence.

"Let it out," he heard himself urge. *Speak through me, Father. Give me the words.*

"It's okay to cry, baby." The endearment caused him momentary concern. But they'd been acting as newlyweds all afternoon and evening, and the word slipped out before he could stop it. Luckily, she didn't seem to notice.

"It's over for them," he added, wanting desperately to console her. "They're free and at peace and together. The world can't hurt them anymore."

Charlotte went still at his words, then she tipped her head back to look at him. Her red-rimmed eyes stared directly into his. Her lungs convulsed as she drew a deep breath.

"I do think of that," she choked out.

He nodded with encouragement.

"My mother loved God. My father never talked about Him but he always went to church," she added.

A clear image of her parents popped into his head.

"I just don't understand why God let them die like that," she contin-ued, anger creeping into her voice and wiping the smile from his face. "Knowing the whole way down that they weren't going to make it?

Why?" Her eyes implored Lucas to give her an answer that might possibly restore her faith.

Lucas listened for the still small voice inside to provide an answer, but all he heard was silence. Raising a hand to her face, he wiped the moisture from one cheek with the pad of his thumb. His gaze fell helplessly to her lips, pink and tremulous. The longing to kiss her welled in him.

"I don't know, Charlotte," he whispered regretfully. "All I can tell you is what I think—that death isn't as awful as we make it out to be. I think this because I thought I was going to die. There's peace in it. I had regrets, but I wasn't afraid. Maybe they weren't afraid, either. You say your mom loved God. Then I have to think that God was with them the whole time. He could have taken them to heaven even before their plane hit the water."

She seemed to hang on his every word. "I never thought of that," she whispered.

"I think death is so much harder for those left behind than for the ones facing it."

She drew a deep, shuddering breath.

"You've suffered more than they ever did, baby. You can stop now."

He only meant to comfort her. Whether he bent his head or she lifted her mouth to his, he couldn't say, but suddenly they were kissing, and it was too late to stop—not that he wanted to. On the contrary, he wanted to convey all the comfort and admiration and attraction he felt for her in a way that she would never forget.

A long time later, he lifted his head for air and to relieve the clamoring in his blood and body.

Charlotte stared up at him with an expression of astonishment. "That was nice," she said, but her tone conveyed it was far more than that.

To his bemusement, she slipped out of his grasp and scooted off the far side of the bed.

"I need a minute," she explained on her way to the restroom.

As the door clicked shut between them, Lucas cleared his thoughts with a deep breath.

He told himself to get up and go back to the chair, but he couldn't seem to move. The taste, the texture of Charlotte's mouth lingered in his memory. His heart thudded, working hard to move the blood that seemed to have turned to glue inside of him.

The light under the bathroom door went out, and his pulse accelerated. The door opened and Charlotte edged out, pausing when she saw he hadn't moved. They regarded each other in the lamplight for what seemed an eternity.

"Do you think you can sleep now?" Lucas heard himself ask.

The question seemed to relax the set of her shoulders. "I think so." She sent him a small smile. "Thank you, Lucas."

Disappointment vied with relief. Apparently, Charlotte was as torn as he was.

"You don't have to thank me." He got up, freeing her to get back into bed.

"Yes, I do," she insisted, as she lay down, carefully avoiding his gaze. "I'm going to find a way to pay you back for everything."

Disappointment clawed at him, but he was grateful for her reluctance to deepen their intimacy. Clearly, she had plans for her future, and they didn't entail getting involved with a SEAL.

"Sweet dreams," he said, settling back into the armchair. "I'll be right over here."

"Sweet dreams." Her tone was distinctly poignant. He could tell she was wishing he would hold her as he had the night before in Saul's guest bed. But they'd moved beyond the stage that allowed for platonic comfort toward something far more complicated—a desire that had no place in the futures they'd carved for themselves.

Closing his eyes, Lucas allowed himself a moment to wallow in pointless longing. Then he rose above his yearnings and focused, instead, on the big picture.

They were here to find out what had brought Lloyd Elwood to

Sabena. With luck, tomorrow they would do so—before the chief of police communicated with his brother-in-law.

~

It was a hot September day. So hot that it would take an afternoon thunderstorm to cool the steaming landscape. But there could be no relief for her and Lucas.

Setting the canoe paddle across her lap, Charlotte rested her tired arms and let Lucas, who sat behind her, row them the rest of the way across the river.

Following breakfast in Magnolia Manor's elegant dining room, they had selected a canoe from the small fleet made available to the guests. Curiosity drove them to get a better look at the warehouse where Saul was undergoing a job interview while getting a look inside. As soon as his interview was over, he had promised to call them.

With workers on the pier preventing them from venturing too close, Charlotte and Lucas turned their canoe upriver and bird-watched. A pair of ospreys circled overhead, diving occasionally for fish. Charlotte spotted a blue heron standing as still as a statue at the water's edge.

Flapping cooling air under her long-sleeved, fuchsia-colored blouse, Charlotte nonetheless basked in the peacefulness that came from being on the water. Even through closed eyes, she could see the sunlight glinting on its sparkling surface. The waves slapped rhythmically on the fiberglass hull, and one of the ospreys let loose with a keening cry that epitomized the sound of freedom.

For the hundredth time that morning, Charlotte relived the kiss she and Lucas had shared, and her heart lifted.

As kisses went, she had to admit she'd experienced nothing like it. The tender pressure of his mouth, almost reverent, had ignited a fierce quickening in her, which demanded something she couldn't give—her heart and soul. Thank God she'd found the wherewithal to retreat into the bathroom in search of her common sense.

She could tell he'd been as shaken by the episode as she had, which was a consolation. At least he hadn't been thinking about Monica while kissing her.

She craned her neck to glance back at him. Lucas was still paddling. Wearing his sunglasses, his hair ruffled by the wind, he sped them across the water with powerful strokes of the paddle. It was hard to tear her eyes off him. Her desire for him was building like the clouds she could see bunching up on the horizon.

Beyond their role-playing, what would be the point of getting involved in a real-life relationship, she asked herself? Her plans demanded all her energy and focus. After nine months of training, she would be sent abroad as a case officer. Nor was it practical to indulge in a temporary fling, certainly not with Lucas, who didn't seem like the type. He'd be better off repairing his relationship with Monica.

The shrill ring of his cell phone fractured Charlotte's painful thoughts. The canoe wobbled as he put the paddle down to answer it.

"Go ahead," he said.

Charlotte looked back at him again. Saul had to be telling Lucas where to rendezvous because he was scanning the shoreline, looking for something.

Charlotte faced forward and looked, too.

"I see it," he stated, just as she spotted a black sock tied to a branch hanging out over the water.

Putting his phone away, Lucas picked up the paddle again. Charlotte pitched in to help, and in less than a minute, they were gliding onto a flat bit of shoreline and into the cool shade afforded by cedar trees. Not a soul seemed to be watching them, but the sock indicated otherwise.

Hopping off the front of the boat, Charlotte tugged it far enough onto shore that Lucas could make his way up the middle and step out.

"Thank you." Taking over, he pulled the rest of the canoe ashore, then turned to assess their environs. A squirrel scampered across the ground, and several birds darted in the branches overhead. Aside from the usual forest inhabitants, the place appeared deserted.

"Is Saul even here?" Charlotte asked, suddenly wary of a trap.

"Definitely," Lucas assured her with a glint in his eyes. "Stick close," he advised. "You're not going to see him unless he wants you to."

Hurt sliced through Charlotte as he turned his back and proceeded into the forest ahead of her. Yesterday, he would have taken her hand.

That was role-playing, she reminded herself, before trailing Lucas into the eerily quiet woods.

～

Fallen leaves crunched under Lucas's tennis shoes, frustrating his ability to hear. It was broad daylight, for goodness' sake, with sunbeams shooting through the branches to brighten the woods around him. He ought to be able to spot Saul before The Reaper could startle him.

To give Charlotte credit, she hung back far enough that she wasn't adding her noise to his. Sensing an ambush, Lucas paused under a massive oak tree and turned in a slow circle, then nearly jumped from his skin as Saul materialized right next to him.

Charlotte, who must have received a signal from Saul not to give him away, chuckled at Lucas's reaction.

Grinning, Saul, who looked like a woodsman, dressed all in khaki with his hair hanging loose about his shoulders, handed Lucas a piece of paper.

"What's this?"

"Sketch of the warehouse. My interview didn't go so well. Once I told them I was from Oklahoma, it was all over. They're leery of outsiders. But at least I got a good look around."

"And?" Charlotte rounded Lucas so she could see Saul's drawing. "Oh, wow," she exclaimed. "You call this a sketch?"

Saul's artistic abilities were well known to the troop, who exploited his talent whenever taking photos wasn't an option. His sketch was, in fact, a detailed blueprint of the parts of the warehouse he had seen. To

Lucas's way of thinking, there was only one reason why Saul would go to such trouble.

"Let me guess," he said. "They're not shipping marine parts."

Saul's hazel eyes narrowed. "Can't tell for sure, but you'd think if they were, I'd at least see some propellers lying around or anchors and stuff, right?"

"But you didn't," Lucas guessed.

"Nope. Everything was in crates. Not boxes, mind you, but crates, the way weapons are packaged. What's more, there's an elaborate security system on all the doors." Excitement tinged Saul's normally laid-back drawl. "Get this. I asked who owned the building and the name I got was Lewis Blanchard, who's cousins with the chief of police, who's the brother-in-law of our very own Commander Dwyer. I think we've found Dwyer's stash, sir."

Lucas swung a stunned look at Charlotte, whose jaw dropped.

Behind the lenses of her black-framed glasses, her cherry-brown eyes went wide. "Lloyd must have realized it, too. No wonder they killed him."

Lucas reeled. If they had, in fact, stumbled on the weapons stolen by The Entity then the FBI deserved to know about it.

"We have to tell Fitz...but not until we're sure," he qualified as plans started to form in his head. "Chief," he said, refocusing on Saul, "do you know if there's a dive shop anywhere in this town?"

"There isn't," Saul replied. "Already thought of that. There's only a general store selling end-of-season swimming equipment. Dang it, I knew you'd suggest we swim in." Even though Saul was a SEAL, he detested dives of any kind.

"Swimming is the only way in if there's a security system," Lucas pointed out.

Saul considered the facts with a long-suffering expression.

Charlotte spoke up suddenly. "I'm going, too, right?"

The question threw a sudden wrench into Lucas's developing plans. "Uh...."

"You can't leave me alone," she reminded him, a distinct flush under the foundation on her face. "Fitz told you not to let me out of your sight."

Lucas looked to Saul for help but got only a sardonic eyebrow lift.

"Charlotte." Lucas reached for her shoulder only to have her shrug away from his touch. "We've been trained to swim in the dark, where there's a current—"

"Catfish and cottonmouth snakes," Saul summed up, causing Charlotte's determined expression to waver.

Then she brightened suddenly. "You could let me in once you're inside the building."

"Exterior cameras," Saul countered, "Little John's right. Only way in is to swim in. Open any doors, and the police will show up in minutes."

Lucas sought to reassure her. "It'll be okay. You're safe at the inn. Dwyer doesn't know we're here." At least, he hoped that was the case.

Eyes glinting dangerously behind her glasses, Charlotte notched her hands on her hips. "If you're wrong and I'm taken again, I will never forgive you."

Saul raised both eyebrows this time and waited for Lucas to say something.

"No one is going to snatch you away tonight," he promised her. He wished he could hug her to reinforce his assertion, but she looked pricklier than a cactus at that moment.

"How do you know?" A bead of sweat rolled from her temple, informing him that the wig was uncomfortably hot.

"Because I'm leaving you my pistol and my HK. Just don't shoot Mrs. Digges by mistake," he added, hoping to bring a smile to her face.

When her mouth stayed in a firm, flat line, Lucas turned his attention back to Saul. "Pick up whatever gear you can get, Chief, and we'll insert tonight. I'll bring the reconnaissance camera."

"Yes, sir."

Charlotte interrupted. "How are you going to bring a camera through the water?"

They both responded at the same time, "It's waterproof."

With a sound of disgust, she wheeled away, pretending disinterest in the rest of what they had to say.

Lucas took one more look at Saul's drawing. When the garage-type doors were raised, big boats could pull up inside to unload without anyone observing them. Sabena, accessible via the Atlantic Ocean and the Chesapeake Bay and situated two hours from Washington, DC, was the ideal spot to harbor the weapons The Entity had been stealing —weapons that were unorthodox and ruthless and normally used by unfriendly countries.

Like the SEALs, The Entity didn't want America's enemies getting their hands on the arms. Unlike the SEALs, they weren't destroying the weapons or dismantling them. They were hoarding them to make America the mightiest nation of all. And that, in Lucas's opinion, was a prelude to war.

"All right, Chief." Having memorized the building's layout, Lucas handed the drawing back to Saul. "Let's rendezvous at the Manor, down where the canoes are kept, at 2200 hours. Call me if you need a pickup. All we're going to do until then is eat and hang out."

"I'll walk there," Saul volunteered. "This entire town is less than three miles across. And there ain't no Uber out here, either," he added with an intentionally thick dialect.

"Just the way you like it," Lucas reminded.

"That's right. See y'all. Bye, ma'am."

"Bye, Saul." By the time Charlotte turned around, he had disappeared. "Wow," she said searching the woods for any sign of him. "You weren't kidding."

"Nope." Lucas's smile faded as he beheld the glint in Charlotte's eyes. She was still stewing over the prospect of being left alone later.

"Come on," he said, starting back to the canoe. "Let's go whip up an appetite. Then I'll take you out to lunch."

CHAPTER 11

The late-summer storm that had been building all day broke soon after they returned from eating pizza. As Lucas kicked off his shoes and sprawled face-first across the bed to take a nap, Charlotte turned the armchair toward the window and watched the storm wreak havoc.

Thunderstorms had always enthralled her. The treetops foamed beneath a powerful breeze. Lightning jagged from a leaden sky, and thunder rumbled, shaking the old house with its force. She caught herself thinking, *God is awesome.*

It had been years since she'd contemplated God, let alone talked to Him. Thanks to Lucas, she had a new perspective about what had happened to her parents. Maybe God hadn't turned a deaf ear to their cries. Maybe He'd been with them in their final moments, comforting them, giving them a sense of peace.

Looking back out the window, she envisioned her parents in heaven. Lucas was certainly right about one thing—they were at peace, now. Nor had death obliterated them completely. She could still feel them, still remember the sound of their voices. Moreover, she was sure that, one day, she would see her parents again, face-to-face. So, despite having blamed God for her parents' passing, she still believed in eternal life, still believed in Him.

She would be forever grateful to Lucas for pointing that out to her. She wasn't as alone as she'd thought she was. Maybe she should start talking to God on a more regular basis.

Bit by bit, the storm outside subsided, drawing in its wake a steady downpour that dimpled the surface of the river and obscured the other side. Guessing that a cool front had moved in, Charlotte touched the windowpane and ascertained she was right.

Lucas's chiming cell phone woke him up. With a sharp breath, he rolled over and reached for it. "It's Saul," he said, looking alert and refreshed as he texted back.

"Are you still planning to go with the weather like it is?" Charlotte asked him.

He lifted his gaze to look at her. "Yes," he said with a hint of apology.

"It's like twenty degrees colder," she pointed out. "You could get hypothermia."

His handsome mouth quirked. "SEALs are trained to withstand cold temperatures. We'll be fine."

"Did you bring a swimsuit?" she persisted.

"No. I'll have to swim in these shorts."

"I just wish there was something I could do," she lamented.

"There is," he assured her. "Stay put and stay safe. I don't want to have to worry about you."

She glanced outside where it wasn't yet dark. "What do we do in the meantime? It's only six o'clock."

Their gazes collided, and the room seemed suddenly much smaller.

"Know any card games?" Relieving the tension, Lucas jumped from the bed and opened the drawer of the old-fashioned secretary, lifting out the deck he'd spotted earlier.

"Oh, you are going down," Charlotte warned, warming to his idea. "Where can we play?"

There wasn't any flat surface in the room besides the bed. They both looked at it, then looked at each other.

"Down here," Charlotte decided, sliding off the chair onto the floor.

With a groan, Lucas lowered himself onto the rug facing her.

With the rain drops pattering the windowpanes and the sky darkening, they played Egyptian Rat Screw with the slap rule and Beggar my Neighbor, both of which got slightly out of hand. In spite of a fair amount of friendly bickering, Charlotte won the majority of the games, proving her boast to be correct.

They ate the pizza left over from lunch, then Lucas packed his suitcase in the event they would be leaving that night. That depended, of course, on what they found.

If The Entity was, in fact, storing weapons in Sabena, they would take their photographic evidence straight back to Virginia Beach, delivering their proof to Fitz's office in Norfolk first thing in the morning.

"You need to pack, too," Lucas said to Charlotte.

"I will."

Packing would take all of ten minutes. Then there'd be nothing to do but stand at the window, straining her eyes in the hopes of glimpsing the SEALs do their thing. Any stray noises coming from the hallway would make her think Jason and Laura Dunn had tracked her down and were coming to abduct her again.

"Here." Lucas passed her his Glock. "Show me what you know."

She proceeded to impress him by removing and engaging the magazine and aiming at a spot on the wallpaper while he gauged her accuracy by standing behind her.

All the while, she was conscious of his proximity, his familiar and comforting scent. The urge to turn around and kiss him made her bite down on her lower lip.

"What about the HK?" she asked. "I could use a lesson on that."

"You're not going to need it," he assured her. Nonetheless, he snatched it up and taught her how it worked before transferring it to her grasp.

Charlotte raised the butt of the surprisingly lightweight subma-chine gun to her shoulder and sighted down the barrel. "Yeah, this thing freaks me out," she admitted, handing it immediately back to him.

He put it by his bag and glanced at his watch. "Ten till," he said, stripping off his short-sleeved polo.

Charlotte went lightheaded at the sight of Lucas's bare chest. She'd honestly never seen anything quite so impressive, not even in under-wear commercials. Defined muscles rippled under a smooth layer of almond-colored skin. He sported no chest hair, apart from a dusky line of soft-looking down that bisected his abdomen.

He's not yours to look at. Tearing her gaze off him, she reached for her water bottle.

Lucas wriggled his feet into a pair of leather-thonged flip-flops, drawing her gaze back to him.

"And I thought I had big feet," she commented.

"Don't hate," he retorted, shooting her an amused look. "Listen, I'm leaving my cell phone in the side of my bag, right here." He leaned over and patted the pocket it was in. "If I need to reach you, I'll call it. You really should charge the phone Fitz gave you, you know."

"I don't like being spied on," Charlotte retorted.

"Then charge it but don't turn it on," he suggested, while glancing at his watch again. "That way you can use it if you have to."

He had a point, she realized. "Okay," she agreed. "I'll do that now. I assume that's waterproof, too?" she asked, pointing at his fancy watch.

"Of course." He smiled up at her, and they both fell quiet. His gaze focused on her face. "Keep your disguise on till I'm back," he added. "We'll probably be leaving tonight."

"I know."

He looked like he might hug her before heading to the door. Instead, he grimaced and spun away, letting himself out quietly.

"Bye," she called as the door clicked shut behind him.

Knowing he planned to sneak out the back of the house, Char-lotte went to stand by the window so she could watch Lucas's shadow streak toward the canoes. But in the absence of moonlight and with the rain falling in a silvery curtain, she never caught sight of him.

She was almost certain they would be leaving that night. That warehouse had to be the reason Lloyd had come here in the first place, the reason why he'd been killed. It occurred to Charlotte there actually *was* something she could do. She didn't have to sit around feeling helpless or hunted, after all.

Even in the dark, Lucas could see Saul shudder as they waded into mud. Grateful for the water's warmth and the flippers that protected their soles from sharp mussel shells, Lucas adjusted his mask and bit down on his snorkel. He'd be even more grateful if the flippers Saul had procured weren't two sizes too small for him.

With no weapons between them except the blade strapped to Saul's thigh, they gripped each other's wrist as the water deepened. When it reached their bellies, they each sucked in a big breath and went under. Lucas gave a squeeze, and they struck out, still holding onto each other and counting every other kick.

Swimming just beneath the surface with the rain drumming their watery rooftop, darkness surrounded them. They kicked in a steady, synchronized rhythm, forging the brackish water swiftly. Lucas noted a small leak in the seal of his mask, but it wasn't bad enough to merit stopping.

Surfacing on the count of thirty, they cleared their snorkels and drew air. Clearing his mask, Lucas estimated they were near the middle of the river. A light current tugged at them. He consulted the compass glowing on his tactical watch and corrected their bearing accordingly. With another squeeze of the wrist, they submerged a second time, counting to thirty before surfacing to assess where they were.

The warehouse pier jutted up in front of them, frosted by the light coming from the scant windows. Lucas would have preferred to insert into a warehouse dark as pitch.

Submerging again, they went all the way under, proceeding past a forest of barnacled pilings. The light from inside the warehouse filtered through the water, turning the dark void into an underwater landscape full of darting fish, sunken branches, and bits of lost tackle, including a crab pot.

Following a trough dredged into the muddy bottom, they swam beneath the garage doors and into the bay inside the warehouse.

Lucas signaled that he would surface first. Pressing himself close to the slimy bulkhead, he peeked above the waterline into an empty berthing area. When no alarm sounded, he signaled the all-clear to Saul and raised his mask, draining the water that had leaked inside. Saul bobbed to the surface next to him. Together, they took in what the halogen lights illuminated—row upon row of crates, stacked clear to the back wall.

No one appeared to be guarding whatever was stashed inside them.

Lucas drifted toward the only ladder with Saul right behind him. Stowing their cheap rubber flippers behind it, they climbed the rusty rungs on bare feet.

The warehouse was exactly as Saul had drawn it, with a docking area capable of housing two large boats. Saul pointed out a crowbar lying atop a pile of crates nearby, and they moved toward it. With the drum of rain on the high tin roof masking their movements, Saul inserted the end of the crowbar under the lid and gave it a yank. The squeak that resulted made them freeze like thieves.

Lifting the lid and the packing material, Lucas gaped at a multitude of crude-looking canisters lined up inside. Improvised explosive devices, he realized, spying coils sticking out of them. They looked like a stash the Marines might have come across in Afghanistan. How they'd found their way to a warehouse in Sabena was a question only members of The Entity could explain.

Exchanging a charged look with Saul, Lucas withdrew from his sodden shorts the camera Master Chief had passed off to him. Using its night-vision feature, he snapped several pictures of the crate's contents. Saul replaced the lid and waved him deeper into the stacks to open a second crate. The lid gave way with a grating sound that made Lucas wince and look around.

"Sir," Saul whispered, directing his attention to the aerosol cans lining the interior.

"What is it?" Lucas asked.

"Agent 15," Saul replied, reading one of the labels.

Lucas immediately thought of Jaguar's stepdaughter, who'd been gassed in the back of a patrol car not too long ago. It was suddenly clear how Dwyer's henchman, a former SEAL-turned-police-officer, had managed to get his hands on the illegal substance. The Entity had stolen it, and they weren't above using some when needed.

Lucas was snapping pictures of cans when Saul grabbed his arm in warning. Dread pegged him as he turned his head to see an enormous Doberman Pinscher peering at them around the end of the aisle.

"Don't look at him," Saul murmured in a quiet, almost casual voice. "Put the camera away."

Lucas jerked his gaze from the dog's glowing eyes and swiftly slid the camera back inside the pocket of his shorts, zipping it shut.

"Back up slowly." Saul tugged on one of Lucas's belt loops, urging him to lower the lid and back away.

"What is it, boy?"

A uniformed watchman materialized behind the dog. Catching sight of the SEALs, he jerked up the rifle he was carrying and bellowed, "Freeze!"

The SEALs were already in retreat. At the watchman's command, they spun and ran, leaping into the water just as a deafening shot rang out. The explosion coincided with a searing sensation by Lucas's right shoulder blade. He flinched from it, twisting down and away as he'd been trained to do to avoid taking another bullet. Two more rounds pelted the water close by. Searching for Saul as he hit the muddy bottom, he was glad to see the chief right behind him. Saul seized his belt loop again and tugged him in the direction they needed to go.

A barnacled column scraped Lucas's left cheek. He jerked away from it, dislodging the mask that had been resting on top of his head.

I've been shot.

He refused to let that circumstance slow him down, but the absence of their flippers most certainly did. It took over a minute, holding their breath all the while, to slip under the garage doors into the safety of the river. Lucas tried his best to keep up with Saul, but with only one arm working and with kicks that grew increasingly feeble, he could tell he was slowing them down.

Saul brought them both up for air.

"Stay with me, Little John," he rasped. "Relax," he added, rolling Lucas onto his back and putting his body under him in a lifeguard's hold.

"I can swim," Lucas protested.

"Save your strength, sir. I got you." Saul started kicking for both of them. In that instant, the wail of a squad car split the quiet night.

Here comes the posse, Lucas thought. But unless the cops jumped in a boat and came after them, the SEALs would get to the other side and away from the Manor before any of the police chief's men could descend on them. He pictured Charlotte waiting in the room for their return. If only there was a way to warn her.

By the time Saul helped Lucas through the muck onto dry land, the rain had subsided, drawing sharply colder air in its wake. Lucas shivered as the air enveloped him.

Saul muttered a string of self-directed epithets. "Didn't do my homework. Didn't know about the dog."

"We got what we needed." Lucas assured him, gritting his teeth to keep them from chattering. "Do I have the camera?" he asked, patting down his pocket. "Yes. Let's grab Charlotte and get out of here."

They both froze at the sound of a twig snapping. With relief, Lucas recognized the glint of Charlotte's spectacles as she hurried toward them, his HK slung over one shoulder and his belt with his holstered pistol tied around her waist. He couldn't have conjured a more welcoming sight.

"What happened?" she demanded.

"We were seen," Saul said. "Lucas took a bullet."

"Lucas!" She ran up to him with gratifying concern, her hands warm and gentle. "Where were you hit? Your face is bleeding."

"That's just a scratch. Upper back, right side."

She ducked under his arm and felt his back. When her fingers slipped in the blood there, she gave a gasp of dismay. Saul, who had found a dry shirt in the bag he'd stowed under a canoe, tore it with one powerful yank and proceeded to bandage his back with practiced efficiency.

"We need to move," Saul said, tying it off.

Blue lights flickered through the trees on the other side of the river. It wouldn't take long for the watchman to give a description that would make the officers think immediately of Lucas, since few men were as tall as he was.

"We're all set to leave," Charlotte informed them. "I've packed the car and pushed it to the head of the driveway so Mrs. Digges wouldn't alert her friends in the force. I even left her the old-timey key so she wouldn't bill us for it."

The men regarded her in mutual astonishment.

"You are off the chain, ma'am," Saul stated.

"Thanks—I think. Where are Lucas's flip-flops?"

"Right here." Saul fetched them from under an overturned canoe.

Cursing his helplessness, Lucas let Charlotte help him slip his sandals on. Then, propping a shoulder under his armpit, she started up the hill with him while Saul changed into dry clothing. The warmth coming off her athletic frame chased away the chills rippling up his back.

"Don't faint on me," she ordered. The HK swung at her hip as she labored under his weight.

"Trying not to," he said through his teeth.

"And no dying on me either," she added on a firm note.

"Not in the plans," he assured her.

Saul caught up to them carrying his duffel bag. Supporting Lucas on the other side, he helped Charlotte get Lucas to the head of the driveway where, sure enough, the Camaro sat waiting for them. After tossing his duffel into the back and snatching up an emergency kit, Saul trundled Lucas into the passenger seat, while Charlotte ducked into the backseat from the driver's side.

"Find gauze," Saul ordered, handing her the kit. "I think he's bleeding through the bandage."

She was still pawing through the kit when Saul jumped behind the wheel and started them forward, adjusting his seat closer to the pedals as he drove.

Having listened to the wail of sirens growing ever louder, Lucas feared they might not even make it out of Sabena. Charlotte ordered him to lean forward, and he issued a groan as she added a layer of gauze under his makeshift bandage.

"Now sit back and use the seat to apply pressure."

He did as she said, just as they reached the intersection with Main Street. He could see blue lights on the bridge, coming from the very direction they needed to go in order to head home.

Saul cursed and glanced at his map. "Sorry, sir. Looks like we need to take a detour."

Keeping the Camaro's lights extinguished, he turned left, hopefully unseen, and rapidly accelerated.

The sudden pressure on Lucas's wound had him swallowing a groan and gripping the arm of the door. He couldn't tell if the sudden darkness around him was because they'd left downtown Sabena or because he was losing consciousness. It was definitely the latter, he decided, as dizziness stormed him.

"I'm going to pass out," he warned in a faint voice.

The last thing he felt was Charlotte throwing her arms around him.

CHAPTER 12

"Talk to me, Saul. What are we doing?" Charlotte heard the edge of panic in her voice and tried to subdue it. If ever there was a time to keep a clear head, this was it.

"This road goes on forever," he answered tensely. "I don't see a way to double back or cut over to the interstate or anything."

With her arms wrapped around Lucas, keeping him from slumping forward, Charlotte studied the map on Saul's dashboard. He was right. The dark, two-lane road they were on headed dead north, with no other road intersecting, at least not close enough that they could see it on the map.

"Can we turn around?"

The twinkling in Saul's rearview mirror provided an instantaneous answer.

"They're coming after us." Saul abruptly accelerated.

Charlotte's heart galloped. They were screaming down a road surrounded by dark trees and almost total darkness, and Saul had yet to turn on the lights.

"How can they even see us?" she cried. They had to be at least a mile ahead of the vehicles chasing them. "Are your reflectors that good?"

"Maybe," he retorted on a grim note. "That or they put a tracking device on my car."

Police Chief Blanchard's voice echoed in Charlotte's head. *You drive a Camaro right? I check all the cars that run through town. It's good to know who's comin' and goin'.*

"Oh, yes, I think they did," she decided. "We need to find it and take it off."

"Can't stop now," Saul retorted, grimly. Glancing toward his teammate, he added, "Reach over him and recline his seat. I'm going to need your hands free."

Eager to help, Charlotte managed to lower Lucas's seatback, so she could let go of him. "What now?"

"Reduce the view on this map," Saul requested, swerving suddenly to avoid the possum waddling across the road. "I need to see our options."

Hitting the minus sign on the corner of his map, Charlotte took comfort from the sound of Lucas breathing. He was still alive. God wasn't going to let him die like this. Zooming out the map's view, she could see some roads coming up, including Rt. 301, the same road she'd been traveling on when Jason and Laura Dunn abducted her. The sight of Patuxent River Military Air Station filled her with relief.

"Look, it's Pax River," she cried, using the commonly used name for it. "They have a hospital there. It can't be more than thirty miles away," she estimated. "We can make it."

"If we can shake our tail," Saul agreed through gritted teeth.

Charlotte glanced at the speedometer and nearly fainted. They were moving at well over a hundred miles an hour in near perfect darkness.

"Since they know where we are, can't we put the lights on?" she pleaded.

"Good point," Saul muttered, switching them on—just in time, as a family of deer stood poised on the edge of the road, waiting to cross.

Saul blared the horn, startling them into retreat. As they tore past the animals, unscathed, Saul blew out a breath of relief, then looked in his rearview mirror and cursed again. "They're gaining on us."

"How?" Charlotte cried. "I thought your car was fast."

"Cruisers have super-charged engines."

His grim tone filled her with dread. "You're saying we can't outrun them," Charlotte guessed.

His only answer was to glance into his mirror.

Heart in her throat, Charlotte twisted in her seat to see out the back window. Second by second, the two patrol cars got closer.

"This is what happened to Lloyd," she realized, trying not to panic. "We should get evidence so we can prosecute," she added, grubbing in her purse for the cell phone Fitz had given her. She had charged it per Lucas's suggestion but kept it powered off. That was about to change, as she needed its camera.

"What are you doing?" Saul demanded.

"I want to film them chasing us. Maybe it'll help me prove they did the same thing to Lloyd."

"Yeah, well I ain't planning to die like Lloyd. You got the HK back there with you?"

"Yes, it's right here." Good thing she hadn't had time to put it in the trunk.

"Full magazine?" he asked as he took it from her, then laid it across his lap.

"Yes. What are we going to do? Stop the car and shoot them when they're close enough?"

"No, there's no stopping," he retorted.

"How are you going to shoot?" she demanded. "You're driving."

"You'll see," he said. "If you want to get that video, now's the time."

Charlotte's phone had finally powered up. Accessing the camera, she put it in video mode and pointed it out the back window.

"This is Charlotte Patterson, intern with NCIS." The words tumbled out of her. "I'm with the two US Navy SEALs tasked by the FBI to guard me. We're being pursued by the Sabena police. As you can see, there are two cruisers closing in on us, and they've silenced their sirens. They're chasing us because we just discovered the contents of the warehouse in Sabena, situated across the river from Magnolia Manor. A group known as The Entity is storing stolen weapons there. The warehouse is owned by the police chief's cousin, and Blanchard is related to Commander Dwyer, who's a member of The Entity."

By the time she'd spoken that last sentence, the two cruisers had narrowed the distance between them to less than a football field.

"They're gaining on us, Saul."

"I know. Put your phone away," he said, shaking off his seatbelt.

"What are you doing?" she cried, as he slid his seat way back. They were hurtling down a slick and hilly but mercifully straight road, with towering trees on either side. This was not the time to be taking off his seatbelt.

"I'm shooting," he replied. "You're going to drive."

"What? I'm in the backseat!"

"Listen to me and keep calm."

His firm tone had her closing her mouth with a snap.

"The car is on cruise control. All you have to do is hold the wheel straight and don't let me bump your arm."

Fear and dread squeezed Charlotte's heart, causing her to balk momentarily. "I can't do that."

"If you want us to shake our tail, you *have* to," he said. "Let's go. Get ready to take the wheel."

Charlotte hesitated. There had to be another way. Peering behind them, she was horrified to see headlights practically on their bumper. The second car had pulled alongside the first, so that they now occupied both lanes. It couldn't be more obvious they meant to nudge Saul's Camaro off the road. At this speed, the results would be deadly.

Saul pushed the button that opened the sunroof and hefted the semi-automatic, thumbing off the safety.

Chilly air blasted into the car, rousing Charlotte to sharp awareness. With no more hesitation, she released her seatbelt and lunged between the two front seats to grip the steering wheel.

Keep your eyes on the road.

Careful not to touch her, Saul gripped the edge of the sunroof and pulled himself straight up and slightly over, sticking his head and shoulders out the window. Twisting his upper body, he put an elbow on the roof to aim behind them. Charlotte kept her eyes glued to the road.

A barrage of gunfire, scarcely audible for the wind roaring into the car, rang out.

Grateful that she couldn't see into the rearview mirror from her current perspective, she cringed at the screeching of tires that followed.

Hold steady! She gripped the wheel so hard her knuckles ached.

Lowering himself back into the car, Saul accidently bumped her arm with his hip.

No! The car jerked, then righted itself with a wobble as Saul dropped into his seat and seized control in the nick of time.

"You can let go," he said.

It took all her strength to pry her hands free. Numb with shock, Charlotte threw herself over a recumbent Lucas, hugging him for comfort, even though he couldn't respond.

"You did good, ma'am," Saul said, ruffling her wig.

"Did we kill them?" she asked.

"No."

Saul's calm tone reassured her enough to sit back and put on her seatbelt.

"One car lost control," he elaborated, "but it didn't hit the trees. I'm sure the air bags kept anyone from dying."

We're not going to die either, Charlotte realized, closing her eyes with profound relief. The sweetness of life broke over her along with a warm rush of gratitude.

"Thank You, God," she whispered, aware that she'd prayed for the first time in three years. She felt immediately better for it.

Saul had slowed their speed to something survivable while still making good time.

"How's Little John's pulse?" Saul asked. "I need to know if we can afford to stop and look for the tracking device."

Charlotte felt for Lucas's jugular. "He's freezing," she realized, wishing they had a blanket. "But his pulse is good," she added as Saul turned up the heat.

"How much farther to Pax River?" she asked, looking at the map.

"Fifteen miles or so. We gotta find that tracker now so they don't realize where we're going."

"Agreed," she said. "Let's be quick about it."

Lucas will make it, she assured herself.

God had many more plans for Lucas Strong before calling him home. She pictured him on harrowing missions with his SEAL troop, then pictured him returning home to a wife who put her husband and her kids ahead of her career. A gust of loneliness blew through her. At least he would be happy.

~

"Welcome back, Lieutenant."

Prying open sticky eyelids, Lucas found himself in what appeared to be a hospital recovery room. The sterile space was crammed with tubes and instruments. Two other patients slumbered in beds nearby. Taking inventory of himself, Lucas found an IV needle imbedded in the back of his left hand. His right arm was strapped to his chest by Velcro strips banding his torso. The last thing he could recall was passing out in Saul's car as they sped away from the Sabena police.

Where am I? he went to ask the behemoth-sized woman looming over him, only he found he had to clear his dry throat first. "Did I have surgery?" he asked instead.

"Mm-hmm."

Blinking her into focus, Lucas noted with puzzlement the frown on her dark face and the disapproving line of her lips.

EVERY SECRET THING

"I'm Rexanne," she informed him.

He found her pretty name at odds with her ferocious appearance. The name T-Rex would have suited her better, even though he would have to borrow it from a former SEAL, a member of Blue Squadron whose foot had been crushed during an op-gone-wrong.

"And I know who you are," she added, reaching for him.

Lucas flinched, but all she did was check his pulse while looking at her watch.

Releasing him, she entered data into the computer on the wheeled table next to him.

"You used to play for the Dallas Cowboys," she continued. Her tone turned downright condemning. "And ever since you left, they haven't gone to a single Super Bowl."

Many of his fans had yet to forgive him for quitting football. T-Rex was apparently among that number.

"Do you know where my friends are?" he asked, trying to sit up.

"Unh-uh!" She halted his ascent with a man-sized hand on his chest. "You ain't goin' nowhere just yet. Give yourself a day or two."

"What day is it?"

"Thursday."

Jaguar's motion hearing was tomorrow. He simply didn't have a day or two.

"Where am I?" he asked with growing agitation.

"Patuxent Naval Air Station. And your friends are waitin' for you in the room I'm about to move you to." She pointed a threatening finger at him. "Don't you even think about leavin' until the hospital commander gives the all-clear." Her dark eyes bulged as she added, "I've dealt with your kind before. You think taking a bullet's like getting stung by a bee. Well, it ain't. We had to dig deep to get that sucker out. You move before you're ready, and you're gonna start bleedin' internally."

Lucas heard her words, but he planned on leaving anyway.

"And just so you know," she added, "Patient Safety's going to want

147

to know how you got shot in the first place. A rep will be stopping by your room to talk to you."

Nonplussed, Lucas wondered what he was going to say to explain his circumstances.

Cranking the handle that had kept his gurney immobile, the nurse proceeded to wheel him out of the recovery room. They moved briskly down a hallway in dire need of renovation and turned into the open elevator where T-Rex pushed the button for the fourth floor.

Lucas struck the option of escaping through a window. He was in no condition to rappel down the side of the hospital from that height.

A minute later, they turned into room 402, and Lucas sighed in relief to see Saul passed out in the armchair and Charlotte sprawled on the bed.

At their noisy entrance, she sat straight up, jostling her wig. "Lucas!" Relief brimmed behind the lenses of her glasses. His own spirits lifted abruptly.

"Off!" T-Rex ordered, pushing the gurney alongside the bed.

Charlotte vaulted off it, and Saul sprang up from the armchair into a position of attention. Lucas looked at him and blinked. Saul's long hair was a tangled mess and his goatee resembled a pin-cushion.

"You look like you survived a tornado," he commented.

"Something like that," Saul affirmed, while sliding T-Rex a wary look. "How do you feel, sir?"

The nurse answered for him. "He needs to rest for forty-eight hours," she instructed, setting the brake on the gurney. "No excitement and no sudden movements."

Transferring his IV bag first, she pulled down the bedding Charlotte had been sleeping on and fluffed up the pillow.

Lucas, who was afraid T-Rex might try to pick him up, wriggled off the gurney into the bed himself, using his good arm. The mattress was still warm from Charlotte's body heat. He was pleased not to feel any pain with the movement, but then he was likely still benefiting from a nerve block, which would wear off soon enough.

T-Rex confirmed his suspicion with her next words.

"Before your nerve block wears off completely, I'll be back to give you a muscle relaxer mixed with acetaminophen. Or would you rather have that now?" she asked, raising an eyebrow at him.

"No." Acetaminophen was one thing, but muscle relaxers made him sleepy.

The nurse propped her hands on her ample hips. "You best not be acting macho for your friends. Soon as your back starts to hurt, you press the call button and I'll take care of you."

He was afraid of that.

T-Rex wasn't done with her instructions. "If you need to use the restroom, you get one of them to help you." She sent Charlotte a pointed look. "If you're here by yourself, hit the call button and I'll escort you myself."

Lucas vowed he was never going to hit that call button.

Saul made a choking sound and earned the nurse's hard stare.

"It's your job to make sure he rests." She pointed a warning finger at him. "I am holdin' you accountable."

Saul saluted her. "Yes, ma'am," he said with vigor.

The nurse scowled at his antics, then turned a narrow-eyed look back at Lucas.

"Like I said, I've dealt with your kind before. Don't try pullin' no tricks on me. I'll be watchin' you." Her eyes opened wide with the threat.

Lucas had met terrorists who scared him less. He murmured something to appease her, then followed her progress all the way to the door. No one said anything until it closed and the sound of her footsteps faded.

"Phew." Lucas expelled a breath. "What happened? Tell me everything."

Moving closer to him, Charlotte gestured for Saul to answer. He reached into his pants pocket and pulled out a smashed bit of hardware. "This is a tracking device. We found it in one of the Camaro's wheel wells."

Given its mangled state, the device wasn't betraying their location anymore.

Charlotte added, "Remember Blanchard saying he likes to keep tabs on who comes and goes? That's how he does it. I'm betting he did the same thing to Lloyd's car."

Lucas looked back at Saul. "So, you outran the cops?"

"Nope." Saul put the device away and crossed his arms. "They caught up to us, planning to run us off the road."

"Just like they did to Lloyd," Charlotte inserted darkly.

"So, how did you lose them?" Lucas asked.

Saul shrugged. "Shot out their tires."

"While you were driving?" Lucas couldn't begin to envision how that was possible.

"Sort of. I set the cruise control, and Charlotte held the wheel so I could stick my head out of the sunroof."

Lucas swung an astonished look back Charlotte. "You held the wheel from the backseat?" He could only imagine her terror.

"Yep," she said, with a brave little smile. "I also videotaped the chase. If I can prove Blanchard put a tracker on Lloyd's car, too, I'm going to see he goes to jail for murder."

Taking in the determined glint in her eyes, Lucas could imagine her succeeding.

Saul summed up the rest. "By the time all this happened, we were fifteen miles south of Pax River, so we brought you onto the base and straight to the hospital."

"Thank you," Lucas said, marveling that he couldn't remember a thing. "I'm sure you saved my life." He focused on what needed to be done now. "Unfortunately, we've got a couple of situations on our hands. First, some rep from Patient Safety is going to ask me how I got shot."

"Taken care of," Saul assured him. "I called Master Chief this morning and told him what had happened. He's going to call Patient Safety and explain that you were injured in a live-fire training exercise, top secret."

Lucas thanked Saul for his forethought. "Our next problem is Jaguar's motion hearing is tomorrow, and they don't want to release me for forty-eight hours. We need to get back to The Beach tonight if we want our evidence approved. Those pictures from the warehouse will destroy Dwyer's integrity."

"I thought we couldn't mention The Entity," Charlotte reminded him.

"We won't. We'll merely make the panel wonder what Dwyer's up to. Wait, where's the camera?" Lucas cried, realizing his shorts were no longer on his body.

"Right here, sir." Saul produced it from the pocket of his camou-flaged jacket. "And your clothes are in a plastic bag in that closet," he added, pointing.

"Can I have it?" Lucas asked, holding out a hand for the camera. "What about my cell phone?" Charlotte produced his cell phone from her purse and put it into his hands.

"Thanks." Looking from his phone to the camera, Lucas added, "I'm going to try to download the pictures from the camera so I can send them to people."

"Are you sure you're up to that, sir?" Saul asked. "You just had surgery."

Lucas looked up at them. Saul's eyes were bloodshot. Charlotte stifled a yawn. "You're the ones who've been up all night. I feel fine," he assured them. "Why don't you leave me here and find some shady place to sleep in the car, or maybe even at one of the motels outside the gate." He knew he could trust Saul to be a gentleman. "Come back for me at seven this evening, and we'll take off then. I don't want to have taken a bullet for nothing," he added persuasively.

Saul nodded in agreement. "I could use some sleep," he muttered.

Charlotte hovered over Lucas. "Do you need anything before we leave? Can we help you get to the restroom?" she asked, worry etched on her face.

Lucas pictured the tiny gown he was wearing. He was almost

certain it gaped in the back. "I'll be fine by myself," he growled. "I've been in worse shape than this."

"Hold onto the IV pole for support if you get up," she advised, fingering his blanket. For a moment, it looked like she might hug him or even kiss him. "Call Saul's phone if you need anything," she urged, patting his arm instead.

Saul was already headed for the door. Charlotte followed him reluctantly.

Watching her walk away, Lucas was struck with a feeling of abandonment. Charlotte's backward glance suggested she felt the same way.

In just a few days' time, they'd gotten used to each other.

Finding himself alone, he eased awkwardly out of bed, leaving the phone and camera under the sheet. Grabbing hold of his IV pole like Charlotte had suggested, he shuffled to the bathroom.

By the time he returned, he was shaky and a little lightheaded. He got back into bed and accessed Fitz's number on his phone, only to have his call go to voicemail. It was all he could do to leave a coherent message about Dwyer's connection to the warehouse in Sabena.

Lowering his phone onto his chest, Lucas closed his eyes and succumbed to lethargy. In a minute, he would rouse himself and figure out how to transfer the photos from the camera to his cell phone.

With no idea of how much time had passed, he came awake knowing someone was standing over him. Opening his eyes, he sucked in a startled breath to find Special Agent Fitz holding the camera and scanning the digital pictures.

"You're here already?" Lucas asked, slurring his words. Groping for his phone, he checked what time it was and discovered he'd snoozed about an hour—not just the few minutes he'd planned on.

Fitz couldn't possibly have driven from Norfolk to Patuxent in only one hour. He must have taken a plane the moment he received the voicemail.

The agent's green eyes focused on him intently. "How are you feeling?" he asked, ignoring the question.

"I'm fine," Lucas managed, though he could tell the nerve block was wearing off fast, and the subsequent pain in his back wasn't going to be pleasant.

Fitz held up the camera. "Excellent work, Lieutenant, but I'm afraid you injured yourself for no reason. I already knew about the warehouse in Sabena. There's no reason for you to have these pictures."

Lucas realized Fitz wasn't simply looking at their pictures; he was deleting them.

"Sir!" he protested, trying to sit up. A sharp pain knifed deep into his shoulder blade, causing him to arch and fall back, swallowing a scream.

"I'm sorry," he heard Fitz say. "But I can't take the chance that you'll be so moved to save your colleague, you'll ruin my investigation in the process. I'm at a very delicate juncture right now."

Fighting waves of agony, Lucas couldn't manage a single word of protest.

Suddenly, Fitz was digging his fingers into the base of Lucas's neck, adding yet another layer of pain to his almost unbearable discomfort.

"Have you made any copies yet? Downloaded the pictures onto your phone or any other device?" he growled, his voice as hard as nails.

Slitting his eyes, Lucas took in the ruthless set to Fitz's foxlike face and realized Charlotte might have been right not to trust him. At every turn, Fitz seemed intent on destroying any evidence that could damage Dwyer's reputation. Was it possible he wasn't investigating The Entity but, in fact, doing damage control for them and protecting Dwyer?

"No, sir," he grated.

His suspicions continued to bubble as Fitz released him. The man stood a moment, looking down his nose at Lucas.

"I'll let the nurse know about the pain you're in," he offered on a kinder note. "Please give my regards to Charlotte. Whatever you do, don't let your guard down. Anything could happen to her."

Is that a threat? Lucas wondered. The pain radiating through him made it difficult to think. Was he threatening to hurt Charlotte if Lucas didn't cooperate with him?

Too angry and confused to speak, Lucas watched Fitz set the camera back on the nightstand. Sending Lucas a sharp nod, he strode away.

What just happened? Lucas asked himself as the agent disappeared.

Had he and Saul been duped from the start? Had Fitz lied to them about shutting down The Entity? Could he be, in fact, protecting its members? Perhaps Charlotte was a better judge of character than either one of them.

I have to call her, he thought, picking up his cell phone. He had to think a minute before realizing he didn't know her number. He started to call Saul, then hesitated at the thought of disturbing the rest they were getting. All at once, the door flew open and in marched T-Rex with a smirk on her face.

"I knew you was just lookin' tough for your friends," she declared, crossing straight to his bed and reaching for the IV. "You ain't nothin' but a big baby."

Lucas's gaze fell to the syringe in her man-sized hand. "Wait," he called out, "I don't want that." Anything with a muscle relaxer in it would put him right to sleep.

"That's not what your friend said," she retorted, scarcely even pausing as she removed the plastic cap from the needle and jammed the syringe into the port.

Lucas realized she was referring to Fitz. "He's not my friend!" He practically shouted the words, but it was too late.

With a pursing of her lips and a rolling of her eyes, T-Rex shot the liquid formula into the tubing that sent it straight into Lucas's veins.

"Don't matter to me if he is or he ain't," she retorted. "These are doctor's orders."

With a muttered curse, Lucas went to pull the IV needle out of the back of his hand, but with his right arm bound to his chest, that effort proved impossible. He cursed again, thrashing his head against the pillow in his frustration. Already, he could feel an insidious tide of lethargy sweeping through him. Whether he wanted to or not, he was going to relax to the point of passing out.

He figured he had just enough time to complete his call to Saul.

He was thumbing the call button when T-Rex slapped his good arm. "Oh, no you don't. Can't you read the sign?" As Lucas followed her nod toward the sign saying NO CELL PHONES, she snatched his phone away and placed it on the stand next to the camera. "You got a landline beside your bed. You can use that."

Closing his eyes, he willed her to leave so he could take his cell back without her seeing. He had to inform Saul and Charlotte what Fitz had done. The agent had destroyed their best hope of freeing Jaguar.

That was Lucas's last thought before the sedative trekking through his bloodstream got the better of him.

CHAPTER 13

"*L*ucas, please wake up. We're missing the motion hearing," Charlotte begged. Not daring to shake him, she lightly tapped his cheek, though in her frustration she was tempted to slap him harder.

His eyelids fluttered, the first sign she'd seen that he was regaining consciousness, but he still didn't waken.

"I think he heard me," she said to Saul, who stood at the foot of the hospital bed with a scowl on his face and his arms crossed.

"Won't make much difference at this point," he stated, glancing at his watch. "We can't get back to The Beach in two hours. And thanks to his watchdog, we're going to have a hard time sneaking out of here before they're ready to release him."

Charlotte heaved a long-suffering sigh. They'd returned to the hospital the previous evening, with the intent of stealing Lucas out of his room. The nurse who'd hounded them that morning had left for the night, giving them the perfect opportunity, except Lucas had been sleeping so soundly they hadn't been able to waken him.

While cooped up in the hospital room, waiting for him to stir, Saul had discovered the photos on the digital camera were gone, completely erased.

"He must have found a way to copy them over to his phone," Charlotte concluded.

"And deleted the originals?" Saul argued. "I don't think so."

Charlotte had to agree with Saul. Lucas had wanted to back up the pictures, not transfer them. Plus, he'd been sleeping like the dead, forcing her and Saul to return to the same motel they'd crashed at earlier. The fact that he was still sound asleep at eight o'clock the next morning suggested he'd been drugged.

When Rexanne had barged into his room that morning, she'd told them Lucas had asked the other nurse for the muscle relaxers last night; then he'd asked for more earlier that morning.

"He ain't nothin' but a big baby," Rexanne had declared, checking Lucas's vitals and then leaving.

Neither Saul nor Charlotte had believed her.

"I swear they're drugging him intentionally," Charlotte raged, pacing to the window and back. "What if someone came in here and deleted the photos while he was sleeping? He never would have known."

"Who would have done that?" Saul countered. "No one knows we're here."

Charlotte stared down at the parking lot, thinking. "Fitz might have known," she reasoned, "either because I turned on the phone he gave me and he's tracking me, or because Lucas called him and told him what happened. Remember, he said he was planning to call Fitz."

Facing Lucas's bed again, her gaze went to the cell phone next to it. "We could find out if you would just hack into Lucas's cell. Are you sure you can't guess the passcode?" she added, repeating the same question she'd asked an hour earlier.

"No," Saul repeated, respecting Lucas's privacy. "Hey, I think he's waking up."

Charlotte hurried to the bed in time to see Lucas slit his eyes. He visibly struggled to rouse himself.

"Lucas, you have to wake up," she repeated. "The motion hearing starts in two hours. We might get our evidence to Carew in time if you get up." *If they still had evidence.*

"What happened?" His voice sounded rusty with disuse. "What time is it?"

"It's eight thirty on Friday morning. You've been asleep for almost twenty-four hours." Seeing his confusion, Charlotte turned to pour Lucas a glass of water from the pitcher by his bed.

Saul approached him on the other side. "You want to sit up, sir?" he asked, pressing the remote that raised Lucas to a sitting position.

"Oh, no," Lucas blurted suddenly, causing them both to look at him in concern.

Charlotte froze. "What?"

Lucas plowed the fingers of his free hand through his thick hair. "Fitz was here," he grated. His entire body went rigid. He gripped the bedrail with a white-knuckled hand.

"Calm down," Charlotte urged, passing him the cup she'd poured. "Drink some water and then tell us what happened."

Lucas gulped down the contents of the cup and handed it back. "Where's the camera?" he asked, looking around. "Are the photos gone?" he added, as Saul produced it from the pocket of his jacket.

"Yep."

Lucas growled in disgust. "Fitz showed up like an hour after you left," he raged.

Charlotte had never seen him so hot under the collar.

"He said he already *knew* about the warehouse. Wait, did he say that?" For a second, Lucas seemed to question himself. "Yes, yes, he did. I remember." Lucas frowned, as if trying to remember. "He said he didn't want us jeopardizing his investigation, so he deleted the pictures. And then, I think he threatened me—or you," he added, looking at Charlotte with an expression of befuddlement.

The words roused her indignation. "Threatened me how?"

Lucas frowned again and shook his head. "Maybe it was more of a warning; I don't know," he amended. "He said not to let my guard down or something could happen to you."

His gray eyes, full of concern, looked up at her.

"I told you I don't trust that man," she reminded him, pacing to the window and back. "He's been throwing up roadblocks for Jaguar's defense from the beginning." She proceeded to list all the instances Fitz had gotten in their way. "First, he took the hard drive from Lloyd's office, making all the evidence Lloyd had disappear, except his iPad, which only I knew about. I personally think he took that from me, too, but I'm not going to convince *you* of that. Then he told Jaguar's counsel not to mention The Entity in any of her arguments, and now he's deleted our proof that Dwyer has been storing stolen weapons in Sabena. How do we know he's telling the truth about shutting down The Entity? It looks to me like he's trying to protect them!"

Lucas shared a dark and disappointed look with Saul.

"I have to agree with you," he surprised her by admitting. "On top of all that, Fitz told T-Rex that I'd asked for pain meds. He's the reason I was drugged all this time."

Charlotte's hands curled into fists. "He told her to drug you?" she railed, while taking note of Lucas's nickname for the scary nurse, who lurked in the hallway even then.

"Wait." Another thought occurred to her. "What if he drugged you to keep you away from Jaguar's motion hearing?"

Lucas tossed back the sheet that covered him. "I'm sure he did. Either way, we're missing the hearing, and our evidence is gone."

"So that's it," Charlotte seethed. "We know where Dwyer is storing stolen weapons, and we can't do anything about it?" She gestured helplessly. "And you got shot for nothing," she added.

"What can we do without proof?" Lucas pointed out.

"I told you Fitz had an agenda," Charlotte reminded him. "And we've been unwittingly helping him. If the FBI is protecting The Entity, then we *have* to turn to the DIA for help. Let's go talk to my godfather," she proposed, warming to the idea. "Don't forget I sent him photos of LeMere's journal. If he still has those, we can use them to reinforce Monica's testimony."

Lucas shot an uncertain glance at Saul. "We don't know for sure that Fitz is working for The Entity."

"We don't know that he isn't, either," Charlotte countered. "At the very least, my godfather could help to protect us. Think about it. If Fitz is protecting Dwyer, then The Entity knows exactly where we are right now. We're not safe. We need protection."

Lucas looked at Saul, who tugged on his beard, clearly undecided.

"Fitz told you not to contact your godfather," Saul reminded her.

Charlotte tried again. "That's because he knows Larry Martin is the only one who can stop him if he's dirty. Don't forget, Lucas, the man stole our evidence and he drugged you. What more proof do you need that he can't be trusted?"

Lucas rubbed his forehead thinking. "I'll agree to visit your godfather on two conditions," he relented. "The first is we say nothing about The Entity. We're there for the evidence you sent him and nothing else. Secondly, we don't mention the FBI. If Fitz is on the brink of bringing down The Entity, I don't want to be the reason his investigation goes south."

"Agreed. We should go soon, then," Charlotte urged, glancing at the clock on the wall. "Uncle Larry knocks off early on Fridays to play golf."

"We'll have to dodge that nurse," Saul reminded them.

Lucas swung his feet off the bed. "Help me get dressed," he requested of his chief.

As Saul turned toward the locker for Lucas's clothing, Charlotte headed for the door.

"I'll find a way to distract T-Rex," she offered, using the nickname Lucas had given her. "Think you can be ready in five minutes?"

"Should be," Saul answered.

Six minutes later, Charlotte slipped back into the room just as Saul was helping Lucas put his shoes on.

"Time to go," she announced with urgency.

In that same instant, a fire alarm started shrieking at the other end of the hallway.

Saul shot her an astonished glance. "Did you do that?"

She strove for an innocent expression. "Not me." It was, in fact, a fork and paper towel sparking in a microwave in the staff's little kitchenette that was causing the billowing smoke.

Lucas's pale complexion gave Charlotte second thoughts. "Maybe leaving isn't such a good idea," she added.

"I'm fine," Lucas insisted, standing up.

As Saul grabbed Lucas's duffel bag, Charlotte went to put her arms around her injured hero. It felt nice to hold him close again, though the circumstances weren't the best.

Five minutes later, they streaked away from Patuxent Naval Air Station with Lucas in the front seat, his eyes closed and lines of pain bracketing his mouth. He tried to raise the headrest with his one good hand.

"Here, let me do that." Charlotte raised it for him.

With a whispered word of thanks, his head fell back. Charlotte caught herself smoothing down the short, soft strands of his hair that were sticking up. The reminder that Lucas wasn't hers to pet had her withdrawing her hand. He didn't want a woman whose career was important to her. He wanted a wife who would stay at home and give him babies—three of them. *And it won't be me,* Charlotte thought.

Barring traffic, DIA headquarters was about an hour-and-a-half drive from Patuxent. With her phone from Fitz powered off, the FBI special agent shouldn't have any notion where they were headed.

She might actually make it to her godfather's office without being abducted this time.

~

At DIA Headquarters' security checkpoint, Lucas suffered a body search, despite his obvious injury. The guard on duty claimed to be a retired Marine master sergeant, and given the search he gave Lucas, he clearly nursed a grudge against SEALs.

"He squeezed my *cojones*," Saul growled, still red in the face from his humiliation. "I almost broke his effing nose."

If he weren't in such terrible pain, Lucas would have laughed at Saul's discomposure, but laughing was beyond him at that moment. Voices echoed off the marble floor of the vast lobby. He leaned against the wall, waiting for Charlotte to be admitted.

She had taken off her wig and glasses and scrubbed the makeup off her face so she could use her NCIS badge. Her makeup-free face was flushed with frustration at that moment since the badge, which Fitz had given to Lucas at their first meeting, was scanned by the security guard and declared inactive. He refused to let her in.

Not to be stopped, Charlotte summoned a guard who recognized her. Lucas heard her persuade the man to telephone the director on her behalf and tell him who was there. In the next instant, Charlotte was talking on the phone with her godfather, her smile of tenderness so beautiful Lucas's heart clutched.

Their time of being stuck with each other was going to end soon. Whether Jaguar succeeded in clearing his good name or ended up being dishonorably discharged, Charlotte was bound to go her own way—provided everything worked out as Fitz had promised them.

Lucas didn't want to believe Fitz had actually betrayed them. If that were true, why would he have coordinated Charlotte's rescue and enlisted the SEALs help in the first place? It made no sense for him to go to such lengths, unless his only purpose was to dupe them into believing in his investigation.

But Charlotte had a point. The man had denied them their best shot of proving Jaguar's innocence. All they'd gotten from Fitz was his promise that Dwyer would be arrested soon and Jaguar's convictions overturned. Was Fitz a man of his word?

Charlotte cut into his thoughts as she breezed up to them, beaming with anticipation.

"Uncle Larry is expecting us," she declared. "He's out of his mind with joy right now. All this time he thought I was dead. It'll probably take him a while to get his emotions under control."

Her dancing eyes focused on Lucas and her smile faded. "Lucas, you don't look so good."

"I'm fine," he assured her, pushing off the wall. "Your godfather's waiting."

In the elevator, a clammy sweat breached Lucas's pores, causing his T-shirt to stick to him. He widened his stance to counteract his unsteadiness as the elevator rose to the fifth floor.

Glancing at him sidelong, Charlotte shifted closer and linked her arm through his good one.

He felt instantly bolstered. She didn't have to touch him anymore. They weren't trying to pass themselves off as honeymooners as they were in Sabena, but she obviously considered him a friend. The realization both consoled and saddened him, making him acknowledge he wanted more from her than merely friendship.

As they stepped out of the elevator, a woman in a chic gray suit jumped up from her desk to greet them.

"Miss Patterson," she cried, embracing Charlotte warmly. "I'm so happy to see you. Gentlemen," she added, acknowledging Lucas and Saul as she backed up and opened a wide door. "Go right on in," she invited. "Mr. Martin is expecting you."

"Uncle Larry!" Charlotte abandoned Lucas to rush into the big office beyond. Lucas and Saul followed more sedately.

The handsome, fifties-something director rounded his desk with his arms flung wide. Charlotte threw herself at him.

"Charlotte!" He pulled her into a bear hug, lifting her briefly off her feet before putting her down again and setting her at arm's length to look her over. If he thought her wardrobe odd, he didn't say anything. His own attire was as sharp as Special Agent Fitz's, with a power tie and glinting cuff links. "I can't believe you're here. And you look incredible, not a scratch on you. You'll have to tell me everything," he added, his speech swift and forceful. "I've been worried sick."

"You've lost a lot of weight," Charlotte commented. She rubbed his flat belly, clearly on familiar terms with him.

"From worrying about you," he admitted, with a grimace. "I thought you were dead, Charlotte," he added gravely. The weight of the world seemed to descend on his shoulders as he regarded her.

"Well, I'm fine," she assured him, "thanks to these two." She gestured to Saul and Lucas. "These are the SEALs who rescued me from the Bahamas."

"Bahamas!" Martin shot her a look of disbelief before stepping forward and extending his hand.

"This is Lt. Lucas Strong," Charlotte said, making introductions.

Mr. Martin, seeing Lucas's right arm strapped to his torso, switched hands and gave Lucas's left hand a firm shake.

"And Chief Saul Wade," Charlotte added.

"I can't thank you men enough," Director Martin clipped, grasping Saul's hand with equal zeal. "Please, have a seat." He gestured to the upholstered armchairs facing his desk, then turned back to his goddaughter. "Charlotte, tell me everything," he commanded, steering her toward the chair closest to his desk. Wheeling his own chair out from behind it, he sat down next to her.

Lucas heaved a sigh of relief to be off his feet. His back throbbed with every beat of his heart. As Charlotte relayed how she was kidnapped and drugged only to wake up in Roger Holden's plantation house, Lucas willed his pain to subside so he could listen better, perhaps even add a word or two. He was grateful to Saul for paying close attention as she went on to explain how the SEALs had rescued her.

Her godfather interrupted, asking the SEALs in his peremptory manner, "How on earth did you know where to look for her?"

Saul spoke up before Lucas could. "We're not permitted to disclose that information, sir," he said quickly.

"No, of course not," the director agreed. "It's just that I had my own people looking everywhere, and we came up with nothing." He regarded Charlotte again and grimaced. "Well, you're home now, and that's all that matters," he relented. "Tell me what happened to you," he ordered.

Charlotte shrugged and said simply, "Obviously, someone didn't want me bringing you that evidence."

"Commander Dwyer," the director guessed, then glanced sharply at the SEALs. "Wait, Dwyer is your commander, isn't he?"

"Unfortunately, he is," Lucas acknowledged, speaking through a jaw clenched in pain. "We'd like to prove he's been stealing weapons in advance of the Teams, but all the evidence disappeared when Charlotte was abducted."

Director Martin frowned at their dilemma. All at once his brow cleared. "Wait, not all of it," he corrected Lucas. "Charlotte emailed me some pictures of a journal with entries that implicate Dwyer's XO of sending unauthorized emails."

He looked back at Charlotte who smiled at him hopefully. "I was just going to ask you if you still have those pictures."

"Of course I have them." Pushing off his feet, Director Martin sent his chair shooting back behind his desk where he performed a quick search on his computer. "Right here. I kept them thinking I'd go after Dwyer myself if you never came back. Should I print them out for you?"

"That would be great," she agreed. "And forward them to my personal email, if you would, but not to my work address," she added with a look of frustration. "Apparently, I'm not an intern for NCIS anymore. They must have fired me when I failed to show up for work."

Martin's blue eyes flashed as he looked up at her suddenly. "That's absurd," he stated with affront. "You were kidnapped. What were you supposed to do? Call in sick? I'm going to make some phone calls about this," he added, reaching for a pen as if to scribble himself a note.

"Oh, no, don't do that," Charlotte begged him. "It's no big deal, really. I don't want to work at NCIS anymore anyway—not when one of the higher-ups is clearly protecting Dwyer."

"Protecting him how?" Martin wanted to know.

Charlotte gestured to Saul. "Well, for one thing, Saul's testimony about what happened between Dwyer and Lieutenant Mills was completely overlooked. And for another, my supervisor's hard drive, along with all his evidence against Dwyer, disappeared within a day of his death."

Martin's lean face flushed with indignation. "I can't believe all this corruption," he muttered, sending the SEALs a sympathetic look. He wrested his gaze suddenly back to Charlotte. "Dwyer doesn't know you're back in the area, does he?" he inquired with concern.

Charlotte bit her lower lip in lieu of answering. Lucas could tell she couldn't bring herself to withhold everything from her godfather. "Um, he might," she prevaricated without giving any details.

Larry Martin waited for her to say more. When she kept mum, he looked back at the SEALs and said in his terse manner, "Please don't take offense, gentlemen, but Charlotte would be better off staying with me for a while—at least until your arm heals," he added, glancing pointedly at Lucas's right arm.

Lucas was tempted to tell him nothing was wrong with his arm, but that would entail explaining how he'd gotten shot in the back, and they'd agreed not to bring up the subject of The Entity or the warehouse.

Charlotte spoke up before he could. "Thank you, Uncle Larry, but I have to stay with the SEALs. Lieutenant Mills is on trial because of Dwyer, and I promised to help him weeks ago, remember? That's what my supervisor would have wanted."

Martin considered her with a long, worried look. "What about bodyguards, then? I can assign two of them for additional security, and you'll never even notice them. They come with their own housing in the form of a Winnebago," he added persuasively.

Charlotte looked to Saul and Lucas for their reaction. "What do you think, guys?"

Lucas balked at first, his pride resisting the notion that they couldn't protect Charlotte themselves. But then he realized The Entity, once they figured out who had broken into their warehouse, might come looking for reprisal. Moreover, if Fitz was protecting Dwyer, not tearing down The Entity like he'd said, the SEALs couldn't count on the FBI to protect them. So, yeah, they could use all the added manpower they could get.

"We'll take them," Lucas gritted, having received a slight nod of approval from Saul.

"It's set then," Martin concluded, wiggling his mouse to bring up something on his desk top. "Galbraith and Stone will be waiting in the lobby to follow you when you leave," he added decisively.

"Thank you, Uncle Larry," Charlotte murmured as Martin finished putting in his request.

He straightened abruptly to look at her. "Have you spoken to your brother yet?"

"Yes, I called him from the Bahamas. "But Fi—" Charlotte caught herself just in time from mentioned Fitz's name. "But I figured," she recovered smoothly, "that Calvin would be safer if I didn't call him from within the USA."

Martin regarded her thoughtfully. Lucas wondered if he'd noticed Charlotte's near slip-of-the-tongue and was wondering what she'd been about to say. "You're probably right," he finally said. "How long do you plan to stick around? We could all go to lunch, my treat," he offered.

Charlotte shot Lucas an assessing look. "I don't think so. Not today, Uncle Larry. Lucas needs to rest."

"Rest where?" Martin demanded. "You're not driving all the way back to The Beach, are you?"

"No, we're going to stay at my parents' townhouse for a couple of days," Charlotte answered for all of them.

This was the first Lucas had heard of such a plan, but Saul's complacent reaction suggested he and Charlotte had discussed it without him.

The director turned a concerned gaze on Lucas. "I hope my men give you some piece of mind so you can recover, Lieutenant," he said kindly. It was clear he was dying to hear what had happened to him but was too professional to ask.

"Yes, sir. Thank you, sir."

"I'd better give them a heads-up." Moving toward his phone, Martin buzzed his secretary. "Donna, make sure Galbraith and Stone received my orders. I want them ready to scramble in five minutes. No, I don't need them at the golf course," he added, countering something she said on an impatient note. "I've gone there a thousand times without incident. Charlotte's safety comes first," he added, on a note that wasn't to be argued with.

"Uncle Larry," Charlotte protested when he released the button.

"I don't want to hear a word." His firm tone was countered by the affectionate look he sent her as he pushed to his feet. "Commander Dwyer has kidnapped you once. I'm not letting him get to you again." He rounded his desk with his arms outspread. "Now give me a hug and stay safe," he ordered her gruffly.

Realizing it was time to leave, Lucas rose unsteadily to his feet.

Charlotte embraced her godfather one more time. "Promise me you'll start eating again," she ordered as she pulled away.

"I'll get fat as a boar now that you're alive," he declared with a tolerant smile. "Gentlemen," he added, shaking both SEALs' hands a second time. "Charlotte means everything to me," he added, implying they had better protect her with their lives. Then he crossed to the door and pulled it open for them. "Don't forget to grab the printouts from Donna," he reminded Charlotte as they all filed out.

Lucas had to concentrate to put one foot in front of the other. Pain shuddered down his spine with every step. He wanted to keel over and die. Instead, he forced himself to pay attention as Charlotte fetched the printed photos of LeMere's journal and carried them into the elevator.

As they stepped inside, Saul put a steadying hand on Lucas's elbow. Charlotte, who was busy scanning the printouts, let Saul push the button for the lobby.

"Little John needs to rest now," Saul said, speaking as if Lucas wasn't there.

Lifting her gaze from the printouts, Charlotte eyed him with

169

concern. The pain Lucas was feeling must have shown in his face for she immediately stuffed the papers into her purse and propped herself under his good arm.

"Don't faint on us," she ordered sternly, sounding just like her godfather with her clipped words. The concern in her eyes, however, warmed him all the way to his toes.

"Too much going on for me to faint. As soon as we get to the car, one of you needs to call Jaguar's lawyer and find out what happened at the motion hearing."

Charlotte patted his hand. "We'll take care of it, Lucas. You don't have to be the man with the plan right now. Just take it easy. Once we get to my folks' house, you can rest."

Lucas had no choice but to relinquish control. As Director Martin had implied, he wasn't of any use to anyone in his present state. It was definitely a good thing Martin had offered them the use of his personal bodyguards. Without them, he wouldn't dare to even close his eyes, not given their uncertain situation and the element of danger still in play.

CHAPTER 14

$\mathcal{C}$arrying a tray of soup and crackers and a few other items she'd found in the pantry of her parents' kitchen to the second-story bedroom she had occupied as a teen, Charlotte paused at the doorway. Affection welled in her as she watched Lucas sleep.

In order to fit on her full-sized bed, he had to lie diagonally. Even so, lying on his stomach and hugging a pillow with one arm, his feet hung off the mattress. She should have put him in her parents' king-sized bed, only she rarely entered that room.

The mellowing sun shone through the cracks of her lowered blinds, painting gold stripes across her mauve quilt. Charlotte hesitated. Was Lucas wearing any clothes? His bare back indicated he was at least shirtless.

Saul must have helped him undress. He'd also removed the Velcro strips that kept Lucas's arm pinned to his chest. A crisp white bandage covered the surgery site, indicating Saul had swapped out the old bandage using the first aid kit in his car. Good thing all SEALs had some medical training, and Saul more than most.

Tiptoeing forward, she carried the tray to the desk near her bed. Despite her stealth, Lucas heard her, raising his head.

"Hi." She put the tray down and faced him. "How do you feel?"

"Better." His voice was gruff from sleep. A two-day growth of beard darkened the lower half of his face. He appealed to her so powerfully, she forced herself to look over at the tray.

"I brought up some food. It's pretty basic. There was nothing but canned food in the pantry."

"What time is it?" he asked, glancing at his bare wrist.

"Almost 8 p.m." Seeing his watch on the bedside table, she went to collect it for him.

"Thanks. I can't believe I slept so long," he lamented, strapping it on.

"It's good for you." With her heart in her throat and anticipating the sight of his bare body, she watched him push to his knees, grimacing with discomfort.

His triceps flexed and his pecs bulged, keeping her spellbound as he painstakingly scooted to the edge of her bed. To her mixed relief and disappointment, he dragged the comforter with him, keeping it around his hips.

Once settled, he looked her up and down with interest. "Is this the real you?"

Charlotte cut a self-conscious glance at her salmon-pink sweat-top and faded jeans. "Sort of. These are just some old clothes I left here."

"I like the look," he said with warmth in his dove-gray eyes. "Much more approachable. You look really young. Full of potential." The observation seemed to depress him.

With a slight shrug at his strange mood, she handed him the tray. "Sorry it's weird."

Lucas regarded the various offerings—vegetable soup with crackers, a bowl of applesauce, and baked beans.

"Trust me, I've had way worse," he told her, then dipped a cracker into his soup.

"The Gallstones wouldn't let me order pizza. Tomorrow, they said."

He stilled for a moment, processing what she'd said, then flashed her a smile. "Galbraith and Stone. The Gallstones. Very clever."

"I amaze myself sometimes."

He laughed at her wit, spooned up some soup, and blew a cooling breath across it.

Charlotte's gaze centered on his lips, and the memory of their kiss blew threw her. The thought of never kissing him again filled her with a deep sense of loss. More than anything, though, she would miss the way they bantered back and forth.

"Tell me more about your godfather," Lucas requested between slurps. "I take it he was a friend of your father's?"

Charlotte eyed the bed, wondering whether to sit or not. "His best friend," she answered, staying on her feet. "He and my dad had two tours together, Japan and Ecuador, so I've known him all my life. Uncle Larry didn't make a lateral shift from the CIA to DIA until I was in high school."

Lucas looked up at her with interest. "You grew up overseas. I just realized that."

"Not the whole time. I spent my teen years in this house. Dad got a job at Langley, and he and Uncle Larry got to hang out again."

"What did your mom do?"

Charlotte thought back. "She accompanied them when she could, but she was busy driving Calvin and me to all of our extracurriculars."

Lucas gave up using the spoon and tipped the soup bowl to his mouth, draining it in seconds. He then tackled the baked beans. "Have you eaten yet?"

"Yes. Does my staring bother you?" she inquired. "I'm supposed to put this ointment on your back when you're done." She pulled a tube of Neosporin out of her back pocket. "Saul's orders."

"Hmm." Lucas studied the tube, then looked up at her.

Charlotte's pulse quickened at the expression in his eyes.

Lucas finished his meal in short order. Neither of them spoke another word until the bowls had all been emptied.

"Guess I was hungry," he commented, patting his mouth with the napkin she'd supplied.

"Guess you were." Taking the tray from him, Charlotte placed it on her desk, then twisted the lid off the ointment and, with a self-conscious smile for Lucas, joined him on the mattress so that she was looking at his back.

"Are you squeamish?" Lucas asked as she peeled back the adhesive and lifted the bandage from the wound.

"Not particularly." All the same, the line of stitches poking out of his red, puckered flesh made her stomach lurch. She squeezed ointment directly onto the wound and rubbed it in with one gentle finger. "Does this hurt?"

"No." His voice was gruff, like a purr. "Feels good actually."

Charlotte didn't want to stop. Lucas's broad back, with its complex interplay of muscle and sinew, was like an irresistible playground. It took all her willpower to re-cover the bandage, rubbing the adhesive tape down so it would stick. The impulse to embrace him from behind overwhelmed her suddenly.

Wrapping her arms around him on a whim, she laid her cheek on the back of his good shoulder. It felt so good to hug him again.

"I'm glad you weren't killed," she murmured.

She would have released him if Lucas hadn't clamped a hand over her arm, keeping her from moving.

Locked against his back, Charlotte ran her free hand lightly over his ribs. "Are these the ones you broke?"

"Other side." He took the wrist he'd pinned and moved her hand over the left side of his rib cage. "Can you feel a bump? The bone is thicker where it healed."

"I think I feel it," Charlotte said, but all she felt was the thudding of his heart, beating like hers was, a tad too swiftly. Touching his warm, silky skin filled her with a clamoring to feel his skin on hers.

"I should go," she said, wriggling reluctantly off the bed.

Lucas released her with disappointment he didn't bother to mask. "I enjoy your company," he admitted, as she put a foot on the floor and stood up next to him.

Her heart lifted at the confession then twisted when she remembered why they couldn't have a future together.

"I enjoy yours, too," she confessed. "I've had a really great time with you," she added, trying to lighten some of the tension in the room. "Despite the high-speed car chase and thinking you might die on me," she quipped.

He drew in a breath and let it out again, causing her eyes to slide to his rippling abs.

"I don't suppose I could talk you out of joining the CIA and sticking around The Beach?"

Her eyes widened at the realization he was asking her to give up her career plans in order to be his girlfriend. Picturing them together —truly together—made her mouth turn dry and her head spin.

Wetting her lips, she answered with regret, "You don't know how tempting that is, Lucas. But I've had this dream all my life. And nobody can talk me out of it. Not even you," she added with apology.

His mouth drooped, and he dropped his gaze to the loose thread he was fingering on the comforter. "I understand."

"I'm sorry," she murmured with lament.

He looked up suddenly, clearly just remembering. "Did Saul find out what happened at the motion hearing?" His voice was suddenly all business.

"Oh, yes," she said, relieved to have something less personal to talk about. "Most of the evidence was approved, with two big exceptions, maybe three. Both Saul and Monica are allowed to testify and so is Jaguar's psychiatrist. Dwyer, of course, is going to testify for the prosecution, along with some doctor from Portsmouth Medical Center and an employee of the skeet-and-trap range. Jaguar's lawyer is feeling optimistic.

"What are the exceptions?" Lucas asked, visibly bracing himself.

"Well, the first was expected. The photos of LeMere's journal weren't presented in time, so they're out. Then, the forensic expert you hired to talk about Lowery's supposed suicide was denied testimony because that had nothing to do with what happened at the range. That doesn't mean Dwyer can't be charged later, however. Finally, the vase was rejected as inadmissible evidence. All Monica can talk about is what Dwyer asked her to do while he was at the skeet-and-trap range with Jaguar."

Disappointment firmed Lucas's mouth. "If Carew is feeling optimistic, it's because she underestimates the prosecutor. Ethan O'Rourke is legendary." He shook his head in lament. "Sounds like our pictures of the warehouse wouldn't have been admissible either. I don't know how we're supposed to help Jaguar when all our evidence of Dwyer's treachery is denied."

Charlotte's own hopes for a good outcome floundered. "And we don't even know if Fitz is on our side anymore," she recollected. "If he's helping The Entity, he's not going to care whether Jaguar is dishonorably discharged or not."

"He promised he would overturn any guilty convictions," Lucas growled. "Gosh, I hope he's a man of his word."

"Me, too," Charlotte agreed, though she had serious reservations. "There's one more important thing I need to tell you."

Lucas looked at her expectantly.

"The actual court-martial starts this Thursday."

Lucas's eyes widened. "That soon? It usually comes weeks after the motion hearing."

"I know, but Dwyer is pushing for haste since he can't retire as long as he's pressing charges."

"And it's all about him," Lucas muttered with disgust. "I guess we'd better get back home."

"We have all weekend, and you need to rest. Saul thinks we're safer up here, where neither Dwyer nor Fitz knows how to find us."

"He's probably right," Lucas relented.

"You should rest," she repeated. Charlotte scooped up the tray she'd brought in and backed out of the room. "Help yourself to the shower, but don't get the wound wet."

"I know the drill," he assured her lightly. "Wait, since this is your old bedroom, don't you want to sleep in here? I can move to your brother's room."

"I told you, that bed's too small for you. You stay here. I'll be fine in

Calvin's room. Call me if you need me," she added, regretting her choice of words as she pulled the door closed behind her.

If Lucas called out for her that night, all she could do was check on him and make sure he had what he needed. Unless she gave up her dreams to be his girlfriend, she would never get to sleep in the same bed with him again.

~

Casey Fitzpatrick punched in the code that unlocked the door of his upscale apartment. The triple deadbolts released with a quiet *click, click, click*, giving him access to a penthouse suite that overlooked downtown Norfolk. Tired from his frantic efforts to hold together his investigation, he was almost grateful for the silence that greeted him.

But not really. Silence made him think of the family vault in St. Raymond's Cemetery, New York City, where the bodies of his entire family—Mary and their three children—lay entombed.

He thrust the memory from his head. It was better to think of them as still living and to recollect the noise that awaited him after a long day's beat in the NYPD. Mary would be herding the children from the bath to their beds, using threats to ensure their cooperation. She was the loudest of all of them, he recalled, his lips twitching toward a smile.

The door to his apartment closed with a soft hiss of air. He punched a button on his door and the door relocked itself. *Quiet again.*

Though the sun had set a couple of hours ago, Fitz kept the lights off, unwilling to chase away the memories of his children greeting him.

Daddy's home!

He imagined the younger ones hiding behind his legs to avoid their ranting mother. Funny, he could still remember their voices, even after all these years. The baby, Collin, had a giggle so infectious no one could hear it without laughing also. Rosy, who was four, could hit notes that shattered glass. Rory, who took after his father, was thirteen. His voice had been about to change into that of a man's when…

Fitz snapped on the lights to keep his thoughts from returning to the day he'd found them all dead—even the baby. Shot in the head.

What had he expected? One didn't lock up the two most powerful men in the Mafia without paying a price, a price so awful he woke up every morning wondering why he bothered to get out of bed. It was only because of Mary that he'd moved on. Even in death, she harangued him.

Don't be a sissy, Fitz. Get up, get moving, and you'll feel better.

She'd been right, of course. After five years, he'd accepted their deaths. He'd grown accustomed to the silence. But he had yet to forgive himself for what had happened.

Light flooded his living room. Dropping his briefcase onto the sofa, Fitz made his way to the kitchen, prompted by the rumbling of his stomach. His work had kept him so busy, he'd forgotten to eat lunch. In many ways, indicting the leader of The Entity was like capturing those kingpins in the Mafia. Knowing whom to befriend and playing both sides of the coin to get the evidence he needed put him in extreme danger of reprisal.

Except now, he had the edge over everyone else. He no longer had a family to lose. No one could touch him, threaten him, blackmail him. He had nothing left to lose at all.

His thoughts went to Charlotte Patterson, who'd unknowingly lost her parents because of The Entity. When she'd used the cell phone he'd given her the other night, Fitz had been startled to learn she wasn't in Virginia Beach as he'd supposed her to be. Angered by the SEALs' irresponsibility, he'd jumped in the car to track her down. Thirty minutes from Pax River, he'd gotten Lucas Strong's message telling him exactly what had happened.

With a shake of his head and a muttered word, Fitz opened the refrigerator and stared at the sparse contents—stale milk, some orange juice, and three-day-old pizza. Pulling out the orange juice, he unscrewed the lid and drank straight from the bottle.

Lucas Strong and his sidekick sniper needed to leave the evidence-gathering to Fitz. They had no idea whom they were dealing with. It pricked Fitz's conscience to have threatened the lieutenant while he was recovering from surgery, but one false move and Fitz's entire investigation could crumble into dust.

Tipping the bottle all the way back, Fitz drained its contents, grateful for the rush of natural sugars that revived him. But then the light draft of air running across the knuckles of his upheld hand made him freeze.

He took one last swallow then quietly put the lid and the bottle both on the counter. Reaching around the wall for the light switch, he turned the lights in the living room back off, then drew his Magnum from the holster under his seersucker blazer. With a stab of concern, he recalled he'd removed his bulletproof vest in the car because of the heat.

Peering into the living room, he scanned the dark sliding-glass doors that opened to his tenth-story balcony, and ascertained they were all shut. The draft was coming from his bedroom, which gave access to a second balcony.

His years as a street cop kept his heart beating steadily as he traversed the short hallway, past his guest bedroom and guest bath to the master. His thoughts raced ahead of him at the possibility that the head of The Entity was already on to him.

The master door stood cracked. Fitz sidled up to it, pushing it farther open with the muzzle of his Magnum. The night-light shining from his bathroom shed just enough light that he could make out his gauzy curtains, lifting and lowering from the breeze coming through the open glass door. He knew for certain he hadn't opened it himself.

Instinct warned him to step back, but he wasn't fast enough.

A pistol discharged. Fitz saw the muzzle flash, felt the bullet strike his upper chest, throwing him back against the hallway wall. A simultaneous sting in his neck confused him. He slid down the wall, stunned to think he'd been mortally wounded.

Landing in a seated position on the floor, he raised his free hand toward the warmth sliding down his neck and realized that, though he'd been shot in the chest, only his neck was bleeding. Blood was also trickling down his throat, forcing him to swallow to keep it from filling up his lungs.

But he wasn't dead yet. The realization that he could still think, still move, prompted him to raise his pistol at the silhouette coming toward him and pull the trigger.

Bang! The Magnum kicked against his palm and sent his attacker staggering backward, struck in the shoulder. As the man transferred his pistol to the other hand, Fitz aimed and fired again, finally killing him.

The Entity's hitman, probably Jason Dunn, was now lying dead in Fitz's bedroom, leaving no doubt in his mind that The Entity was on to him. A dozen epithets vied for articulation, but he couldn't speak with blood pouring down his throat. Spitting it out onto his Berber carpet, Fitz rolled onto his hands and knees. He fished his cell phone from his pocket and calmly dialed 911.

There was still a way left to retain the upper hand.

When the dispatcher answered, he found he still couldn't speak and not only from the blood. His vocal chords must have been damaged by whatever had sliced his throat.

"Sir, I can hear you on the other end. Tap the phone once if this is an emergency. One tap for yes, two for no."

Fitz tapped his phone against the wall, once.

"Would you like us to send an ambulance to your location?"

Tap.

For the next two minutes, without him saying so much as a word, the woman had located his address and dispatched an ambulance along with the police. Fitz got up and staggered toward the door to unlock it. He also turned the lights on.

Choking on his own blood, he dropped to his knees again, keeping his head lower than his chest so the blood drained out of his mouth onto his marble-tiled entryway.

As his St. Christopher medal swung against his chin, Fitz reached up to finger it, astonished to find the once-smooth medallion jagged and chipped.

"This is going to save your life one day," Mary had declared when she'd given it to him after they first got married.

Instead of piercing his chest, the assassin's bullet had struck the platinum medallion, cracking it in half and sending the chipped piece, like shrapnel, into Fitz's neck.

He had to laugh at the irony, only he couldn't make a sound. Tears of humor mixed with grief and gratitude.

Mary was right, of course. She had always been right. The medallion had saved his life when The Entity clearly meant to end it. Despite the quantity of blood pooling in the foyer around him, Fitz was certain he would live.

What surprised him was the realization that he actually wanted to.

CHAPTER 15

*L*ucas did not call Charlotte out of her brother's bedroom that night.

For eight hours, she tossed and turned on Calvin's rock-hard mattress scarcely able to sleep. In her head, Lucas's offer replayed over and over again, inciting pointless longing.

I don't suppose I could talk you out of joining the CIA and sticking around The Beach?

When she finally did sleep, she dreamed she was trapped in a foreign country being chased by people who wanted to kill her, all the while trying to find her way back home. At dawn, Charlotte rolled off the torture rack and went downstairs to shake off her nightmare.

Saul, who was sprawled across the couch with Lucas's HK across his chest, cracked an eye as she came down the steps. "What time is it?"

"Six," she said tersely. "Tell the Gallstones they need to go pick up some food for us. I want eggs, milk, bacon, and bread. Oh, and coffee. If they won't get it, I will."

Saul swung his feet to the floor and dragged his hair out of his eyes to better consider her. "What side of the bed did you roll out of?"

"The wrong side, obviously," she retorted, going back upstairs to shower.

She realized as she was drying off that her clean clothes were in with Lucas. She sent a stern glance into the fogged bathroom mirror. *Don't even think about* it, she ordered herself, then wrapped the bath towel securely around her nakedness.

As large as the towel was, it covered her modestly. She would go in quickly, grab her clothes, and leave.

Lucas's eyes sprang open at her quiet entrance.

"Sorry," she apologized, leaving the door open behind her. "I just need to get some clothes."

He didn't say a word as she crossed to her old dresser and pulled it open, plucking underthings and a T-shirt from various drawers.

"How'd you sleep?" he finally asked, his gruff voice like music to her ears.

"Terribly," she admitted, clutching the garments to her chest.

He glanced at his watch. "It's only six thirty. Why don't you go back to bed?"

The offer made her look at the space next to him with pointless longing. All at once, the phone on the nightstand started buzzing.

"Someone's calling you," she said, stating the obvious.

His groan of pain as he reached for his cell phone prompted her to cross to the bedside table and picked it up for him.

"Thanks," he said, frowning at the number as he took it. "I don't recognize the caller."

"Answer it," she urged.

He hit speaker so she could also hear. "Hello?"

"Lucas, it's me."

The voice Charlotte remembered from her confrontation with Monica hit her like a slap in the face. But this time it was tinged with fear.

"Is something wrong?" Lucas asked, flicking Charlotte an uncomfortable glance. "Why aren't you calling on your own phone?"

"Because I don't have it. I'm using my sister's phone."

"What happened?" he prompted again.

"You're not going to believe this, but someone broke into my house last night. I'm pretty sure they came to kill me."

With difficulty, Lucas pushed himself to a seated position. "What?"

"Thank God I wasn't in my bed or I doubt I'd be talking to you right now." Monica hurried on, unaware that Charlotte was listening. "I'd gotten up to use the bathroom. All of a sudden, I heard my bedroom door open—you know how it squeaks."

Charlotte took immediate note of the intimate reference.

"When I heard the squeak, I locked the bathroom door, but the intruder knew I was in there, and he started messing with the lock, so I crawled out the little window over the toilet and fell all the way to the ground, spraining my wrist." A sob ruptured Monica's tale.

"That's when I heard the door crash open. I hugged the house so I wouldn't be seen, then I turned the corner and jumped the fence in my nightgown. I ran through a few backyards until I got to a friend's house. You remember Cathy? I pounded on her back door until her husband let me in. Oh, my God, Lucas, I was so scared!"

Her genuine terror took the edge off Charlotte's jealousy.

"Where are you now?" Lucas asked.

"Cathy called an Uber to take me to my sister's house. Becky didn't think we were safe there, so we jumped into her car, and now we're at a lake house belonging to a friend of hers, up near Charlottesville."

"Good thinking," Lucas praised. "You did what you had to do."

"Lucas, I don't think the break-in was a coincidence," Monica stated.

Lucas shared a dark look with Charlotte.

"I think it was because I agreed to testify. I can't believe Dwyer would hunt me down like some kind of animal after all I've done for him!"

Like what? Charlotte wondered, intrigued by her choice of words.

"I believe it," Lucas answered grimly. "I'm just glad you weren't hurt."

Charlotte turned away and walked out of the room. The concern in Lucas's voice tore at her heartstrings.

All along, she'd suspected he might patch things up with Monica. That time had evidently come. Monica's frightening experience would summon Lucas's protective instincts. He would offer to rescue her and protect her until Jaguar's court-martial was over, perhaps even longer. That was what superheroes did.

Dressing swiftly in her brother's room, Charlotte listened to Lucas's conversation through the wall. She couldn't hear his words, only his soothing tone, which stirred her jealousy. He had used that tone with her on the rigid inflatable boat after rescuing her, then again after she'd seen Jason Dunn in the tree. She had thought that voice was reserved especially for her.

Still feeling out of sorts, Charlotte tromped down the stairs to the galley kitchen at the back of the nineteenth-century townhome and found Saul whisking eggs in a bowl while bacon sizzled on the stovetop.

"They got what you asked for," he said, glancing at her briefly. "Must be nice having a security detail who also does the shopping."

When Charlotte didn't say a word, Saul took closer stock of her.

"What's wrong?" he demanded.

Charlotte stuck to the facts as she opened the lid of the coffee maker and pulled out the filter basket. "Someone broke into Monica's house last night and tried to do her in. Lucas is talking to her now."

Scowling thoughtfully, Saul flipped the bacon. "You think she's telling the truth?"

Saul's dubious tone wrested Charlotte's attention. It hadn't even occurred to her Monica was lying.

"Don't you? The defense found out yesterday that Monica's testifying," she reminded him. "Dwyer obviously doesn't want that happening."

Saul grunted noncommittally.

"What have you got against Monica, anyway?" she asked him,

opening the fresh bag of coffee and breathing in the crisp, tantalizing scent.

"She's an opportunist," Saul stated, sliding the griddle off the burner. "Every guy in the squadron could see it but Lucas. In my opinion, the only reason she's agreed to testify against Dwyer is because he transferred her to a different office, and she hates her new job."

"Really?" Charlotte poured coffee grounds into the filter.

"Why did *you* think she agreed to testify?" Saul asked.

"To prove to Lucas that her career isn't more important than he is."

Saul grunted again, and Charlotte turned to fill the coffeepot with water.

The sound of stairs creaking alerted them both to Lucas's approach. Charlotte snatched up the loaf of bread, preparing to make toast, and Saul turned his attention to the stove again—both of them acting like guilty children.

"Something smells good in here," Lucas commented as he loomed at the doorway

Charlotte darted a look at him. He had managed to dress in jeans and a T-shirt without anyone helping him. With his hair sticking up and his jaw darkly stubbled, he almost passed for a normal human being. She was glad to see his coloring back to normal.

Saul didn't waste time on pleasantries. "Don't tell me we're protecting Monica now, too," he said, then dumped the bowl of whisked eggs into a heated pan.

Lucas sent Charlotte an uncomfortable glance. "Just so you know, this wasn't my idea. I called Jaguar's counsel after talking to Monica, and she recommended we pick her up on our way back to The Beach. Carew considers her testimony critical to Jaguar's defense. Monica has to be there."

And someone has to protect her until the trial on Thursday. Charlotte dropped bread in the toaster, thinking hard.

"We're already protecting Charlotte," Saul pointed out with disapproval in his voice.

"I don't need your protection anymore," she countered, just real-

187

izing that fact. "I've got the Gallstones to protect me. Monica doesn't have anybody. Go get her. I'll go home with my godfather's bodyguards."

When silence was her only reply, Charlotte turned around to see Lucas standing at the doorway looking torn. Saul, scrambling the eggs with vicious strokes, said nothing more.

"We can protect both of you," Lucas argued, but the look on his face told Charlotte the mere idea made him uncomfortable.

"Listen." She strove to put him out of his misery. This was the right thing to do. "I'm not actually a threat to Dwyer anymore—or, by extension, The Entity. I can't remember enough of Lloyd's files to be a threat. There's no point to my wearing a disguise anymore, either, because Dwyer already identified me. Therefore, I don't need protection."

She held up a finger as Lucas went to cut her off. "If the bad guys still come after me, I've got the Gallstones to defend me. I'll be fine," she added, turning back to the toast so she wouldn't cave in and offer him a reassuring hug.

Lucas sought Saul's opinion. "What do you think, Chief?"

With the eggs done, Saul turned off the stove with a decisive snap. His gaze went from Lucas to Charlotte and back to Lucas. "I think two women to protect is too much," he said shortly. "Especially with you being injured."

Charlotte, who knew what Saul was really saying, thanked him with a quick glance for being ambiguous. Lucas heard what he wanted to hear—that Charlotte could defend herself while Monica now needed their protection. She hoped he wasn't gullible enough to fall for her antics anymore.

"Breakfast is ready," Saul added, turning his attention to plating the food.

As they sat down to eat a moment later in the nook at one end of the kitchen, Charlotte found it difficult to eat. The food, while perfectly cooked, seemed tasteless, as the prospect of parting ways with Lucas hit her harder than she had thought it would.

Glancing at Lucas and experiencing an immediate tug of attraction, she acknowledged to herself she was a tiny bit concerned he would fall for Monica again. Despite how strongly he'd condemned Monica's actions, Charlotte did not underestimate her ability to charm him again. After all, she had managed to pull the wool over Charlotte's eyes during their one brief encounter.

That's not going to happen, she comforted herself. Lucas knew he deserved better than a woman who used him. What he deserved was someone… She caught herself thinking *more like me,* then remembered her own job and the three kids he wanted.

The sad truth was, she wasn't any better for Lucas than Monica was. Bowing out of the picture now was the best thing she could do for him.

~

It was late by the time Lucas shut and locked his bedroom door in his condo in Virginia Beach. He stood a moment in the dark, listening for indications Monica was done with her shower and was settling onto the futon in his guest bedroom. He had shooed Saul home in time to pick up Duke from the dog sitter's. Given the state-of-the-art alarm system in Lucas's condo, Saul's presence seemed redundant. What's more, Saul was barely civil to Monica, which made being around both of them even more stressful than being around only her.

How Lucas had gone from protecting Charlotte to protecting his ex-fiancée still puzzled him.

Hearing the water turn off in Monica's en suite, Lucas crossed toward his dresser where he unbuckled his belt, sliding off the paddle holster and laying it, with the gun still inside, on his dresser. With some difficulty moving his right arm, he shucked his jeans and socks, dropping them into his laundry hamper. Wearing only his T-shirt and boxers, he picked up the holster and carried it to his bedside table. Then he pulled back the tightly tucked sheet and climbed into bed before turning off the lamp.

After so many nights away from home, it felt strange to be lying in his own bed. He kept his eyes open, refamiliarizing himself with the dimensions of his dark room. Moonlight filtered through his blinds illuminating the walls, the glinting rectangles of his framed Ansel Adams' photos, and his coffered ceiling with the high-end paddle fan twirling lazily overhead.

Had it always been so quiet in his house?

After sleeping in older homes for the past few nights, he couldn't help but notice how his newly constructed condo didn't creak or groan. It was, in fact, a little too quiet, like something was missing. His gaze fell to the empty half of his king-sized bed and, all at once, he realized what that was—Charlotte wasn't with him.

His heart clutched with sudden longing.

I miss you, baby.

They had gone their separate ways around noon—Saul and Lucas in the Camaro and Charlotte in the Gallstone's Winnebago. Watching the Winnebago until it turned a corner and disappeared, Lucas had wrestled with the feeling that he had made a grave mistake. Fitz had ordered him and Saul to keep an eye on Charlotte until he told them she was safe. That hadn't happened yet.

What's more, that might never happen if Fitz was, in fact, protecting the vigilante group rather than arresting its members. Lucas hadn't heard from him since their encounter at the hospital.

Not once in his military career had Lucas ignored a direct order. Yet, somehow, Charlotte had talked him into it, with reasons that had struck him as sound at the time. Apart from seeking petty vengeance, The Entity had no more reason to want to grab her. Her memories of Lloyd's files had faded. They'd already discovered the warehouse in Sabena. What's more, she'd revealed that, in her phone call with her brother made in the Bahamas, he had claimed he hadn't eaten or slept when he'd thought her dead. The young man probably needed her. She had to get back to Calvin.

It hadn't occurred to Lucas until the Winnebago disappeared with

Charlotte inside it that she had actually shrugged off his protection because Monica was back in the picture.

But it's only temporary, he wanted to tell Charlotte as he lay alone in bed. Even though Monica had greeted him with gratitude and relief and had clung to him like a burr, Lucas felt no satisfaction in having her underfoot. Unlike Charlotte, she wasn't clever or droll. What he had once admired about Monica—a mysterious beauty that kept him guessing—now struck him as duplicitous.

Not trusting her, he had kept her at arm's length all day and would continue to do so. He had promised her his protection in exchange for her testimony. And nothing more.

Even so, when he'd put Monica in his guest bedroom that evening, he'd seen the hurt and disappointment on her face, and he honestly hadn't cared. Had she really thought he would let her back into his life after what she'd done?

What's more, she wasn't the one Lucas wanted lying next to him. Charlotte was.

Closing his eyes, Lucas envisioned her snuggled close, and his entire being yearned for her.

I'll call her, he thought, only to realize, though he had the number of the phone Fitz had given her, she never kept it on. Leaving a message she might never hear would be pathetic. And what would he say, anyway? *Hey, I miss you.*

What was point to making that confession? He'd already asked if he could talk her out of going into the CIA, and she'd turned him down, albeit gently. He couldn't fault her for wanting to proceed with her plans. Everyone had the right to pursue his or her destiny.

The sound of a door opening down the hall pricked Lucas's ears. Monica was stirring. Listening over the thud of his own heart, he tried to determine what she was up to. In the next instant, he heard his doorknob jiggle. Ah, so she was hoping to join him in his bed. Too bad for her. He'd locked his bedroom door and wasn't about to unlock it.

Her sigh of frustration was audible, bringing a cynical smile to his lips.

Ironic, wasn't it? The woman whom he'd thought he loved had shown her true colors, making him realize he didn't love her, after all. While the woman who'd shown her true colors from the start had won him over without ever intending to.

Hearing Monica retreat in defeat, Lucas took a cleansing breath and cleared his mind. He would pray for forgiveness for shirking his duty first, then for protection for all of them. Lastly and most fervently, he would pray for the possibility that, one day, Charlotte Patterson would somehow turn into the uncomplicated woman he was looking for and put him before her career plans.

All things are possible with God, Lucas reminded himself. So maybe, one day, Charlotte Patterson would come back to him.

Thankful she'd subscribed to an actual newspaper while working on her master's thesis, Charlotte organized the pile of newspapers littering her kitchen table. Without them, she would have had no way of catching up on the news she'd missed these past few weeks. Digital news didn't come with that option. And, thankfully, it hadn't occurred to Calvin to toss the papers out.

Apparently, it also hadn't occurred to her brother to clean up after himself in any way at all.

Sorting the papers by their dates, she put them in a neat pile from oldest to newest and started skimming quickly through them, while sipping a cup of coffee that slowly went to room temperature.

At one point, she tore her attention from the news she was reading to watch her brother empty his cereal bowl in the sink. He rinsed it and was about to walk away when she told him, rather tersely, "Put it in the dishwasher."

If she hadn't come home to a pigsty, she might have used a kinder voice. For a young man who purportedly hadn't eaten the whole time she was gone, he'd sure gone through a lot of dishes, and they'd all been piled in the sink waiting for her.

"And don't forget to brush your teeth," she added as Calvin duti-fully put his bowl where it belonged.

"I'm not five," he muttered. Nonetheless, he went obediently into the bathroom, and seconds later she could hear his electric toothbrush humming.

It's good to be home, Charlotte thought. After weeks of uncertainty and living out of a suitcase wearing clothes she hoped never to wear again, she was back in her own apartment doing her own thing— except she no longer worked for NCIS. She had called to verify that was, indeed, the reason her badge was invalid. Sure enough, she'd been let go for not showing up at the office.

The real reason, Charlotte decided, was someone at NCIS consid-ered her a threat to Dwyer.

She had considered fighting for her position and taking advan-tage of her godfather's influence to get her job back. Instead, she had decided to let it go. Her internship hadn't paid much anyway, and, thanks to her parents' life insurance policies, money wasn't an issue. Provided Calvin managed to land a job right out of college, she was going into the CIA the same month he graduated —though grades had apparently suffered when he'd thought her dead.

Moreover, she had plenty to do before committing herself to her new career, like hunting down Lloyd's wrecked Taurus in the hopes of finding a tracking device on it. If she found it, she could pair it with the disabled tracking device Saul had given her and pair it with her video of the high-speed chase to bring a suit against the Sabena police department.

Later that week, she would attend Jaguar's court-martial. Her spirits lifted abruptly at the prospect of seeing Lucas there. Shaking her head at her impractical feelings, she went back to poring through the newspapers.

So much had happened in the world in the past few weeks! Some of it she had overheard when Saul watched the news on his cell phone at her parents' house. The United States had shot down another hostile Iranian drone. The president's immigration policy was under attack. Talks with North Korea had failed abysmally.

Reading the international news left a body thinking the end of the world was imminent. No wonder The Entity wanted to be prepared. However, a handful of powerful men weren't going to keep America safe, regardless of how many weapons they stockpiled.

Skimming the headlines of the local news, she read that a former state delegate had been charged with defrauding the federal government. Students at an area high school had all walked out in protest over the firing of a teacher. And a former Navy SEAL and FBI special agent had both died in a shoot-out.

What? Charlotte read the article quickly, gasping out loud as she encountered two familiar names—Jason Dunn and Casey Fitzpatrick.

Flattening the paper as it started to curl, she read it one more time, more intently.

Jason Dunn, a former Navy SEAL, was declared dead on the scene after breaking into the penthouse apartment in Norfolk belonging to FBI Special Agent Casey Fitzpatrick. Investigators have confirmed that Dunn shot and mortally wounded Fitzpatrick while the latter survived long enough to return fire, killing his assassin. The FBI refuses to comment whether the break-in was related to any completed or ongoing investigation.

"Bye, Charlotte."

Unaware of her absorption, her brother loped past her with a backpack slung over one shoulder.

Charlotte tore her stunned gaze off the paper. "Be careful," she called, but it wasn't really him she was worried about. It was the rest of them.

Fitz wouldn't have been targeted by The Entity if he'd been protecting them. In other words, she'd been totally wrong about him.

And now he was dead. Mortally wounded, the paper had said.

"Dear Lord," she said, aware that her words were a plea for protection.

She had to tell Saul and Lucas what had happened, though perhaps they already knew. Was it possible The Entity intended to snuff out anyone and everyone who knew enough to oppose them? Surely not. Fitz had held all the evidence. She, Saul, and Lucas could only claim that Dwyer had stolen and stored weapons in Sabena. Once those weapons were moved elsewhere, The Entity had nothing to fear from them.

All the same, it would pay to be vigilant.

Getting up to fetch her purse, Charlotte took out the phone Fitz had given her and turned it on. It was still holding a charge. Suffering remorse for having misjudged the special agent, she dialed the Gallstones while carrying her cell to her third-story window. She could see their Winnebago parked in the lot immediately below her.

"Hey," she said when Stone picked up on the second ring. "I need Lucas Strong's phone number, and I remember he gave it to you."

Stone, ever efficient and professional, recited the number to her.

"Thanks," she said, and promptly hung up on him.

Her heart beat with anticipation as she keyed in Lucas's number, memorizing it in case the phone Fitz gave her suddenly stopped working.

"Hi."

Simply the sound of his voice flooded Charlotte with emotion. For a second, she couldn't speak.

"What's up?" he prompted. His casual tone let her know someone else was listening to their conversation—Monica, of course.

"I just read something from last Thursday's paper. You may already know. Fitz is dead."

"What?"

His alarm made her own scalp tighten. "Jason Dunn broke into his apartment. They had a shoot-out, and both of them are dead."

"No way."

Charlotte whirled from the window and paced to the kitchen and back. "I was wrong about him, Lucas. He wouldn't have been targeted if he was helping The Entity. He really was going after them, but now he's dead, which means they're winning."

"Like heck they're winning," Lucas growled. "We can't let that happen."

"I don't see what we can do," Charlotte lamented. "All our evidence is gone. My memory is a blur. We'd have to start all over again."

He thought a moment. "The FBI has to realize Fitz was targeted for his investigation. Someone in the Bureau will take over."

"Possibly," she agreed. "But Fitz was going to help Jaguar, and now he can't." The finality of Fitz's death hit her suddenly, causing her to drop abruptly onto her couch.

"You good?" Lucas asked, perhaps overhearing her movements.

"Don't worry about me. What are we going to do about Jaguar?"

"The only thing we can do," he replied on a grim note. "Convince the panel he's innocent."

Charlotte considered the evidence they'd been allowed and their witnesses. "Do you really think he has a shot? Maybe we should bring up Dwyer's connection to The Entity after all," she suggested.

"With what evidence?" Lucas countered. "We don't have any."

"Right." Plus, it was too late at this juncture to present evidence that hadn't been approved.

Charlotte's shoulders fell. "There has to be something we can do."

"We can still pray."

He sounded so certain prayer would make a difference that Charlotte figured she'd give it a shot.

"All right. I'll pray, then," she agreed. She drew in a breath and let it out again. "Lucas, you don't think The Entity is going to target us next, do you?"

Thoughtful silence followed her question. "I don't see what it would gain them."

"We know about the warehouse."

"And we've told other people. The only way to contain that leak is to move the weapons elsewhere, which they've probably done by now."

"True," she agreed. "Unless the police chief didn't want to alarm his brother-in-law."

"I'm sure he told him. And I'm sure they've figured out I was one of the men who broke in."

In the background, she heard Monica vying for Lucas's attention with words that weren't quite audible over the phone.

"I should let you go," Charlotte offered, annoyed by the intrusion.

"I'll see you at the trial, though, right?"

Lucas had asked the question as casually as possible, but Charlotte still heard his eagerness to see her, and her heart immediately warmed.

"Of course," she said. "Thursday at one o'clock in the courtroom down the hall from where I used to work."

"You mean they really let you go?" His tone let her know he thought NCIS was crazy.

"Sure did. But that's all right," she added. "I've got other plans."

"Yes, you do."

"Besides, someone in NCIS works for The Entity, it would seem, so I wouldn't go back there anyway."

"I don't blame you."

She wanted to reach through the phone for one of Lucas's all-encompassing hugs. She missed everything about him—the low timbre of his voice, his clean scent, his faith that everything would work out.

With an ache in her throat, she added, "See you soon, Lucas."

"See you," he repeated, hanging up.

Charlotte closed her eyes and held the cell phone against her empty heart. *Am I doing the right thing, God?* Lucas was a one-in-a-million kind of man. Walking away from him felt so wrong. But what choice did she have? She couldn't be a field operative for the CIA while dating a Navy SEAL who lived in the USA. The only time they'd ever see each other was…never.

That wasn't what Lucas wanted or deserved. He'd said his wife could work, but he and any children needed to come first. That was never going to happen as long as Charlotte was a spy.

With a long sigh, she put her cell phone away. At least she knew Lucas's number now. Perhaps they could talk from time to time, remaining friends.

I'll see him on Thursday, she cheered herself. In the next instant, she thought of the stressful conditions under which they would meet. With Fitz dead, Jaguar could be sentenced to three years in prison and fined, all on top of being dishonorably discharged.

"Not going to happen," she muttered, remembering to pray. God's mercy was Jaguar's only hope at this juncture. Clasping her hands, she sent a silent but heartfelt prayer upward.

The urge to expend some pent-up energy had her jumping up from the couch in search of her running shoes. Recalling the possibility that The Entity might be gunning anyone who knew about their facility in Sabena, she decided to run in the workout facility of her apartment and not on the boardwalk as she usually did.

If only she could run from all of her present uncertainties.

CHAPTER 16

With one eye trained on the courtroom door, Lucas spotted Charlotte the second she entered, with less than a minute to spare before the trial was due to start. Pleasure flooded him at the sight of her out of her disguise. Wearing a lemon-yellow pantsuit, with her red hair recently trimmed into a sassy-short cut, she reminded him of a luminous flame.

"Here she is," he murmured to Saul.

Rising partially, he caught her eye and waved her over. Her face lit up, and she started in his direction, only to slow her steps as she caught sight of Monica. With a sardonic tilt to her lips, she slipped into the space Lucas had saved for her. Monica stiffened on his other side. The two women exchanged looks while he sat between them, uncomfortable with the fact that Monica was still sporting his engagement ring.

The latter hissed into his ear, "You have a new girlfriend already?"

Wishing very much that he could answer, "Why, yes," Lucas sent her an impassive look and said, "She's a colleague."

As Monica drew a sharp breath and averted her face, Lucas turned his attention back to Charlotte.

"How's it going?" he asked, squelching the impulse to hug her.

Her gaze caught and held his. "Good," she said breezily, but the quick glance at his mouth betrayed the desire to kiss him. The telltale sign that she had missed him, too, made his heart skip.

"I'm glad you're safe," he said. In the past two days, he'd fretted something would happen to her, making him regret letting her take off with just the Gallstones for protection.

"Are you safe, though?" she asked, widening her eyes and glancing pointedly at Monica's left hand.

Lucas had to laugh. "Don't worry. I've got my armor on," he assured her under his breath.

"Shield," Charlotte corrected. "Captain America has a shield."

"Ah," he said, grinning.

His smile abruptly faded as Jaguar, looking sharp in his dress whites and, thankfully, free of handcuffs, stepped into the courtroom accompanied by Counselor Carew, whose big blue eyes made her look terrified in Lucas's opinion. Jaguar, taking in the great number of SEALs present, drew to a halt as he realized his entire former troop was there to support him. Sending them all a nod of gratitude, he then went to greet his family, seated in the front row. He had only just torn himself away from them when the prosecutor stepped out from the opposite door, papers tucked under his arm and a confident smirk on his face.

"That's O'Rourke," Lucas murmured into Charlotte's ear. Tall and angular, with a large beaked nose, the military lawyer had a reputation for being ruthless and thorough.

Charlotte assessed him a moment, then whispered into Lucas's ear, "O'Rourke the Stork."

A snort of amusement escaped Lucas, causing Monica to glance at him sharply.

"All rise," intoned the naval ensign who was serving as the bailiff.

Lucas and everyone else in the room stood as panel members filed out from the deliberations chamber. Lucas recognized the five men from the printout Counselor Carew had shown them at the pretrial hearing. He reminded himself that Rivera had vetted all of them as best he could, but any one of them could still have ties to The Entity.

Captain Englert, the military judge, followed right behind them. Short and balding, he took his raised seat, prompting the panel members to sit, as well.

"You may be seated," he intoned, and in one accord, everyone in the courtroom sat, including the two lawyers. An expectant hush fell over the white-walled chamber.

The judge's dour expression worried Lucas. He wondered whether Holland, the current base commander, might have prejudiced Englert to get this unpleasantness over with. Holland abhorred the fact that Jaguar's charges reflected poorly on his naval annex.

Addressing the panel members, Englert introduced the accused as Navy SEAL Lt. Jonah Michael Mills and his counsel, Lt. Commander Claudine Carew. He then instructed the court reporter to begin recording the events of the hearing.

Englert addressed Jaguar next, asking if he wished to challenge any members of the panel.

"No, sir," Jaguar said, seemingly content with the lineup.

Englert then gave his attention to swearing in the panel members.

"Do you affirm that you will well and truly try and determine, according to the evidence to be disclosed between the United States of America and the person to be tried, that you will duly administer justice, without partiality, favor…." Lucas tuned out the remainder of the lengthy oath until it concluded. "So help you God."

"I do." The courtroom echoed with the panel members' affirmation.

At long last, it was time for the trial to get underway. Captain Englert gaveled in, calling the court to order. Then he eyed the two lawyers. "You have five minutes each in which to give your opening arguments."

The prosecutor rose and addressed the panel. "Gentlemen, during the course of this trial, I will demonstrate that the defendant, Lieutenant Jonah Mills, is guilty of violating Article 128 of the Uniform Code of Military Justice for the reason that he was goaded by his Post-

Traumatic Stress Disorder to willfully assault his commanding officer by firing a shotgun at him with the intent to injure him. Both men were off-duty at the time. This will be proven by his medical records, by forensic evidence gathered at the scene of the crime, and by the testimony of said commander and a firsthand witness. Prosecution will show this evidence is substantial enough to support a conviction of Lieutenant Mills and will call upon witnesses, Commander Daniel Dwyer and retired Navy SEAL Robert Fripp. If it please the court, I will reserve the remainder of my time for rebuttal."

Englert nodded. "Let the record show the prosecution reserves one minute for rebuttal." He turned an expectant eye on Jaguar's lawyer.

Carew rose and gave her own opening argument, her voice ringing out with confidence Lucas suspected was counterfeit.

"Your Honor, the defense will show that Lieutenant Jonah Mills is innocent of the offense of which he is charged. We will prove that the accusations brought against my client are all falsehoods meant to cover up his accuser's blackmailing tactics. We will show my client fired only one shot and that it was in self-defense, that he was of sound mind, and that he acted in the best interest of the nation and the world at large."

Englert's eyebrows rose as if Carew's opening remarks struck him as over-the-top.

"Indeed," he said, looking back at the prosecutor. "The court will now hear from the prosecution's first witnesses, Commander Schmidt, doctor of traumatology at the Portsmouth Medical Center."

Lucas elbowed Charlotte in order to convey, "Here we go."

Shooting him a quick smile, she promptly leaned against him so that their arms continued to touch. That simple contact, layered with her warmth and her familiar scent, rendered him utterly content. If only their present circumstances, including this gut-wrenching trial, would miraculously resolve, allowing him and Charlotte to remain together always.

At long last, a full hour into the proceedings, it was Dwyer's turn to take the stand. Charlotte had to admit the man looked every inch a Navy SEAL commander as he approached the witness box. At well over six feet, Dwyer cut a fine figure in his dress white uniform. Colorful service medals vied for space over his left front pocket. If he'd worn cowboy clothes, she mused, he would look very much like John Wayne, apart from the bushy mustache he sported, dyed several shades too dark to match his graying hair.

The prosecution's first two witnesses had just finished testifying. Dr. Schmidt, who was the first doctor to treat Jaguar following his reappearance, had summarized his medical reports stating that Jaguar had been diagnosed with Post-Traumatic Stress Disorder following a year-long captivity. Carew, in cross-examining, had asked him how long he had treated Lieutenant Mills.

"Three days," he'd said.

Carew had just looked at him. "No more questions, Your Honor," she'd said and sat down. Charlotte already knew Jonah's psychologist, Dr. Branson, would refute Dr. Schmidt's diagnosis, and Branson had worked with Jaguar for weeks.

The next witness had been Bob Fripp, a former SEAL who worked at the skeet-and-trap range where the altercation between Jaguar and Dwyer took place. Fripp claimed he had opened the range for Dwyer on Labor Day, as a favor to his former leader. After identifying Lieutenant Mills as the accused, he'd explained how he'd kept score and triggered the remote while Mills and Dwyer shot a round of five stand. And then he'd testified that Dwyer had offered Lieutenant Mills the opportunity to return to active duty, a circumstance that prompted the lieutenant to go suddenly berserk, firing on the CO without provocation.

All lies, Charlotte had thought, fuming inwardly.

Carew had cross-examined Fripp by holding up a poster with a huge hole in it. "This is what skeet shot does when it's fired at a distance of twenty feet," she stated. "Mr. Fripp, how is it that Lieutenant Mills went 'berserk,' as you said, and fired at his CO without killing him?"

Fripp had shrugged. "I never said he was tryin' to kill him. I guess he just wanted to scare him."

The charge, Charlotte had recalled, was assault, not attempted murder. Carew had sputtered, "No more questions," and sat down.

Now Dwyer was beginning to spin the same yarn as his witness, while the prosecutor paced before him, feeding him well-rehearsed questions.

"How would you describe the defendant's demeanor that morning?" O'Rourke inquired.

"Lieutenant Mills was jittery," Dwyer said, shooting what might have passed for a look of apology at the very man he was accusing. "Not that I blame him, mind you. Can't say I would have held up any better after a year of captivity and torture."

The Stork whirled to face his witness. "Then you were aware of Lieutenant Mills's medical diagnosis regarding his PTSD?"

"Of course."

"Yet, even in light of his diagnosis," O'Rourke continued, "you offered Lieutenant Mills the chance to return to active duty. Is that right?"

"Yes, I did. I informed him I was in need of a new executive officer, and I expressed my hope that he would take that position."

"Surely, he was grateful for such an offer."

"Objection," Counselor Carew said again. "Prosecution is leading the witness."

"Sustained," Englert decided.

O'Rourke changed his comment into a question. "How did Lieutenant Mills react to your offer, Commander?"

Dwyer shook his head, looking suddenly overwrought. "He started screaming nonsense about how he'd been abandoned and left for dead. And then he stalked off. When I called him back, seeking to placate him, he turned around and fired his weapon at me."

Dwyer lifted his bandaged right hand for everyone to see. "Nearly blew off my finger at that point."

Charlotte clicked her tongue in annoyance, prompting Lucas to lay a restraining hand over hers.

"Did you then fire your own weapon to defend yourself?" O'Rourke prompted him.

"Yes, of course, while taking cover to keep from being injured again. I knew he only had five shells in his shotgun. I figured if he used them all up, he'd pose less of a danger to himself, as well as to Bob and me."

Aware of Saul's mounting tension, Charlotte glanced over and found him staring at Dwyer with such intensity, she half-expected Dwyer to detonate.

"Did Lieutenant Mills continue to fire, using every round at his disposal?" O'Rourke queried.

"Yes," Dwyer said, avoiding eye contact with Jaguar.

"Liar," Saul murmured under his breath.

O'Rourke addressed the judge. "Your Honor, calling your attention to Exhibit A, you have a written statement from our forensic expert pairing spent shells with the shotgun that was fired by the accused."

Carew's fraying bun popped up again. "Objection to the admissibility of evidence on the basis that it is unduly prejudicial, Your Honor. There are literally thousands of spent shells at a skeet-and-trap range and no fail-proof method of linking spent shells to my client's weapon. Later, defense will show Exhibit B, a letter written by our own forensic expert stating as much."

"Objection noted," Englert answered. "Is the prosecution finished?" Receiving a nod, he added, "The defense may cross-examine."

Carew stood up and opened her poster again with the gaping hole in it. "Commander, again, how could a Navy SEAL wielding a shotgun have managed not to put a hole this big in you?"

Dwyer held up his bandaged thumb. "He nearly blew my hand off."

"Uh huh." Carew put her poster down and changed tactics. "Commander, kindly express for the court your views on national defense."

With a puzzled glance at his lawyer, Dwyer supplied an answer anyone would expect of a squadron commander.

Charlotte sighed inwardly. If only they could bring up Dwyer's ties to The Entity. Even knowing of Fitz's death, Carew still refused to bring it up. For one thing, they had no evidence. For another, the FBI wouldn't thank her for disrupting an ongoing investigation should another agent pick it up.

"Did you or did you not tell Lieutenant Mills on the day of the incident that what our nation needs are more operators like you and less politicians running the country?"

Dwyer shrugged. "I may have said something along those lines."

"Did you then say Washington, D.C. needed to be burned to the ground for that to happen?"

Dwyer waved a negligent hand. "Retired Navy SEAL Dick Marcinko wrote that in a book. I never said it."

"But didn't you say, and I quote, 'Our enemies can't strike at us if we steal their weapons first. We amass them and we control them because, in the end, power means peace.' Are those not your words, Commander?"

"Objection, Your Honor," O'Rourke intoned. "This line of questioning is irrelevant!"

Englert beetled his thick eyebrows. "Denied. Answer the question, Commander."

Dwyer shrugged. "I may have said something like that. So what?"

Carew looked him in the eye. "Did you then offer to make Lieutenant Mills your executive officer, provided he agreed with your radical political beliefs?"

Dwyer expressed puzzlement. "What's so radical about wanting to make the world safe again?"

Carew tried again. "What happened to your last executive officer?"

Dwyer dropped his gaze and shook his head sadly. "I'm sorry to say he took his life two weeks ago."

"How unfortunate." Carew raised eyebrows at the panel as if to suggest there was more to Lowery's suicide than met the eye.

Englert interrupted. "Counselor, need I remind you to stick to the events occurring on Labor Day?"

Chastised for seeming to stray off-topic, Carew lost momentary traction. An uncomfortable silence fell over the chamber as the young lawyer scanned her notes, looking for the best way to continue. Charlotte found herself holding her breath.

At last, Carew looked up with confidence, and Charlotte was free to exhale.

"Commander, are you aware that your late executive officer, James Lowery, sent top-secret information via emails to unauthorized recipients?"

Dwyer darted a nervous look at his lawyer, who sang out on a victorious note, "Objection. I believe we just established we are sticking to events occurring on Labor Day."

"Sustained." The judge's voice held an edge of impatience.

"Yes, sir. Let me start again. Commander Dwyer, on *Labor Day* morning, when you went to the range to meet with Lieutenant Mills, did you send your secretary, Miss Monica Trembley, to your office with instructions to break into Master Chief Rivera's office and remove from his locked desk a journal belonging to the deceased SEAL Blake LeMere?"

Charlotte whispered to Lucas, "Where is Rivera?"

"Couldn't come. He's in charge with Dwyer out."

Dwyer's expression turned cautious. "Of course not. I would never violate Master Chief Rivera's sanctum."

Carew sent him a thin smile. "And yet I have Miss Trembley's written testimony stating exactly that—Exhibit C, Your Honor."

Dwyer flicked a dark glance at Monica who folded her arms across her chest.

Carew continued. "Miss Trembley's written statement says she delivered the journal into your hands that same day. Can you tell us what was in the journal you didn't want anyone to see?"

Dwyer's jaw jumped. "No, I cannot. I don't know what you're talking about."

"Were you aware that your late executive officer sent classified information via email to unauthorized recipients?" Carew waved the printouts that Charlotte had gotten from her godfather.

"Objection," O'Rourke protested yet again. "How is any of this relevant to the charges?"

This time Englert agreed with him. "Sustained. You will drop this line of questioning, Counselor."

"Yes, Your Honor." Carew didn't look too put out that she'd been derailed. The printouts in her hand had managed to serve their purpose, raising questions in the panel members' minds as to whether Lowery, now dead, had sent illicit emails on Dwyer's behalf.

"No more questions, Your Honor."

Charlotte heaved a silent sigh. If only the panel could be told about Dwyer's association to the weapons being stored in Sabena. Then they would know how conniving and dishonest he was.

The thwack of Englert's gavel gave Carew a reprieve before the defense stated its case.

"Court will take a brief recess, reconvening in thirty minutes."

With a general murmur of relief, people got up to stretch their legs. Saul startled Charlotte by bolting out of his seat. Leaving the pew to let others out, she watched him close in on a drab woman sitting near the prosecution.

"Who's Saul talking to?" Charlotte asked as Lucas sidled up beside her.

"I don't know," he said, following her gaze. "Wait, is that LeMere's widow? Wow, she looks really different."

Offering her hand to Saul, the painfully thin woman shot a wary look at the prosecutor.

Charlotte could tell, even from a distance, LeMere's widow had the potential to be beautiful but took no pains with her appearance. Her hair was lank, and she wore no makeup.

"Don't tell me she's married to O'Rourke now," Charlotte commented.

"No. I would have heard about that," Lucas assured her. Then, with

Monica demanding to speak with him a moment, he rolled his eyes and then left Charlotte standing in the aisle by herself.

Giving up on Saul, who looked completely absorbed, Charlotte left the crowded chamber in search of a water fountain.

Given Jaguar's lineup of witnesses, things didn't look too bleak from the present vantage.

CHAPTER 17

*T*hirty minutes later, Charlotte watched Counselor Carew blow out a steadying breath before approaching the stand to question Saul, the first witness. The visual impact of Saul in a crisp white uniform, resplendent with service medals and wearing a neatly queued ponytail, kept the onlookers riveted as Captain Englert swore him in.

"Chief Wade," Carew began, "kindly tell the court what happened on Labor Day morning when you accompanied Lieutenant Mills to the skeet-and-trap range."

In his laid-back drawl, Saul proceeded to explain how he'd been denied entrance at the clubhouse door.

"In that case, Commander Dwyer and Mr. Bob Fripp were the only two people actually on the range with Lieutenant Mills. Is that correct?"

"Yes, ma'am. I was sitting on the hood of my car when I got a text from my troop leader advising me to keep an eye on Lieutenant Mills."

"Did he say why, Chief?"

"No ma'am. But the circumstances of Lieutenant Mills's disappearance the year before might have played into it."

Lucas glanced at the Stork, expecting him to object, but he didn't. "Please continue, Chief."

Saul nodded. "Only way to see Lieutenant Mills was to get on the roof of the clubhouse. I took my hunting rifle with the scope so I could see him better and went up the trellis. I'd just located them on the range when I saw Lieutenant Mills go rollin' off the edge of the platform, grabbing up his shotgun before he fell. The CO fired at him and missed, and Lieutenant Mills dived under the platform looking for protection."

"Are you saying you saw Commander Dwyer fire the first shot?"

"Yes, ma'am. And the second one, too, straight down at the lieutenant, who was underneath him, pinned. I knew if I didn't deter the CO, he'd hit his mark, so I shot at a spot close to his feet, distracting him and giving the lieutenant a chance to slip out of there."

"Did Lieutenant Mills know it was you who took the shot?"

"Don't think he could see me, but we've gone hunting together, so he recognized the report of my rifle. Soon as he heard it, he bolted out of there. I covered him so he could get from one trap to another and use them for cover on his way to the fence."

"Did Dwyer fire at him again?"

"Yes, ma'am, five more times. Seven total."

"Are you sure that number is accurate?"

"I'm a sniper, ma'am. Counting bullets is second nature. He was shooting a pump-action riot shotgun with a standard choke. They hold up to ten shells. Lieutenant Mills's shotgun only held five."

"How many times did Lieutenant Mills fire back?"

"Only once."

"Did you, at some point, shoot Dwyer's weapon out of his grasp, causing injury to his hand?"

"Yes, ma'am, to give Lieutenant Mills a chance at getting over the fence. Needing both his hands free to climb it, he put his shotgun down. And, even though I injured the CO's right hand, he managed to get another shot off."

"Please clarify. Commander Dwyer shot at the back of an unarmed man?" Carew expressed astonishment even though she knew the story.

"Yes, ma'am."

A murmur of disapproval rolled through the rows of Navy SEALs.

"Thank you, Chief." Carew swung a triumphant look at Captain O'Rourke. "Your witness, Counselor."

O'Rourke stood up, meandered over to the defense's table, and picked up the same poster Carew had used earlier. He showed it to Saul. "You say Commander Dwyer fired seven times at Lieutenant Mills? How is it that Dwyer is the only one injured, while Lieutenant Mills appears in perfect health?"

The question didn't appear to faze Saul. "Because every time he went to shoot, I laid a bullet at his feet. You can't shoot and dance at the same time, sir," Saul added, drawing snickers from the SEALs in the audience.

O'Rourke didn't look at all amused. "Chief Wade, if you were, in fact, on the roof of the skeet-and-trap range, why is there no record of your testimony in the investigation report?"

Saul sat back, folding his arms across his chest, and sneered. "'Cause they ignored my testimony. 'Cause someone at NCIS is in bed with Dwyer."

The Stork cocked his head in disbelief. "Or," he added, supplying another explanation, "you came up with this story after the fact, in order to help out your teammate."

O'Rourke looked back at the judge. "Your Honor will see for himself, there's no mention in the original investigation, or any subsequent investigation, of Chief Wade having ever been present at the skeet-and-trap range. We can assume, therefore, that he has made up his entire testimony."

Saul began to scowl. His face turned a dull shade of red, causing Charlotte to catch his eye and will him to keep his cool.

The Stork wasn't done with him. "I have one more point to make. Chief Wade, how long have you been in the service?"

Saul regarded him through narrowed eyes. "Over fifteen years."

"Fifteen years," the prosecutor repeated. "How is it, after all that time, you are not aware that bringing a personal firearm onto a military installation without prior approval of the installation commander is punishable under Article 92 of the UCMJ, by two years' confinement, dishonorable discharge, forfeiture of all pay and allowances, and reduction to pay grade E-1?"

Saul's jaw muscles jumped. "I have prior approval," he said stonily.

O'Rourke held up a finger. "Correction. You have approval to carry a personal handgun on the installation, not your hunting rifle. I thought I'd remind you of that, lest you end up facing some charges of your own."

"Objection." Carew shot to her feet. "Your Honor, the prosecutor is talking apples and oranges. If the convening authority wants to bring charges against my witness, that is his priority, but his point does not change the validity of my witness's testimony. Moreover, our forensic expert has confirmed the existence of spent rifle shells on the roof of the clubhouse."

Charlotte wanted to applaud Carew's indignant retort. O'Rourke merely smirked at her and said to the judge, "I've completed my questions, Your Honor."

As the panel members watched Saul leave the witness box, Charlotte wondered who among them had believed his testimony. It was hard to tell from their thoughtful expressions. O'Rourke had done his best to discredit Saul's testimony, but he wouldn't be able to discredit that of Jaguar's psychiatrist.

A minute later, Dr. Bartholomew Branson was sitting on the witness stand being sworn in. Saul slipped back onto the bench next to Charlotte, who grimaced consolingly and squeezed his hand.

Carew wasted no time establishing Branson's relationship to the accused. The psychiatrist had treated Jaguar soon after he'd been brought into Portsmouth Naval Medical Center, showing signs of starvation, torture, and amnesia.

"What was your professional opinion of Lieutenant Mills when you first encountered him?" she inquired.

Branson scratched his clean-shaven face. "He was still in shock, a bit disoriented. It was clear to me he suffered memory loss. I assumed his amnesia was due to stress, possibly Post-Traumatic Stress Disorder, as Dr. Schmidt already testified, but a CAT scan subsequently revealed damage to his prefrontal cortex, and that can also cause amnesia."

"Are you a trauma specialist, Doctor?" Carew inquired.

"No. I'm a cognitive behavioral therapist. Commander Dwyer asked me to treat Lieutenant Mills as a personal favor."

"You owed him a personal favor, Doctor?"

"Well, yes." Branson sent a disapproving look at Dwyer, who was seated behind the prosecutor's table. "Daniel Dwyer and I went to high school together. When I was looking for a job, he fast-tracked my application with the DoD and helped me get hired. Thus, when Lieutenant Mills returned from the dead, so to speak, and Daniel requested that I treat him, it didn't occur to me to refuse him. I realized why he chose me, though, when he later asked me for the lieutenant's clinical notes. The Military Command Exception rule allows commanders access to medical records in order to determine fitness for duty. I figured that was why he wanted to see the notes, to decide whether Lieutenant Mills was ready to return to active duty. Strangely, though, he also demanded I tell him everything the patient was starting to remember. When he saw that I had *not* diagnosed Lieutenant Mills with Post-Traumatic Stress Disorder, he insisted I do so. Otherwise, he said, the Navy wouldn't continue to give Mills his disability pay."

"Was that true?"

Branson shook his head. "Not at all. I conferred with my supervisor and was told Commander Dwyer had no right to tell me how to diagnose my patient, let alone to be told the patient's memories."

"Then, Lieutenant Mills does *not* suffer from Post-Traumatic Stress Disorder?"

Branson leveled a benevolent gaze at Jaguar and said, "In my professional opinion, there's nothing wrong with Lieutenant Mills apart from memory loss due to a mild brain injury."

"Thank you, Doctor."

Charlotte's nervousness returned as Carew thanked Branson and handed him over to O'Rourke to be cross-examined.

O'Rourke clasped his hands behind his back and slowly paced the length of the floor.

"Dr. Branson, you were hired by the Navy after two years of unemployment. Is that correct?"

Branson stiffened, his face suddenly expressionless. "Yes."

"How kind of your long-time acquaintance, Commander Dwyer, to fast-track your application. Tell me," he said before Carew could object, "what was keeping you from finding a job outside of the DoD?"

Branson, breaking eye contact, looked suddenly flustered. "I was...I was sick."

"Sick, hmm." O'Rourke pondered the word thoughtfully. "To treat your illness, you spent twenty-four months checking in and out of the Stern's Rehabilitation Center in Richmond, Virginia, am I right?"

"Yes." Branson's reply was barely audible.

"That must have been quite an illness. You were addicted to pills, I understand—Vicodin and Dilaudid. Is that all?"

Carew tried desperately to deflect the prosecutor's impeachment of her witness's competence—to no avail. By the time O'Rourke said, "No more questions, Your Honor," he had shredded the doctor's reputation so completely the panel eyed the doctor with pity and very little confidence.

Jaguar's only hope for proving his innocence now rested on his third witness, Monica.

Charlotte glanced at Lucas to gauge whether his dismay matched her own. Given Lucas's grim expression, Jaguar didn't have a snowball's chance in hell.

∼

Sweat breached Lucas's pores as Monica was called to the stand to provide her testimony.

"Ms. Trembley," Carew began once it was established who she was and why she was testifying, "Please describe to the court why you were sent to SEAL Team Six Headquarters on the morning of Labor Day."

Strangely, Lucas got the impression Monica rather enjoyed the spotlight. Looking poised, she lifted her chin and said, "Commander Dwyer asked me to enter Master Chief Rivera's office via the commander's office—they share a connecting door—and to use one of my keys to get into Master Chief's desk. He said he wanted the blue journal that Master Chief had forgotten to give him."

"Did you know that journal detailed how his late executive officer was leaking top-secret information to unauthorized personnel?" Carew prompted her.

"Objection, Your Honor," O'Rourke intoned. "The journal's mere existence is in question, not to mention the contents therein."

"Sustained." Englert nearly rolled his eyes. "Stick to the facts, Counselor."

"Yes, Your Honor. Did Commander Dwyer tell you what was in the notebook?"

"Of course not." Monica tossed a lock of dark hair over her shoulder. "It's not my job to ask questions."

"Can you tell me where the journal is now?"

Monica shrugged. "I gave it to Commander Dwyer at about twelve o'clock that afternoon." She described how she had gone to his home, handing over the journal at his front door.

"That would have been about two hours after the incident at the skeet-and-trap range," Carew pointed out. "Did the commander tell you what had happened that morning?"

"Not at all. He thanked me for getting the journal, and that was it."

"Yet he claims he has no recollection of the journal. Did he appear upset at all by what had allegedly happened that morning?"

Monica tipped her head and thought back. "Nope. He seemed rather cheerful, actually."

"Cheerful," Carew repeated. "Interesting. How would you explain his inability to recollect the journal or even recall asking you to fetch it for him?"

"Isn't it obvious?" Monica directed her jewel-like gaze at Dwyer and smiled thinly. "He's lying."

A murmur of surprise rippled through the courtroom. Recognizing Monica's determined smile, Lucas realized, with a twinge of concern, she was ready to do battle.

Carew had to raise her voice for her next question to be heard. "Miss Trembley, it sounds as if you speak from experience. Has Commander Dwyer ever asked anything else of you that was possibly unethical?"

"Objection," O'Rourke droned, looking bored. "The witness is not an ethics expert, and her testimony to such a question is an impermissible form of character evidence."

"Sustained," Englert agreed. "Need I remind you, Counselor, who is on trial here?"

"No, Your Honor." Carew, having been denied her line of questioning, yielded the floor reluctantly to the prosecutor. "No further questions, Your Honor."

Drumming his long, thin fingers on the table, O'Rourke took his time getting up.

"Ms. Trembley," he said as he finally approached her, "tell the court, if you would, your current position within Spec Ops. Do you still work as Commander Dwyer's civilian secretary?"

Monica's chagrin was apparent for all to see. "No, I do not. I work in the administration building across the street."

"Is that a promotion?" O'Rourke asked with a guileless manner.

Monica glared at him. "No."

O'Rourke gestured to where Dwyer was sitting. "Are you upset with Commander Dwyer for transferring you?"

Monica kept quiet, no doubt sensing a trap.

"Is that why you've testified against him?" O'Rourke pressed. "Is it because you detest your new position?"

Monica's eyes flashed with indignation. "Yes," she agreed, answering the prosecutor's question.

Shifting to the edge of her seat, she gripped the railing in front of her so fiercely that her knuckles turned white. "I detest my new position, and I didn't deserve a demotion." She turned her baleful gaze on the CO. "You." Her voice shook with sudden fury. "You punished me for doing exactly what you asked me to do. You want to get nasty, Daniel?" Her eyes narrowed to glittering slits. "Well, two can play that game."

Lucas's stomach gave an unpleasant lurch at the realization that Monica had just called Dwyer by his first name.

She stood up suddenly, drawing a look of outrage from Captain Englert. "The truth is Daniel Dwyer and I were lovers."

Lucas had realized the truth a split second before she confessed it. All the same, a sound of dismay escaped him, causing Charlotte to reach out and squeeze his hand consolingly.

Monica was just warming up. "Not only did he take advantage of his position to exploit me, but he used me to help him bug a conversation between Lieutenant Mills and his teammates, so he could find out what Mills was starting to remember. Moreover, when he discovered I was going to testify today, he sent some *minion* to my house to try and kill me. If you think I'm making that up, Your Honor, just call the local police."

"Calm down, Miss Trembley," Englert ordered her. "Counselor O'Rourke, are you done cross-examining?"

"Not quite, Your Honor." O'Rourke gave one last stab at trying to paint Monica as a vindictive secretary of questionable character, but Dwyer's reputation, now linked with hers, remained sullied. Seeing he wasn't gaining any traction, the lawyer sat down, and Englert dismissed the witness.

With a polite nod at the panel members, Monica descended the raised platform with unhurried elegance.

Carew sat back in her seat looking as shocked as everyone else, though not exactly displeased. At last, one of her witnesses had managed to impugn Dwyer's character.

Dwyer himself was shaking his head in denial, but the expressions on the panel members faces—not to mention Captain Englert's—suggested they believed Monica's story.

She added to her credibility by mouthing *Sorry* to Lucas as she headed toward the exit, her back rigid, her head high.

The courtroom buzzed with speculation. Englert had to beat his bench with the gavel.

"Order. Order now! As we've concluded all cross-examination, I will hear your closing arguments," he said to the lawyers.

O'Rourke, who had remained standing, proceeded to give an award-worthy monologue in which he ridiculed the defense's witnesses and their paltry attempt to sully the word of a renowned military leader. He then dismissed Monica's testimony as a dramatic, last-ditch effort.

When it was her turn, Carew reminded the court that too many inconsistencies existed for Commander Dwyer's testimony to be accepted at face value. Truth beyond a reasonable doubt was the standard demanded by law, and the prosecution had failed in any way to demonstrate that Lieutenant Mills was the least bit guilty of the charges leveled at him. One man's word against another should never lead to conviction. As for the supposed Article 128 violation, the prosecution had failed to prove Lieutenant Mills had, in fact, assaulted his superior officer. If anything, Commander Dwyer had assaulted his lieutenant first, for refusing to perform duties unfitting to an officer of the United States Navy. The panel clearly had no choice but to declare Lieutenant Mills innocent.

Englert wrapped up the trial with one last address to the panel on their duties to weigh the evidence. If they were unable to find that the prosecution had proved its case beyond a reasonable doubt, they were required to bring in a verdict of not guilty.

"The reading of the verdict will take place tomorrow morning at

0900 hours." Beating his gavel one last time, Englert brought an end to the hearing and pushed to his feet, compelling the bailiff to yell, "All rise!"

Lucas watched the panel members follow the judge out of the room. Dwyer and his supportive peers departed immediately after them.

Just like that, Jaguar's court-martial was over without Jaguar ever taking the stand himself.

Standing respectfully where they had sat, Jaguar's troop members watched him take leave of his family, then surrender himself to the MPs, who cuffed him and led him away. Watching him disappear, Lucas could only imagine Jaguar's hopefulness that he would spend only one more night in the brig. However, a guilty verdict tomorrow might lead to several more years of incarceration.

Charlotte tugged at Lucas's arm, recapturing his attention.

"Did you know Monica was going to do that?" she asked. Pity and concern shone in her wide eyes.

"No." He had to laugh at his mixed disgust and relief. *Monica and Dwyer!* Thank God he'd broken off their engagement when he had.

"You're not upset?" she queried, searching his face.

"Not really." While he'd never suspected Monica of being in cahoots with Dwyer, it made perfect sense, in retrospect. Not only had she helped Dwyer bug his house, but she'd gone back for the vase at Dwyer's request, exactly as he'd suspected.

"Are you still planning to protect her?"

"What for?" he asked, scanning the uncertain faces of his teammates. "She's already admitted the truth to everyone. If something happened to her now, Dwyer would be the first man arrested. Excuse me a second," he added, raising his voice to address the other troop members. "Hey, who wants to go to Rascal Jack's to blow off some steam? First drink is on me. You can buy your own food."

"Hooyah, sir," many of them responded, including Theo and Bambino.

Lucas turned back to Charlotte. "Rascal Jack's is a bar and pool hall. I know you play pool," he added, inviting her with his smile.

She propped her hands on her hips. "How do you know that?"

"You just confirmed it," he pointed out. "Come on. Let's go tell the Gallstones where we're going next."

CHAPTER 18

Charlotte sat at the edge of the L-shaped bar, between Saul and Lucas, polishing off her burger. Eating in silence, they devoured an early dinner while members of Alpha Troop enjoyed a free first round of drinks. Several men played pool in the area behind them. The clatter of billiards and the music coming from an authentic jukebox made talking unnecessary, but Charlotte was full of questions.

She put down her half-eaten burger, licking a drop of ketchup off one finger. Eyeing first Saul's thoughtful scowl, then Lucas's self-absorbed expression as he chewed the end of a french fry, she asked him, "Are you guys okay? You're awfully quiet."

Lucas's gray gaze snapped up to meet hers. He slowly dropped the rest of the fry onto his plate. "Sure. I'm sorry. I didn't mean to ignore you."

"I don't care if you ignore me. I care if you're feeling bad. I'm sure you had no idea about Monica and Dwyer...you know."

He made a face and shrugged casually. "No, I didn't know but—" He glanced at Saul "Now I know why none of my friends liked her."

Saul shook his head in denial. "We weren't sure, sir. Otherwise we would've said something."

Lucas forced a smile. "I'm not blaming you, Chief." He reached for the lemon on the lip of his club soda and squeezed it.

"Thanks," Saul muttered. Then he went back to eating.

Charlotte sighed, took another bite of her burger, then tried again. "I, for one, didn't see that coming. I thought she wanted to testify so she could win you back."

A seed flew out of Lucas's lemon wedge. "Who said I wanted to get back together with her?"

Charlotte sent him an approving smile. "Well, I'm glad you didn't," she admitted. "And I'm glad Monica made Dwyer look like the scum he is. No one else managed to do that. Thanks to her, I think Jaguar has a shot of beating his charges, don't you? She's the only witness O'Rourke didn't manage to eviscerate."

Lucas gave a hopeful grunt. Saul took another bite of his burger.

"Speaking of O'Rourke," Charlotte continued, turning her attention to Saul, "why was Blake LeMere's widow sitting with the prosecution? Her husband died because of Lowery, and Dwyer likely ordered Lowery to kill him."

Saul put his burger down as if he'd suddenly lost his appetite. "Her brother asked her to come sit near him."

"Her brother?" Charlotte repeated.

"O'Rourke. He wanted her to see how Dwyer, even though he may be lying through his teeth, will still get off."

"Wait." Charlotte had too much to process at once. "First off, O'Rourke the Stork can't be Mrs. LeMere's brother. They look nothing alike."

Saul's eyebrows pulled together. "Maybe Rachel's adopted," he suggested.

Charlotte shrugged while taking note of the woman's first name. "Secondly, why would O'Rourke represent Dwyer if his sister lost her husband because of the man?"

"I asked her that," Saul answered, staring into the amber depths of his beer. "She told me her brother doesn't care what's right or wrong. He only cares about winning."

"Wow." Charlotte shared a look with Lucas. "Nice brother she's got there.

"Yeah." Avoiding eye contact, Saul picked up his glass and drained it. "She lives with him," he added, putting the glass down with a thud.

"Lives with him? Why?"

"I don't know."

Charlotte cocked her head, thinking. "Why would anyone live with their brother as an adult?" She realized what she was saying and added, "I mean, I live with my brother, but that's because he's helpless. I'm sure her brother knows how to clean up after himself."

"Probably for financial reasons," Lucas suggested.

"Plus, she has a son," Saul pointed out.

Charlotte winced as the tragedy of Blake LeMere's death confronted her again. "How old?"

Saul looked at Lucas and guessed, "Nine?"

"At least ten now," Lucas said.

Having lost her parents at twenty-two, Charlotte could only imagine how LeMere's death had affected his young son. "That's awful."

It suddenly occurred to her that Dwyer was responsible for that child's heartache, for his mother's emaciation. In her rising agitation, Charlotte slapped a hand on the bar and stood up.

"I swear if Jaguar is found guilty tomorrow, I'm going to lose it."

Lucas shared a dark look with Saul. "Well," he said, "we don't have Fitz to do damage control, so let's pray that the panel members have enough doubts about Dwyer to find Jaguar innocent."

Charlotte wasn't finished. "When I think of how many people's lives have been ruined by that man...I just—I just want to *hurt* him," she growled.

Lucas heaved a heavy sigh and reached for his Perrier.

Saul demolished another french fry.

"I need to hit something," Charlotte declared, looking around. "Who'll play pool with me? Lucas?"

Lucas pointed wordlessly at Saul, who froze with a fry sticking out of his mouth.

"Are you good?" Charlotte asked him. "I need a challenge right now."

"He's the best," Lucas answered for him. "The reigning champ in all of DEVGRU."

"Hmph. We'll see about that. Come on." She urged Saul off his stool.

He gestured at his fancy attire. "I can't play in this monkey suit."

Charlotte lifted a foot in the air. "If I can play in these heels, you can play in your uniform. Come on. The table's free."

Eager to vent her frustrations, she strode toward the open pool table. Like Moses parting the Red Sea, the throng of Navy SEALs stepped aside, making way for her. Maybe after trouncing Saul at a game of pool, she'd feel better.

~

Following Charlotte and Saul with his gaze, Lucas found himself shaking his head and smiling wryly. She stood at least as tall or taller than any man in the room, incandescent in her yellow pantsuit. Everyone watched as she produced a quarter from her purse. Calling heads, she flipped it to see who would go first, her or Saul.

Lucas could tell by her flashing grin that she won the coin toss. While Saul racked the balls, she selected precisely the stick she wanted, rubbed chalk on the tip, then leaned over the table and prepared to break.

With a dozen pairs of eyes admiring her long, athletic frame, Lucas felt a prick of jealousy, but mostly admiration. He doubted he would ever again meet a woman as complex and fun as Charlotte Patterson.

She might be the antithesis of the uncomplicated woman Lucas was looking for, but he loved her just the way she was.

I love her. The recognition of his feelings took his breath away.

With a powerful jab, Charlotte struck the clustered balls so forcefully that the crack and subsequent clatter sounded clearly over the cheering of her audience. Lucas stood up so he could see better. Not one—but two—balls dropped into opposite pockets. Charlotte claimed solids.

On her second turn, she sank a third ball.

Every SEAL in the place, besides himself, went ballistic. Pulling a twenty-dollar bill from his pocket, Theo caught Bambino's eye as he fluttered it in the air, then pointed to Charlotte. With a loyal glance at Saul, Bambino nodded and the bet was on.

As Charlotte orbited the pool table considering her options, her bright hair bounced and shifted. The recollection of its silkiness slipped through Lucas's memory, making him yearn to run his fingers through her hair and kiss her again. Taking her fourth then fifth turns, she sent two more solids cleanly into the pockets she designated. Lucas glimpsed a flash of gold on her finger and realized, with a rush of warmth, that she was still wearing the ring he'd bought for her in Sabena—in fact, wearing it proudly on her left hand, like it was a wedding band.

As the realization lifted his hopes, Charlotte sent the cue ball ricocheting like a bullet off the far side of the table and striking a solid purple, sending it in the general direction of the middle pocket, but not quite cleanly enough to drop in.

An outburst of lament came from Charlotte's supporters. Bambino offered Saul a high five.

Saul now had his opening.

Taking over, Saul started sinking balls, one ball after the next, much the way Charlotte had. His supporters cheered him on. Lucas watched Bambino lick one end of the twenty-dollar bill he'd produced and stick it to his forehead. It was only at such times Lucas remembered how young the junior SEAL was.

Shifting his attention back to Charlotte, Lucas could tell from her wry expression she had to suspect Saul might beat her. That didn't seem to bother her. Her equanimity, like everything else about her, impressed him.

She's the one for me.

The thought came out of nowhere, prompting Lucas to put his glass down before he dropped it. *No, no. She couldn't be.* He had just prayed that she would give up her career in order to stay with him.

But what if that prayer had been a selfish one?

He sank back onto the stool, thinking. The reason he loved Charlotte was exactly *because* of her complexity. She amazed him! What right did he have to expect her to change her plans for him—she shouldn't have to. She was meant to do incredible things with her life, to channel her energy into making the world a better place, in precisely the way he had been called to do.

As the one who loved her, his job was to support her in every way possible. Could he do that? Could he cope with having a girlfriend whom he saw only a few times a year? He was a Navy SEAL—of course, he could. The sacrifice would be well worth it if they could be a couple—if not always physically together, then emotionally and spiritually.

A unison sound of lament drew his gaze back to the table where Saul had just flubbed up, giving Charlotte the opportunity to still beat him. Bambino took the twenty-dollar bill off his forehead. Glimpsing the table, Lucas saw that Saul and Charlotte had two balls left apiece.

Charlotte stepped back up to the table with a determined grin. Indicating the far-left pocket, she leaned way over the table and banked a red solid off the long side, sending it smoothly on its journey into the corner pocket.

"Ho, ho, ho!" Theo celebrated his impending victory.

There was only one solid left, the green ball nestled against the short side of the table. But the eight-ball stood between it and her cue ball.

Charlotte studied her options from all angles.

Come on, baby, Lucas thought, cheering her on silently.

As if hearing her, she looked up abruptly, meeting his gaze through the crowd of uniformed men. *Don't call me that,* Lucas imagined her saying. Then she looked back at the table, frowning as she returned her focus to the game.

Amused, Lucas basked in the glow of his love for her.

The SEALs grew hushed, considerate of the concentration required to keep her lead. Even the music blaring from the jukebox seemed to dim.

Seated behind the wall of bodies, Lucas lost sight of the table, but the roar of disbelief that followed on the heels of Charlotte's shot let him know she'd won.

Determination spurred him to approach her. The members of his troop roared at the upset, ignoring their troop leader as he elbowed past them. Only Saul noted Lucas's approach and snapped into a rigid posture with his arms tightly at his sides. "Attention!"

Conditioned to respond, every man jerked to attention, which was utterly ridiculous under the casual circumstances, not to mention embarrassing. Charlotte was the only person standing at ease, a hand on her hip and one eyebrow raised.

"Can I talk to you outside?" Lucas asked, ignoring the others and causing her eyes to widen.

"Sure." But her expression asked, *What is happening?*

"Good." He cupped her elbow and steered her swiftly toward the exit, while growling over his shoulder, "As you were."

Lucas's stomach churned with mixed fear and hope as he held the heavy door open, escorting her out into the cooler evening air. The late September sky had mellowed to a color not unlike the juice they'd sipped by Eric's pool in the Bahamas.

The Gallstones had parked their Winnebago under the pine trees on the far side of the parking lot. Lucas was glad to see them keeping watch. The last thing on his mind at that moment was any lingering threat presented by The Entity. Then again, who would be so stupid as to target them here, with two DIA bodyguards and fifteen SEALs to call on for help?

Lucas searched for a place for them to sit. His legs felt a bit like they did right before high-altitude, low-open parachute jumps. What if Charlotte rejected his offer?

Rascal Jack's shared a parking lot with a tattoo parlor and a dry-cleaning shop. It wasn't the most romantic spot to ask Charlotte to forge a relationship with him. There weren't any benches, and the curb was littered with trash, spilled beer, and other stuff he didn't want to think about.

Homing in on the back of his pickup truck, he lowered the tailgate, then wiped the dust off the bed liner with the handkerchief in his pocket.

"These always come in handy when you wear dress whites," he pointed out, then tossed the soiled linen square off to one side. "Have a seat," he offered.

"Okay." She swung athletically onto the tailgate and watched him lower himself gingerly next to her. "What's up?"

Pondering the best way to start, Lucas directed his gaze across the street, past the chain-link fence that separated them from Naval Air Station Oceana's landing field. A cargo plane, a C-5 Galaxy the size of a whale, lumbered up the runway in preparation for takeoff, its twin engines flaring. With the crimson sunset beyond it, the view was almost picturesque. If that darn plane could get off the ground, Lucas thought, so could his relationship with Charlotte.

The engines roared, giving him the added time to organize his thoughts. The nose of the Galaxy went up. For the longest time, it seemed to hover above the tarmac before climbing ponderously into the sky. Charlotte waited.

"You know, we've talked about what I'm looking for, and I told you I want a woman who'll put her husband and kids before her career. Remember?"

Her cherry-brown eyes looked almost red with the sunset reflected in them. "Of course."

"I think I misspoke. I should have said, 'I'm looking for the woman God thinks is right for me—someone amazing and smart and fun to be with.' I think I'm meant to be with you, Charlotte." It took all his courage to spit the words out.

She looked stunned, completely bowled over.

"I guess you didn't see that coming," he added, tempering his expectations.

"Not really, no." Looking away, she blinked several times as if trying to come to terms with what he'd said.

He tried again, covering her hand with his. "I'm not asking you to give up your plans. I want you to be exactly who you are and to do exactly what you feel called to do. Just know that I would always be there for you. We could make it work if we're both committed."

She drew a deep, shuddering breath, clearly touched by his words. "Oh, Lucas."

Turning her head, she looked deeply into his eyes, but then her gaze slid up to his forehead and her eyes flew wide before she yelled, "Get down!"

Shoving him onto the bed of his truck, she threw herself over him as a hiss and *thunk* made Lucas realize a bullet had punctured the truck's lining mere inches from his head. Charlotte lay on top of him. He threw his arms around her and rolled toward the inside of the bed, hoping it would shield them and keep her safe beneath him.

"Where'd that come from?" he demanded.

"Shooter on the roof," she said in a thin voice.

Crap, where were Martin's bodyguards? Lucas struggled to dig his cell phone out of his pocket.

Thunk. A second bullet embedded itself in the liner right next to his exposed thigh. With a strangled curse, he concentrated on putting his call through. Stone's cell phone started ringing.

That's when Lucas saw the blood. On Charlotte's head, in her hairline above her temple. Not even her bright red hair could disguise the scarlet stain oozing into her roots.

His look of horror had her reaching up with her fingertips to touch it.

"The bullet only grazed me," she said, but her face went instantly pale as she beheld the blood on her fingers.

Lucas ignored his shock long enough to peek over the edge of the truck bed. He could see the shooter standing on the roof, half hidden by the Rascal Jack's sign. If his eyes weren't playing tricks on him, the ponytail suggested he was looking at a woman. Perhaps Laura Dunn?

Unbelievable that The Entity would come after them at this late juncture.

"Yes, sir." Stone's cheerful answer suggested he hadn't heard either gunshot.

With a few choice words thrown in, Lucas summarized their situation. Not five seconds later, Stone and Galbraith came bursting out of the Winnebago, firing shots at the roof. Lucas braved a second peek. Laura Dunn was retreating. Lucas pushed to his knees.

In that same instant, Navy SEALs poked their heads out of Rascal Jack's, clearly drawn by the sound of gunfire. Lucas spotted Saul and shouted, "Over here!"

Saul sprinted to the truck and, with a look of consternation, peered down into the bed. "What the hell happened?"

"Laura Dunn shot at us from the roof." Torn between wanting Saul's help and wanting the woman apprehended, Lucas made a quick decision and pointed. "Go after her. I've got Charlotte," he added.

With a parting glance at her, Saul ran toward the trunk of his car to collect his weapons.

Ignoring Charlotte's insistence that she could walk, Lucas gathered her gently into his arms. Taking great pains not to jostle her, he scooted them off the tailgate, touched a foot to the pavement, and swung her clear of the truck. In the same instant, he spotted Saul darting out of sight behind the building. Even in his polished dress shoes, he moved like he was wearing moccasins. A couple of SEALs took off after him. The rest took note of Lucas's predicament and rushed over.

"She's shot," Bambino exclaimed.

"Barely," Charlotte managed.

"Yes," Lucas said. "Theo, call 911. Bambino, get the door. It's time to put your medic training to the test."

"Yes, sir!"

As Theo whipped out his phone, Bambino ran ahead to open the door and yelled at the milling SEALs to make way.

In the bar's cool interior, the jukebox was still blaring. Theo and Bambino followed Lucas to the nearest pool table, then hovered with concern as Lucas laid Charlotte on the table's velveteen surface. The bar manager materialized to offer aid.

"I need a first aid kit," Lucas barked at him. "Tell me you have one."

"Sure." The manager hurried into the kitchen.

"What do you think, Tony?" he asked Bambino, who was peering at Charlotte's head wound.

"Looks superficial," Bambino declared, his Philadelphia accent suddenly apparent. "All we can do is disinfect the wound and bandage it and treat her for shock," he added.

Lucas leaned over Charlotte, resting his forearms on the table. "Talk to me, baby," he requested.

She pretended to glare at him, but with her face so pallid, she couldn't pull it off. "I told you not to call me that."

The manager's return with the first aid kit gave Tony something to do. He pawed through its contents, pulling out bandages and disinfectant. Lucas realized Charlotte had started to shiver. He caught the manager's eye. "Do you have any clean towels?"

"Yes, sir."

As that man went to fetch them, Lucas clasped Charlotte's cold hand and caught her eye.

"I can't believe what just happened," he said, staving off his own shock. "How did you know she was about to shoot us?" he demanded. "Your back was to the building."

"Not us," Charlotte whispered back, confusing him.

"What?"

"She was aiming for you." Her eyelashes started to flutter. "I saw the laser dot on your forehead."

Two things occurred to Lucas at once. The first was that Charlotte had thrown herself on top of him to protect him. The second was that she was about to lose consciousness.

Lucas put his face closer to hers. "Stay with me, baby. Don't sleep," he begged.

"I'm just closing my eyes," she whispered, as Tony used adhesive to keep the gauze stuck to her forehead.

"You can't. You have to keep them open." He lifted an imploring look at Tony. "What do we do?"

"Just keep talking to her," Bambino suggested. Taking the towels the manager had just run out to them, he moved swiftly to Charlotte's feet, propped them up with several towels, then draped two more over her to keep her warm.

Thankful for Tony's calm efficiency, Lucas cradled Charlotte's hand between both of his in order to warm it. As he lowered his lips to kiss her knuckles, fearful tears rushed into his eyes.

She was watching him through her lashes. "You really need to work on that, Lucas," she whispered.

"Work on what?" he choked out.

She managed a weak smile. "Never mind. I like that about you."

He had to believe she did more than merely like him. She'd taken a bullet for him, for heaven's sake. Thank God—thank *God* it hadn't hit her more directly. But she wasn't out of the woods yet. She'd clearly sustained a concussion, which could still result in complications like a brain bleed, even death. *Don't think that!*

God wouldn't let that happen when he'd only just realized she was the one for him. The mere idea was appalling.

"I'll be okay," Charlotte murmured.

But in the next instant, her eyes rolled back in her head, and her lids drifted shut.

"Charlotte!" Lucas called, but she didn't stir. He squeezed her hand harder, willing her to wake up. "Where is the ambulance?" he shouted, with a desperate glance over his shoulder.

"On its way, sir." Theo, who had been standing guard just inside the door, spoke with calm reassurance. "I can hear the siren now."

Drawing a shaky breath, Lucas took in Charlotte's still, pale form with gut-wrenching helplessness. He'd been in situations where teammates had been shot, injured, even killed. But this was different.

This was his future, hanging by a thread.

CHAPTER 19

$\mathcal{E}$ ven with her eyes closed, Charlotte was conscious of the sun streaming through the hospital window. She awakened to it by degrees, turning her head slowly so as not to exacerbate her pounding head. The bandage secured so tightly over her brow seemed to make the headache worse. Over the thud of her own heart, she could hear the hospital staff bustling about, tending to their patients. It had to be midmorning or so—her phone was in her purse, which was in the locker, she recalled, along with a change of clothing.

The reading of Jaguar's verdict, followed by sentencing—or extenuation and mitigation as it was called in the military—would be happening at any moment, she realized. That was why Lucas had left. Prior to that, he'd remained steadfastly by her side, from the moment she had roused in the ER to the wee hours of the morning when she'd finally been permitted to sleep. His steady presence had made the unpleasant ordeal nearly tolerable.

Somewhere between her CAT scan, which revealed only a mild concussion, and the suturing of her scalp, Lucas informed her that Laura Dunn had been apprehended. With her arrest, the threat posed by The Entity seemed to be lessened. All the same, Galbraith and

Stone had reached out to her godfather, who received hospital permission to let them stand guard in the hallway. Lucas, himself, had occupied the reclining chair by her bed.

As she'd drifted off to sleep, the words Lucas had shared with her so earnestly before the incomprehensible shooting replayed themselves in her head. He'd said she was amazing and smart and fun to be with. He'd said he thought they could work out a relationship, despite her career plans. She knew he was waiting for her answer.

As much as she wanted to belong to Lucas, heart and soul, she could not—would not—condemn him to the kind of hit-or-miss relationship he'd described. He'd said he wouldn't ask her to give up her plans and that he would always be there for her. But Lucas didn't deserve a long-distance love affair. He deserved a woman who curled up next to him every night and gave him beautiful babies.

Sadly, that wouldn't be her.

She had nurtured her plan to join the CIA since adolescence. Come hell or high water, she intended to see it through. Knowing Lucas was somewhere thinking about her wouldn't help her concentration. Knowing he was missing her would leave her feeling torn. He deserved better than what she could give him. A tear of regret leaked from her eye and dropped to the pillow.

Pressured by her bladder, she tossed back the sheet and sat up, putting her feet tentatively to the floor. Her head, she discovered, hurt far less in a vertical position. Out in the hallway, she could hear Galbraith flirting with a nurse.

Worried about Jaguar's fate and eager to be cleared for dismissal, Charlotte used the restroom. Appalled by her bandaged reflection, she gave herself a cat bath, then dressed in the khaki slacks and patterned blouse her brother had brought for her. The thoughtful gesture must have been Saul's idea, since Saul had been the one to give Calvin a ride. Checking her phone for an update on Jaguar, Charlotte groaned to find the phone dead, uncharged.

As she eyed the clock on the wall, she could only imagine how Jaguar had to be feeling with his fate about to be announced.

Please, oh, please, God, let the court find Jaguar innocent, Charlotte prayed.

She was wriggling her feet into her pumps when a sharp knock preceded her door opening. Peeking in, her godfather looked astonished to see her standing and dressed.

"Charlotte!" he exclaimed, stepping inside and approaching her with concern in his eyes.

"Uncle Larry." She accepted his familiar hug with relief, then looked up at him. "You didn't have to come all the way down here."

He put her at arm's length to inspect her. "Of course I did. My bodyguards failed to protect you. I can't believe they almost let you die. They're fired," he declared, sounding sincere, though she knew he had to be joking.

"It wasn't their fault," she insisted. "Besides, it wasn't me who was being shot at, it was Lucas. Dwyer must have wanted to punish him for reconning his warehouse."

Her godfather went suddenly still, his gaze intent. "What do you mean, darling?"

Too late, Charlotte remembered her godfather knew nothing about The Entity. Now that Fitz was dead, though, perhaps he ought to know. If anyone could put an end to a ring of extreme right-wing vigilantes, it was the director of the DIA.

Ignoring how weak she was feeling, she explained how The Entity was a highly organized group of top-level officials in both the military and the government. "And Dwyer is a key member. He's been stealing weapons in advance of his SEALs and, instead of destroying them, he's been storing them in a warehouse in Sabena. Special Agent Fitzpatrick of the FBI was just about to shut down the syndicate when he was killed."

"Fitz?" her godfather repeated, clearly recognizing the name.

"Yeah, you've heard of him?"

"Of course. He's a legend. You mean he's dead?"

"Yeah, he was shot by The Entity's hitman, Jason Dunn. Dunn and his wife were the couple that abducted me, and she's the one who tried to shoot Lucas last night."

Uncle Larry's eyes had taken on a horrified light. He rubbed his stomach as if it were hurting him. "I can't believe all this," he muttered, looking ill-at-ease. "It sounds like something straight out of a spy thriller."

"You can put an end to The Entity, though, can't you, Uncle Larry? It'll take the FBI way too long to pick up where Fitz left off."

Her godfather's mouth crimped and his jaw hardened. "Yes, I can," he said in a strange voice, then nodded. For a moment, he stood lost in his thoughts before focusing on her again. "I need to get you somewhere safe."

"No, you don't. I doubt I'm in danger anymore. Laura Dunn was captured last night, and The Entity knows I can't remember anything else at this juncture. I'm not a threat to them."

"All the same, it wouldn't hurt to take a vacation until this group is dismantled."

Charlotte frowned. "That's what I was told at NCIS. I don't *want* to take a vacation. I want to hear Jaguar's verdict and find out whether he's being sentenced or released."

Uncle Larry considered her with his head cocked. "That's happening right now?"

Charlotte checked the clock on her wall. "In like fifteen minutes."

"All right then." His jaw muscles jumped as he thought for several more seconds. "Let's go there. I'll take you," he offered.

"Really? But I haven't been released yet."

He waved a hand. "I'll take responsibility for that. You look fit as a fiddle. Come on, let's go. You don't want to miss the excitement."

The prospect of joining Lucas at the reading of the verdict followed by the sentencing filled Charlotte with nervous energy. She knew she would have to answer Lucas's proposition with words that would hurt him. But a clean break was the most painless one. She would bid him good-bye, the sooner the better, before they became even more emotionally entangled than they already were.

Sitting in what was obviously a rental car, Charlotte had to close her eyes against the blinding sunlight. Her head hurt, but not too badly. As long as she held nice and still, she felt almost normal. Her godfather drove with care, braking slowly and taking leisurely turns. Out of consideration, he didn't force her to converse with him.

Even with her eyes closed, Charlotte knew precisely when they approached Oceana's main gate. She'd gone this way to work every day for the past year. Fishing her driver's license from her purse, she ascertained with a peek that it wasn't the one for Justice Strong, then gave it to her godfather to show the guard.

"Oh, I won't need that." He waved it off.

Sure enough, the MP took one look at her godfather's ID and waved them through.

With a smile, she closed her eyes again and put her license away. After several more turns, she opened them again to assess where they were.

"Wait, the courtroom is in my old building," she protested, seeing they'd passed it.

Uncle Larry slanted her a pitying look. "I'm sorry, but you can't make it to the sentencing."

She blinked at him. "What? I thought that was where we were going."

He shook his head and grimaced. "I can't take the chance something might happen to you. I lost your mother, I can't lose you, too."

"Uncle Larry," she protested. Immediately, her head started to pound. "I told you, I'm not the one who was targeted. The Entity has no reason to come for me."

"All the same, we can't take chances."

She protested again, only to have her argument fall on deaf ears. Her godfather was speeding now at well over the limit. With a sense of shock, she realized they were headed toward the airfield.

"You're not flying me out of here," she stated. Every muscle in her body went rigid.

"Just relax," he retorted. "You've had a concussion, and you're not thinking clearly."

"The hell I'm not!" She regretted her outburst immediately. Compounding her headache by shouting wasn't going to help her cause any. She needed to keep calm and find a way to avoid leaving. If her godfather steamrolled her decision, she would bolt when he wasn't looking.

Her godfather drove right onto Oceana's tarmac for private planes and pulled alongside the King Air 350, which she recognized as his private jet. He must have flown it down to Virginia Beach that morning. His pilot sat under the wing, reading a book in its shade. Noting their arrival, he jumped up and put the book away as her godfather slowed to a stop nearby.

"Change of plans," Uncle Larry called to the man as he pushed out of the driver's seat. "We're going to the Bahamas."

"Sir, some FBI agents were just here looking for you," the pilot informed his boss on an anxious note. "They told me if I fly you out of here, I'll be arrested."

"Don't worry about it, Gibbs. Go start the plane or I'll find someone to replace you."

With a grim nod, Gibbs tugged the chocks from behind the plane's wheels, preparing them for takeoff.

Charlotte didn't have time to process the implications of the words she'd overheard. All she knew was she had to escape at once. Reaching for her door handle, she ignored the certainty that she couldn't outrun both men in her current condition, but she gave it a shot, anyway, thrusting the door open and taking off. She hadn't taken ten steps when her godfather halted her flight abruptly as he grabbed her arm. He then dragged her, fighting him feebly, toward the entrance to his plane.

"You'll thank me later," he promised, his gentle voice at odds with the painful pressure on her arm. "I know how to look after my own."

"I don't want to leave," Charlotte insisted, bracing herself on the plane's exterior as her godfather tried to pull her in after him. "I'm afraid of flying." Appealing to his compassionate nature, she fully expected him to back down.

Instead, he snapped at her, "Get in the plane, Charlotte. You don't know what you want."

His powerful tug spilled her onto her knees just inside the rear entrance and resulted in such a splitting headache, she could do nothing but crouch on the floor with her head in her hands, certain she was going to vomit.

Sliding her foot out of the way, her godfather pulled the door shut and sealed the cabin by securing the airlock.

"Let's go!" he shouted down the length of the eight-seater to the pilot up front.

With the feeling she had to be hallucinating, Charlotte prayed for her headache to subside while performing a reality check. The rough rug under her knees and the whine of the plane's engine both assured her she wasn't imagining things. Her godfather had prevented her from attending Jaguar's sentencing and forced her onto his aircraft. Why? Because he thought her life in danger?

But was that really the reason? His erratic behavior suggested there was more going on here.

One glaring clue gave her somewhere to start. He'd said they were going to the Bahamas.

"Come on, Charlotte. I'm sorry if I hurt you. You have to get up now and take a seat."

Compliant for the moment, Charlotte let herself be helped into one of the seats at the back of the plane. Her godfather secured the seatbelt around her waist for her.

"There you go. Close your eyes and rest," he urged.

"You're friends with Roger Holden, aren't you?" she accused, watching his reaction through half-closed eyes.

He froze a moment, then dropped heavily into the seat facing hers and buckled himself in. Charlotte realized with dismay that the plane was moving. She couldn't believe she'd allowed her godfather to abduct her—again.

"The time has come to be honest with you, Charlotte." His regretful tone did little to mitigate the anger starting to simmer inside of her. "You got yourself in way over your head taking over Agent Elwood's investigation. Dwyer is difficult to manage when he's backed into a corner. He killed your supervisor against my wishes, and he would have killed you, too."

Charlotte reeled. She could scarcely process her godfather's betrayal. What on earth did he mean by *against my wishes*? Uncle Larry didn't even know Commander Dwyer.

"But why not just protect me? Why send people to grab me and drug me? They took the iPad...," she trailed off as it occurred to her the iPad she'd been delivering to her godfather must have ended up in his hands anyway, yet he'd done nothing about it.

"You promised you would have Dwyer arrested." Yet, he hadn't. Instead, he'd pretended to search for her while holding her captive until her memories of Elwood's files faded. There could only be one reason for him to want her to forget.

She gasped at her epiphany. "You're with The Entity, too?" Ignoring her aching head, she searched his pained expression for the truth. His words about managing Dwyer suddenly made more sense.

His sad smile was all the acknowledgment she needed. But his next words said otherwise.

"Not anymore," he assured her. "I promised you I would put an end to the organization, and that's what's happening right now. We'll put the past behind us and start over."

A frisson of fear swept through her. "Start over? You mean, you're not ever going back?" Shifting her gaze toward the window, she was horrified to see them turning to line up with the runway.

"No, I can't ever go back," Martin admitted with regret. "Ironic, isn't it? I gave everything I had to keeping my country safe and, in the end, this is how she thanks me."

Too stunned to argue with his thinking, Charlotte watched in disbelief as the plane gained speed. Faster and faster it went, turning the grassy field into a blur. The nose of the small plane lifted, then the rest of it.

"We're going to the Bahamas?" she asked, thinking that would be the first place Lucas would look for her. She wouldn't be missing for weeks this time.

"Well, to start with," her godfather qualified. "Roger will make arrangements for us. We'll get what we need from him and then go farther afield. Switzerland, maybe."

She remembered making a joke about that once.

No way on earth was she going to Switzerland. Her godfather had to be crazy to think he could get away with skipping the country. Then again, with Fitz dead, by the time the FBI realized the head of the DIA was a member of The Entity—if not its leader—Larry Martin would have long since disappeared. And his goddaughter with him.

"What about Calvin?" she asked, desperate to retard their delay. "We have to go back for Calvin. He can't take care of himself."

"Of course he can. The boy is smart, so much like your *father*."

For the first time in her life, Charlotte heard an underlying hatred in Martin's voice when speaking of her father, Alan Patterson. That made no sense. He and her father had been lifelong friends, right up to her father's death.

"But I'm smart, too," Charlotte insisted. "I can look after myself. I don't need to go with you."

Martin's jaw tightened. "You're all that's left of your mother," he stated on an odd note. "If she hadn't gotten on that plane with Alan, she would still be alive. Stupid woman," he muttered to himself, looking out the window.

An awful suspicion pegged Charlotte to her seat. Her mother wasn't supposed to be on the fated flight that had killed her parents. At the last minute, wanting to be included in the fun, Vickie Patterson had found a way to join her husband. And she had subsequently perished with him.

What if their deaths hadn't been an accident? What if Uncle Larry had tampered with her father's aircraft, hoping he would die? Only, his plan had backfired when her mother, unsuspecting, hitched a ride.

Tell me you didn't kill them, Charlotte thought, regarding her godfather in a whole new light. How much of a leap was it between kidnapping and murder, if all he'd had to do was to compromise some component on an aircraft?

~

"All rise."

Lucas, anxious to hear Jaguar's verdict—almost as anxious as he was to return to Charlotte's bedside at the hospital—rose in the same company that had occupied the pews the day before, minus Monica and Charlotte.

Surely, after all the discrepancies the panel had heard the day before, they hadn't met the two-thirds majority vote necessary to convict Jaguar. But Captain Englert's scowling face as he entered the courtroom from his recess chamber filled Lucas with sudden dread. The panel did not join him. It was the judge alone who would announce the verdict, then determine Jaguar's sentence if he was found guilty.

"The spectators may be seated," Englert instructed.

Lucas sank onto the hard bench with his stomach churning.

Clearing his throat, Englert looked at the page in his hand and began to spout legalese that was a mere formality and prelude to Jaguar's verdict.

Lucas held his breath waiting for the words that would either free Jaguar or wreck his life. Suddenly, Englert was saying them.

"… finds Lt. Jonah Michael Mills *guilty* of violating Article 128 of the Uniform Code of Military Justice."

A murmur of dissent rose from Jaguar's supporters, including Lucas, who couldn't believe that between Englert and the five panel members, two-thirds of them honestly believed Jaguar had attacked his CO. Cutting a horrified look at Jaguar, Lucas saw him widen his stance as if absorbing a blow. A second glance at Eden's bowed head made Lucas suspect Carew had shared the bad news with them of Fitz's demise.

"We will proceed with the extenuation and mitigation," Englert continued. "Counselor O'Rourke?"

As O'Rourke's dramatic baritone filled the chamber, Lucas tuned it out by thinking of Charlotte, whose presence he sorely missed. He couldn't wait to get back to her so he could hear her decision in regards to their future.

Sadly, he would now have to inform her that their efforts to help Jaguar had failed.

At last, it was the defense's turn to argue for a lenient sentence. Carew reminded Englert of the discrepancies that existed between the testimony of the prosecution's witnesses and the defense's. She then pointed out Dwyer's dishonesty regarding the journal of which he had no recollection, stolen by the secretary with whom he was having an affair.

"In circumstances where the truth is told, there is never doubt," she pointed out, her gaze imploring. "But where doubt exists, someone had to be lying, and that person, Your Honor, is not the man whom you have declared guilty."

The young attorney regarded her client for a moment and said, "My client was held prisoner by an enemy nation for twelve months and eleven days. He has been subjected to electrical torture. He has had his fingernails ripped from his fingers. He was apart from his family and believed dead. With all that he has endured, I request the court abstain from sentencing him to any more time than that already spent incarcerated. He has been punished more than any man deserves."

Bravo, Lucas thought when Carew was finished. Shooting Saul a raised eyebrow, he received Saul's nod of approval. Carew's passion had made up for her inexperience.

Come on, Lord, let Englert's eyes be opened to the truth!

The judge, clearly unsettled by Carew's moving words, regarded

Jaguar with a troubled gaze. To Lucas's surprise, he addressed Jaguar directly.

"Lieutenant Mills, while it is unorthodox for a sailor who is found guilty to speak during mitigation, I'm willing to make an exception. Is there something you wish to say that might impact your sentencing?"

Jaguar visibly swallowed. "Yes, Your Honor," he replied, locking eyes with the man who was free to throw the gravest of punishments at him—dishonorable discharge. "I respectfully request that you consider my family." Jaguar gestured toward Eden and his stepdaughter, Miriam, present for the first time, who sat hugging each other in the first row. "They were without me for a year while I was held captive. My family needs me, and my country needs me, Your Honor." Jaguar nodded to signify that was it. "Thank you."

A solemn quiet followed Jaguar's plea. As he lowered himself back into his chair, the door at the back of the courtroom flew open, startling everyone present. Englert beetled his brow at the intruder.

"What now?" he demanded on a peevish note.

Looking over the heads of those behind him, Lucas did a double take. Special Agent Fitzpatrick was almost unrecognizable in a black suit and black tie with a bright white bandage on his neck, but he was obviously very much alive. He strode into the room followed by four burly men wearing the iconic blue FBI windbreakers. Rather than answer Englert's question, Fitz marched up to him and handed him a piece of paper.

Baffled, Englert skimmed it, his expression shifting from one of disbelief, to outrage as he glanced up at Dwyer, and then, finally, to chagrin.

"Go ahead, take him," he said, handing the paper back. The courtroom seemed to collectively hold its breath as the FBI agents walked toward Commander Dwyer who sat on the side of the prosecution, looking as tense as a rabbit, eyes wide and fixed on the agent who was supposed to be dead.

In the astonished silence that followed, Lucas heard a rasping voice say, "Daniel Dwyer, you are under arrest for defrauding the Department of Defense and for hoarding stolen weapons."

Fitz's voice, Lucas realized, must have been ravaged in his attack, but his death had proved to be a false rumor, likely meant to mislead The Entity into letting down its guard.

Watching the four FBI heavies humiliate Dwyer by slapping cuffs on him and dragging him out of the courtroom, blustering in protest, was one of the sweetest moments of Lucas's life. He and Saul exchanged grins and slapped each other on the back. As the door thudded shut, the SEALs in Lucas's troop clapped and cheered.

"Order!" Englert shouted, then lost control of the courtroom as Fitz approached him a second time. "Right, right," Lucas heard Englert utter as they shared a brief conversation. The judge frowned fiercely, his face turning red.

Snatching up his gavel, he struck it once, twice, thrice, and, finally, the ecstatic SEALs simmered down, eager to hear what Englert had to say with Dwyer now arrested.

With a stony expression, Englert proclaimed, "The United States Navy finds Lieutenant Jonah Michael Mills not guilty. His conviction has been overturned!"

Red in the face, Englert stood up, prompting everyone in the courtroom to do likewise, and stormed off the bench, disappearing through the door by which he'd entered.

As it slammed shut after him, the SEALs erupted once more into noisy excitement. Lucas found himself the focus of Fitz's intent regard. The man was heading toward him, peering to the right and the left of him as he approached, obviously looking for Charlotte.

Lucas slipped out of his seat and into the aisle to meet him halfway. Forgiving the man for his heavy-handedness back at Pax hospital, he stuck his hand out, pleased by the agent's reincarnation and especially by his impeccable timing.

"You're alive! I thought you were dead."

"Where is she?" Fitz demanded, ignoring his comment and clasping his hand only briefly.

The grating quality of his voice was hard to listen to.

"You were supposed to keep an eye on her. She's here, isn't she?"

The agent's edginess made Lucas instantly nervous. He glanced over at Saul, who was standing right behind him, tugging on his goatee.

"Um, no, sir," Lucas answered with reluctance. "She's at Princess Ann Hospital." He knew the minute the words were out of his mouth they'd screwed up royally—mostly him, since he'd let her talk him into going their separate ways.

"Her godfather's bodyguards are protecting her," he added, knowing that was no excuse. Fitz had given him and Saul one job— protect Charlotte Patterson until further notice—and they'd let him down.

"Her godfather's bodyguards?" Fitz's freckled face tightened with fury. "I assigned you to watch her because I knew her godfather wouldn't skip the country without her." He pointed a threatening finger in Lucas's face. "You've done enough damage. You're relieved of duty where Miss Patterson is concerned."

Lucas gaped at him as he turned away. "Wait, are you saying what I think you're saying?"

Fitz wheeled back around. "Yes," Fitz hissed. "Larry Martin is president of The Entity. We went to arrest him at dawn this morning only to learn he'd flown down to NAS Oceana. I'd suspected he would come for Charlotte, which is why I tasked you two with her protection. But she's not even here!" he grated, throwing his hands up in frustration. "And don't bother calling her either. Her phone is dead." With that, he stalked out of the courtroom.

Lucas grabbed Saul's arm. "Come on, we're going, too."

"To the hospital, sir?"

"The airfield. If Martin hears about Dwyer's arrest, he's going to try to leave the country." *Taking Charlotte with him*, he added silently, too afraid to give voice to his fears.

With guilt shackling his chest, Lucas chased Fitz and his minions out of the building. Fitz might have relieved him of his duty, but that wasn't Fitz's call. Only God, who'd brought Lucas and Charlotte together, could ever relieve him of the need to look after her, to care for and to cherish her.

Once outside, they headed straight for Lucas's truck, then squealed out of the parking lot in pursuit of the official black SUVs belonging to the FBI.

With Saul shooting him worried glances, Lucas articulated the questions in his head. "I wonder how Fitz knew Martin wouldn't leave the country without Charlotte."

"I don't know," Saul replied.

"I guess she was right about Fitz in one respect," Lucas reflected.

"In what way, sir?"

"She felt like he had an agenda, and he did. Think about it," he added, shooting Saul a look. "Fitz said he knew Martin would come for Charlotte, which was why he tasked us with her protection. He was using her as bait knowing Martin wouldn't skip the country without her. The question is why she matters so much to Martin," he added, thinking to himself. "I mean, I know they're close but..."

Saul broke into his thoughts by calling his attention to the small plane strafing the treetops up ahead of them. "Tell me that's not Martin's plane."

Lucas ducked and peered from under the roof of the car. The sudden acceleration of the SUVs ahead of him supplied an answer.

"Oh, no," Lucas breathed, suddenly stricken. "We're too late," he stated in disbelief.

The SUVs veered toward the control tower, and Lucas did likewise.

"Don't worry, sir," Saul soothed. "The FBI can order them to turn around. You'll get Charlotte back."

Oh, I plan to, Lucas thought. *And when I do, I'll never let her slip away again.*

CHAPTER 20

"Sir!" Larry Martin's pilot called through the opening from the cockpit to the cabin. "Control at NAS Oceana is hailing us. The FBI is demanding we return to base or they'll scramble jets and force us down."

With an exclamation of dismay, Charlotte's godfather shook off his seatbelt and powered his way up the aisle of the steeply rising craft.

"They're bluffing," she heard him say. "No one's going to force us down. I'm the director of the DIA, for God's sake."

Charlotte watched with a sinking heart as he reached into the cockpit and snapped off the radio, silencing the insistent voice on the other end.

Looking pale and tense, Uncle Larry shot a glance back at Charlotte, then dropped into a seat up front. Charlotte watched him close his eyes and rub his stomach, which was clearly hurting him.

"Turn around!" she shouted from her seat in the rear, but both men ignored her. Mustering her strength, Charlotte unbuckled her seatbelt and fought her way up the aisle to join them. Her head throbbed with every beat of her heart. The plane was still climbing steeply into the sky.

Noticing her advance, Martin tensed, his eyes flashing as they did whenever he spoke of hostile countries. "Sit down, Charlotte," he barked at her.

The suspicion that he'd killed her parents fueled her determination to stand up to him. "No," she retorted. "We're turning around. I am not going to the Bahamas again."

Martin rose from his seat to confront her. "I said, sit down!" He started toward her, intent on grappling her into the nearest seat.

Using the angle of the plane to her advantage, Charlotte grabbed him and tugged him abruptly toward her. As he pitched forward, she plowed her knee into his midriff, then chopped him hard on the back of the head, stepping out of the way as he dropped face-down into the aisle, unconscious.

"Hey!" Startled by her actions, the pilot's hands wobbled on the control yoke. He gawked over his shoulder at her. "You can't do that."

"I just did," Charlotte gritted, then bent over her godfather and searched under his jacket for the 9-millimeter pistol she knew he kept holstered there. Finding and retrieving it, she turned and bore down on the pilot, pointing the gun at him.

"Turn this plane around," she commanded through her teeth, "back to Oceana." Then she reached cautiously into the cabin with her left hand and switched the radio back on.

With a wary look at her, the pilot leveled off the plane, but he didn't turn them around. Charlotte flipped the gun's safety and aimed it at closer range at his head.

"Are you going to fly this plane back to base, or would you like me to fly it while you talk to your Maker?"

She was bluffing of course, but he had no way to know that. To her relief, he pulled the plane into a banking turn. Charlotte snatched the copilot's headset off the hook and worked it onto her head in time to hear, "King Air, do you copy?"

The raspy voice uttering the question sounded vaguely familiar.

"This is Charlotte Patterson," she announced. "Who is this?"

"Casey Fitzpatrick," said the odd voice.

It *was* him, she realized, though he sounded dreadful. "You're alive?" she exclaimed in amazement.

"We'll talk about that later. What's your status?" he rapped.

She flicked a worried look over her shoulder. "Larry Martin is down for the moment. The pilot is turning around under duress."

An audible cheer went up on the other end. Charlotte thought she heard Lucas's rich baritone. "Is...is Lieutenant Strong there?" she stammered, chest suddenly tight.

There was a pause on the other end. "Charlotte."

It was Lucas. Her nose prickled with the urge to cry.

"Are you okay?"

More than anything, she wanted to be in his arms right then. "Uncle Larry's with The Entity. He was the one who abducted me. He was trying to leave the country and take me with him."

"I know, baby," Lucas crooned. "As soon as you get back, the FBI will arrest him."

"I should have realized," she lamented, forbearing to scold him for calling her baby. She peered anxiously over the nose of the plane for any sign of Oceana's airstrip. In the distance, she spotted a pencil-thin line that looked like it. *I think he killed my parents,* she thought, but she couldn't bring herself to say it.

"Hey, guess what? Fitz arrested Dwyer, and Jaguar was declared innocent."

A weight seemed to slip off Charlotte's shoulders. "Oh, that's great. What a relief!"

"I screwed up, Charlotte. I was supposed to protect you from Martin. I didn't realize."

"That's not your fault, Lucas. I didn't realize either."

Hearing movement behind her, she turned to find Martin pushing groggily to his knees.

"Stay right there!" she ordered, turning the weapon on him as he turned a malevolent glare over his shoulder at her.

"Charlotte?"

Lucas's anxious calling of her name coincided with the pilot reaching back with his right arm and grabbing for the pistol. As they wrestled over its possession, Martin came to his feet and charged her. Whether she squeezed the trigger or the pilot caused her to, Charlotte wasn't sure, but the 9-millimeter discharged suddenly.

Martin screamed and staggered back, blood blooming on the fabric of his slacks as he collapsed into a seat, hands clapped to his groin.

Horrified, Charlotte continued to fight the pilot for control of the pistol. Ripping off his headset, she grabbed his full head of hair and slammed his head with all her strength against the side of the cockpit. Knocked unconscious, the pilot released her and slumped over the control yoke. The plane started into a dive.

"Charlotte, what's happening?"

Charlotte flashed out a hand to keep from losing her balance. God help her, the plane was descending and the pilot was out cold!

Sparing a glance at her godfather, who was hunched over trying to stem the blood gushing from his groin, Charlotte tried to rouse the pilot.

"Wake up!" She shook him as she shouted into his ear. Eyeing the windscreen, she was horrified to note the angle of the plane.

The pilot didn't stir. *Oh, no. Oh, help. This can't be happening.*

"Charlotte," Lucas repeated with urgency. "Tell me what's happening."

"I'm in big trouble," she blurted. "Uncle Larry's been shot, and the pilot is unconscious. The plane's going down," she added. "We're going to crash."

"No, you're not."

He said it with so much certainty that she eyed her situation one more time. *Oh, yes, they were.* The plane was headed straight for the ground.

How ironic that she'd dreamed a similar scenario, over and over again. "I'm going to die," she said, resigning herself to the inevitable. For a split second, she thought of Calvin and what this would do to him. Could Lucas patch her through to her brother in time to tell him how much she loved him? To tell him goodbye?

"No," Lucas stated on a stubborn note, cutting through her thoughts. "I won't let you. Listen to me, Charlotte. You need to get the pilot off the yoke and take over the plane. Pull him back and cinch him in tight with the harness belt."

She hesitated, then sprang into action. She had nothing to lose by trying. "All right."

Hauling the pilot off the controls, she was relieved to feel the nose of the plane lift instantly. Cinching his belt as tight as possible, she then dropped into the copilot's seat and eyed the display in front of her. Her father had taught her years ago what most of the instruments were, but that was in an older plane with analogue displays. The digital ones looked completely unfamiliar.

"Tell me what to do," she begged. "Hurry."

"Find the throttles with the black handles," Lucas instructed, "and pull them all the way back. Then pull back on the control yoke."

"This isn't going to work," she informed him. It had never worked in her nightmares.

"Do it, baby. We have you on radar. You're not that far off-course. Just bring the nose up twenty degrees, and I will talk you in."

Yeah, right. It couldn't be that easy, but at this juncture, she had no choice but to try.

God, please don't let me die like this.

As she drew back the black handles, the engine noise diminished. Next, she pulled the control yoke, fighting the increasing pressure. To her amazement, the tops of the trees disappeared from view, but then she was looking at pure blue sky as she soared straight up. A moan of terror escaped her.

"Not too much," Lucas cautioned, his voice remarkably calm. "Ease back down until the nose reaches the horizon and add some power back in with the black handles."

She pushed the yoke forward until the horizon came into view and timidly added power.

"How fast are you going, Charlotte?"

"I don't know." Even to her own ears, she sounded terrified.

"Look at the airspeed indicator. It's right in the middle of the instrument panel, clearly marked."

Charlotte frantically searched the gauges in the middle of the dash and finally found the one for airspeed. "One hundred ten," she said.

"More throttle!"

Responding to Lucas's urgency, she jammed the throttles forward. The plane lunged, and the propeller noise became a scream.

"Easy, baby. Keep the handles about two-thirds of the way forward."

Charlotte reduced the power. She was having a hard time holding the plane level. Each increase or decrease of power made the nose rise and fall, and the pressure of the yoke was tremendous.

"I can't hold it!" she cried.

"Are you buckled in?"

"No." The plane was all over the sky, rising and falling like a roller coaster.

"Do that first." Lucas's steady tone reined in her runaway panic.

"Done," she said a second later.

"Now, do you see a big wheel sticking halfway out of the center console, close to the throttles?"

"You mean the trim wheel?" she asked, remembering it from her father's lessons.

"Yes, that one. First, which way is the plane trying to go, up or down?"

"Uh...down."

"Okay. Push the wheel away from you until you feel the pressure on the yoke ease off to nothing."

Charlotte obeyed and, to her amazement, it worked. The control yoke was blessedly pressure-free.

"That's better," she said.

"Now, find the rudders on the floor," Lucas added, "and push the left one until I tell you to stop. You're a little off course."

She did as he said, and the whole plane started skidding through the air. *Oh, God.*

"That's it. Now release the pedal and have a look. Do you see the airstrip ahead of you?"

She'd kept one eye on it the entire time. "I see it."

"Tap the right rudder with your toe and line yourself up exactly. Make small movements. You have plenty of time."

She heard him muffle the radio and issue orders to have the airstrip cleared and to have emergency vehicles standing by. Her heart clutched with dread at the thought of approaching the ground."

"I'm scared," she confessed.

"Don't be scared," he said. "Think of what Isaiah wrote: 'Do not be afraid, for I am with you. Don't be discouraged, for I am your God. I will strengthen you and help you. I will hold you up with the righteousness of my right hand.'"

In that life or death moment, the words were a balm to her terrified soul. "I so much want to believe that," she admitted.

"Then believe it," he urged. "All things are possible with God. Besides, flying is easy in a turboprop. I'm going to talk you right through it. Okay?"

She expelled a shaky breath. "Okay. I'm a believer."

"That's my girl. Now that you've sped up, I need you to slow down. Pull back on the throttle handles until they're about halfway back. As you slow down, the nose will drop. When that happens, pull the yoke back and roll back the wheel until the pressure's gone again."

As tense as a trapdoor, Charlotte followed his instructions. Like he'd said, the nose began to drop. She pulled back the yoke, bringing the plane level, then adjusted the wheel to reduce pressure, and the nose returned to the horizon. The white needle on the airspeed indicator began to drop.

"It's dropped below one hundred fifty," she relayed.

"Perfect. Now look way over by the pilot's seat and find the landing gear. It looks like a pin with a lollipop on top."

"Found it."

"Pull it out and then push it all the way down. Then nudge the throttles forward just a bit."

"Right now?"

"Yes, now."

She did, and a mechanical sound followed. She sensed the plane slowing down, and she responded by nudging the throttles forward.

"What's the airspeed now?" he asked.

"One hundred."

"That's a little slow."

He tried to mask the tension in his tone, but she still heard it, prompting her to add more power and to roll the trim forward. The airspeed indicator began a slow climb up, allowing her to release the breath she was holding and inhale another one. Her blouse was sticking to her back.

Surely, her father had done this very thing while trying to keep his plane from crashing into the ocean. *Don't think of that!*

"I'm back to one twenty," she volunteered.

"Perfect." Lucas's voice was soothing again. "Now look along the top of the instrument panel. See the three green lights lit up?"

"Yes."

"Good. That means the gear's down. Look on the face of the instrument panel near your left knee. Do you see the small handle marked FLAPS?"

"Yes."

"Pull it down to the first notch in the slot."

She did, and the plane began to slow again. The nose rose slightly.

"How's the airspeed" Lucas asked again.

"Down to one hundred ten again."

"Hold it right there. If it tries to go slower, roll the trim forward to make the nose go down. If it tries to go faster, trim up. Remember this," he added. "It's important: You are going to control the speed by moving the nose up or down. You're going to control your altitude with the throttles. Got it?"

Speed nose. Altitude throttles. "Got it."

"If you pull off power, the nose will drop, and the plane will start to speed up. You have to counter that by raising the nose and holding speed at a hundred ten."

There was so much to think about at once!

"Lucas?" she added, thinking this might be her last chance to communicate with him.

"Yes, Charlotte?"

She hesitated. What could she say to convey how much she'd loved every moment with him? How much she loved him, as she realized at that moment with the horizon bouncing up and down ahead of her, that she did love him with *all* of her heart.

"If I had to do this all over again, I would, just so I could spend these past few weeks with you."

"You're not going to die, Charlotte," he retorted on a determined note. "It's time to push the flaps down one more notch. Trim the nose so your speed stays at one hundred. Fortunately, wind's not a factor today. See, God's on your side."

"Uh huh." Charlotte pushed the flaps down, and the plane reacted by raising its nose. The airspeed indicator started down, and she hesitated, thinking first, before rolling the trim wheel forward to increase her speed.

Looking out the windscreen, she cringed to see how close the ground was getting. At least she was centered on the runway. She tasted salt on her upper lip.

"Time to pull the flaps to the last slot," Lucas instructed. "You're going to slow down to ninety. Remember, control your speed with the trim and your distance from the ground with the throttle. Do it all very gently."

With her heart in her throat, Charlotte lowered the flaps all the way. The plane reacted as it had before, slowing down and raising its nose. Rolling the trim forward, she tried to make the speed settle on ninety. Looking up, she saw she was much too close to the ground, and the runway was still some distance away. Panicked, she shoved both throttles forward.

The engines roared, and the nose rose abruptly. *Oh, God, I'm losing control!*

Lucas's calm voice penetrated her panic again, making her focus. "Pull the throttles back a bit."

She did, and the nose dropped again. She let it fall. Miraculously, the airspeed indicator settled on ninety. The ground came closer. She made a slight correction with her feet.

Suddenly, the nearest end of the runway seemed to be approaching at blinding speed.

"You're doing great, baby." Lucas's soothing voice freed her to breathe. "You have a huge, long runway in front of you. Just let the plane settle in. When you get about twenty feet up, pull the throttles back more. Then as you sink toward the runway, pull back on the control yoke gently. Use the rudders to keep yourself going straight. You're doing great, Charlotte. I love you."

Concrete was flashing underneath her now, and she seemed to be going so fast that there was no way she could survive contact with it.

"Throttles back," Lucas instructed as the ground rushed up under her. The engine noise died away. "Control yoke," he added seconds later, "gently."

She pulled back on the yoke, and then back some more. The pressure was tremendous, but she didn't dare let go to use the trim wheel. The runway disappeared under the nose of the plane. The screeching of rubber sent her bouncing in her seat, but it was the loveliest sound imaginable.

Her plane was on the ground! One of her feet almost slipped off the rudder, but with supreme effort, she kept the plane from veering off course.

"You did it, baby!" The jubilation and relief in Lucas's voice made the tension rush out of her. "The brakes are on top of the rudder pedals. Push them gently, and make sure you keep going straight."

Charlotte depressed the brakes, and the plane began to slow. The end of the runway came into view, but it wasn't close enough to frighten her. She pumped the brakes until the plane slowed. At last, it stopped.

Charlotte closed her eyes and sagged limply in her seat. Tears of relief flooded her eyes. She clasped her hands and lifted them to her lips.

"Thank You, thank You, thank You, God. I'll never doubt you again." The cheers and whistles still sounding in her headset seemed to support her decision.

Suddenly, the plane began to move again. She jammed her feet back on the brakes and yelped. "Help! How do I keep it stopped?"

Her question prompted uproarious laughter from the control tower, which annoyed her.

Lucas's voice, choked with emotion, responded. "Sorry, baby. We're a little hysterical up here. Look on the far-left side of the throttle console for two mixture controls. Pull them all the way back."

"You mean the choke?" she asked, remembering her father's instructions.

"Yes, the choke. Pull them back." She did, and the whine of the turboprop descended like a musical scale. The not-too-distant sound of sirens grew louder, taking its place.

With a tremor in her hands, she followed Lucas's final instructions to turn off the ignition. The instruments jumped and the digital display went dark. Charlotte swallowed convulsively. With her adrenaline receding, she was suddenly aware that her head pounded mercilessly. Nausea roiled in her all at once.

She had fully expected to die. But with Lucas holding her hand, metaphorically, and with God holding her up with His righteous right hand, she'd just given her recurring nightmare a different ending.

It suddenly occurred to her Lucas had slipped a rather profound confession into his last few directions.

I love you, he'd said.

She closed her eyes again, letting the warmth of that message steady her heart. *Oh, Lucas, I love you, too.*

She didn't have the strength to hide from that truth. Nor was she above basking in it while she could.

She was only human. And more than anything in the world, she needed to feel Lucas's arms around her, to know that she was safe and sheltered in his care.

Freeing herself from the copilot's seat, she headed for the exit at the back of the plane, moving past the comatose pilot then pausing to regard her godfather, who had passed out, likely from loss of blood. It was all over the seat he lolled in. He was still breathing, though.

She realized, looking at him, she was seeing a stranger.

"Did you kill my parents?" she demanded, not expecting an answer.

He cracked an eye at her. For a long moment, there was just the sound of sirens and his labored breaths.

"I'm sorry," he finally whispered.

The words were a confirmation of her worst suspicions.

"She wasn't supposed to fly with him. I loved her. I wanted her to myself."

The words tore open Charlotte's grief anew. "How could you do that to your best friend, to my mother, to us?" she cried, pressing a fisted hand into her stomach.

Martin lowered his gaze in shame and shook his head, unable to answer.

Dashing the tears from her cheeks, Charlotte pulled herself together. Eager to see Lucas, she

moved to the airlock on the rear exit. It took all her remaining strength to push the door open.

She leaped out onto the tarmac several feet below her, rolling to prevent injury when her knees folded on her unexpectedly. Sitting on the ground, touching its blessed firmness, she watched a black SUV bear down on her. It screeched to a halt fifteen feet away, and Lucas exploded out of the passenger seat, running as if he were still a tight end for the Dallas Cowboys, while Fitz and several agents followed.

"Charlotte," Lucas cried, hauling her off the concrete and lifting her off her feet in a full-body embrace. "You're okay. You're okay," he murmured, his face buried in her hair.

In that perfect moment, wrapped up in Lucas's powerful arms, she was more than okay. She was whole.

CHAPTER 21

"*H*ow's your head?" Lucas asked, placing his hand over Charlotte's atop her dinette table.

They'd just come from the hospital where he'd insisted she return to be checked over. After several hours of observation, she'd been released, loaded up with Tylenol for her headache, and strict orders not to fly any more random airplanes.

Arriving at Charlotte's apartment, they'd discovered a surprise waiting in her reserved parking space. Fitz, as he'd promised at their first meeting, had her Mustang brought down from Quantico, its back end still crumpled and the keys under the floor mat. Retrieving the keys, Charlotte had led the way, using her keyring to let them in.

Lucas had hoped to meet Charlotte's brother, but he was secretly pleased to find the young man gone from the shared apartment. The time had come for Charlotte and him to finish the conversation he'd begun the day before. Lucas wanted her to remain in his life, no matter what.

He'd swept an interested look around her apartment, not surprised to find it filled with merely the barest necessities. Charlotte had never intended to stay in the area for long.

"I feel okay," she said, sending him a wry smile. Turning her hand over, she interlaced her fingers with his. "Thank you for taking such good care of me."

He was about to segue into their unfinished conversation when she added with a far-off look, "I can't believe that The Entity's no longer a threat."

Fitz had assured them that every known member of The Entity had been rounded up and incarcerated, including its leader, Larry Martin, who'd been taken off the plane straight into surgery to repair his femoral artery. In critical condition, there was reason to believe he might die. Fitz had assured Charlotte she would not be charged if that happened.

The United States was reeling that evening as the FBI had leaked news of its multiple high-profile arrests to Headline News, The Associated Press, and United Press International. Sabena, which had been overrun with special agents over the weekend, had been especially affected. As it turned out, the police chief had, in fact, told Dwyer about the break-in. Efforts were underway at the warehouse to move the stolen weapons elsewhere, but the FBI had descended before the majority had disappeared.

Even NAS Oceana and Dam Neck Base had seen their share of arrests, including two senior members of NCIS and half a dozen officers, two of whom had been on Jaguar's panel, no doubt influencing the remainder of the panel to find Jaguar guilty.

Lucas shook his head in amazement. "It's hard to fathom everything that's had us spun up for the last month is over. Jaguar's home with his family, the stolen weapons are in FBI control, and all is well with the world—except for you," he added, stroking her thumb with his. "How are you feeling about your godfather's betrayal?"

While still at the airfield, Charlotte had shared her horrible discovery—that Larry Martin had caused her parents' plane to crash with the intent of killing her father so he could have her mother to himself.

Pain furrowed her forehead. But then she sighed with acceptance.

"I'm okay now. Like you told me once, my parents are free of this world, and they're together. I heard what you told me on the plane," she added, meeting his gaze and holding it.

He squeezed her hand reflexively. "And?"

She kept silent for several seconds, though her gaze softened. "And I love you, too."

Euphoria seized him. Tears of heightened emotion moistened his eyes as it appeared that all his hopes for the future were about to come true.

"But I'm not going to condemn you to the kind of relationship you described," she added, eviscerating his happiness in one succinct sentence.

Distraught, he couldn't bring himself to speak.

"Don't look at me like that." Charlotte turned her body so she was facing him and, lifting his hand, clasped it between both of hers. "Don't think for a second that what I'm saying isn't killing me, too, because it is. But if I take you up on your offer, I'm only being selfish. I know what you need to be happy, and it isn't me—".

"Yes, it is, Charlotte." He cut her off firmly. "It doesn't matter where your job takes you. It doesn't matter that you don't want to have a family right away. I can't give you up. You've become my best friend." He had to stop before his voice broke.

"And you're my superhero," she countered, her eyes bright with unshed tears. "But I love you too much to make you miserable. You would come to resent me. I'm sorry. I can't do that."

"Charlotte." This wasn't at all how he'd envisioned celebrating Jaguar's exoneration. "Please, just date me until your brother graduates, and then see how you feel."

He could see her picturing what that would be like. Yet she shook her head, dousing the stubborn hope still flickering inside him.

"That would only make it harder on both of us." She drew a shuddering breath and released his hand. "You should probably go now," she added miserably.

He couldn't believe this was happening—not after what she'd survived that morning.

"Charlotte, don't do this," he pleaded gruffly. A tear breached his lower lashes and streaked down his cheek.

Her own eyes glimmered. "I'm doing it for you, Lucas," she whispered. Then, leaning forward, she kissed him.

Their chemistry was immediately evident, sweet and intoxicating. However, the sorrow that laced their kiss overpowered it.

She drew back. "We're both going to be okay," she assured him.

He strove for levity—anything to reduce the pressure in his chest. "It's been a wild and crazy ride," he said as he pushed to his feet.

Smiling crookedly, she also stood. "Thanks for rescuing me more than once, Lieutenant."

"The pleasure was all mine."

She led him toward the door where they stood a moment looking at each other.

Charlotte broke the silence. "Maybe one more hug," she said with a sound like a sob in her throat.

Folding her into his embrace, Lucas closed his eyes and savored the feel of her plastered against him. Why couldn't she see they belonged together?

"I'm going to have to start charging for these," he teased through the lump in his throat.

Her answer was a watery laugh.

"If you change your mind," he added, with his arms still around her, "you have my number."

Charlotte simply stared at him. In other words, he'd be wasting his time if he sat around waiting for her.

"Good-bye, baby," he rasped.

"Good-bye, Captain America."

With a wrenching in his chest, he let himself out and blindly descended the exterior stairs toward the parking lot.

$\sim$

Lucas had never seen the ballroom at the Shifting Sands Club as filled to capacity as it was that night. Every member of Blue Squadron, along with their date, had put in put an appearance at the annual Christmas party. The party was also a means of welcoming Lieutenant Mills back to active duty.

True to his word, Fitz had leaned on the right people and accomplished what had seemed an impossible request merely two months earlier. Not only had Jaguar been reinstated into the squadron, but he'd been made executive officer, filling Lowery's shoes. Their new commander would be onboarding sometime that same week.

The tables stood decked in snowy linens, chinaware, and shimmering crystal. A buffet of roast beef, Cornish game hen, green beans, pasta, rice, and a seemingly endless array of pies and cakes had been laid out, making sure no guest went hungry. With Christmas only three weeks away, evergreen centerpieces and the enormous decorated tree twinkling in the corner added a festive touch.

As dinner ended, the floor became awash with lights reflecting the mirrored ball revolving over it. The tasteful background music was a misleading indication of the pounding beats that were bound to come later. Already, the long lines at the open bar had caused the volume to swell. The guests were having a good time.

Seated at the end of the high table, Lucas watched Master Chief Rivera dance with the ballerina he had married privately and unexpectedly, shortly after Jaguar's trial. Seeing the way they gazed into each other's eyes, there wasn't any question they belonged together. His thoughts went immediately to Charlotte.

With the feeling he'd been knifed in the chest, Lucas reached for the tumbler of scotch he'd ordered from the bartender but had yet to drink. He took a small sip, and the liquid burned his throat familiarly, but it didn't ease his heartache. He set the tumbler down. Drinking wasn't going to help.

He had hoped time would lessen his constant misery, but it hadn't yet. Over two months had passed since he'd laid eyes on the woman he loved. A harrowing, two-week mission in October had brought him momentary relief. Fear, it seemed, was the only emotion powerful enough to temporarily keep her from his thoughts. But then the mission ended, and she'd haunted him anew.

Her only communication arrived in the form of a note: *Told you I would find a way to pay you back. Keep what you want; donate the rest.*

The note was accompanied by a shipment of furniture, which he'd recognized as coming from her parents' townhouse. He'd accepted it, if only to have something by which to remember her. Yet, every time he walked into his house, marveling at how good it looked, bittersweet pain came with the memories of their time together.

Lord, how long do I have to feel this way?

Suddenly edgy, Lucas excused himself from the empty table and, ignoring Jonah and Eden's worried glance, stepped off the dais and left the ballroom, headed for the nearest exit.

A whipping wind hit him squarely in the face. Finding himself on the veranda, Lucas stalked to the cement railing and gazed out over the dunes to the dark, inhospitable ocean. It was here he and his team-mates had first discussed Jaguar's predicament and how they could help him. It was here Master Chief had told him the FBI had located Charlotte Patterson. Lucas hadn't realized at the time how much she would invade his existence.

Cold, salty air pinched his cheeks. He welcomed the discomfort.

Charlotte. The surf seemed to say her name as it crashed onto shore on the other side of the dunes. *Charlotte. Charlotte*

How long was he going to feel like he'd lost a part of himself? The thought pushed tears into his eyes, which the wind quickly dried.

The sound of approaching footsteps had him turning around alertly. With dismay, he recognized Monica, silhouetted by the lights shining in the window behind her. She had raised more than a few eyebrows by attending the ball as Petty Officer Ryan Larsen's date. Lucas stiffened at her approach.

"Hi, Lucas." Her voice sounded different with the waves crashing in the background. "I saw you step out, and I wanted to tell you something in private."

"Go ahead." Regarding her in semi-darkness, Lucas wondered what had ever drawn him to Monica in the first place. She reminded him of a little bird that flitted from one branch to another. Her ambition had gotten her nowhere, as she still worked in the administration building.

"I wanted to apologize for putting the vase in your house for Dwyer. I honestly didn't know it was bugged. I guess I should have wondered, though, when Dwyer asked me to get it back for him."

"Water under the bridge," Lucas assured her, though the bug in the vase had obviously led to Dwyer sending Jason Dunn to climb Saul's big oak tree in the hopes of identifying Charlotte. "Don't worry about it."

"Well, I do," she countered, shivering from the cold but still holding her ground. "I feel terrible for my actions. You're a really good guy, Lucas, and I know I screwed up. Here," she added, opening her clutch and pulling out what he realized was the engagement ring he'd given her. "I should have given this back a long time ago."

Lucas looked at the one-carat, princess-cut diamond and felt nothing. He hoped Charlotte was still wearing the ring he had bought for her in Sabena. "Keep it," he said, not wanting to touch it for some reason.

Monica squared her shoulders. "No," she said in a tone that brooked no argument. "I have to give it back. It's the right thing to do."

Far be it for me to get in the way of her doing the right thing, Lucas thought, holding out his hand. The ring fell heavily into his palm. He slid it into his pocket thinking he could sell it somewhere, then give the money to a charity.

"Goodbye, Lucas." With a sob in her voice, Monica spun away and hurried inside.

Lucas watched her go. He wished he could walk away from himself so easily. But there was no escaping the emptiness yawning inside him. How could this have happened? He'd found his best friend in the world and then he'd let her walk away.

~

On the first day of the New Year, the weather was typical for northern Virginia—just above freezing and inhospitably humid, so the cold went straight to one's bones.

Why, Charlotte wondered, had she chosen to jog along the Potomac River, to Jones Point Park and back? Her lungs ached, her nose was running, and despite the light sweat she'd worked up under her thermal sweatshirt, her extremities were turning numb. Was this really the best way to decide what she wanted from her life?

Veering off the running path she jogged back into Old Town, Alexandria, making her way back to her parents' empty townhome on Princess Street. But she was no closer to making a decision than when she'd set out on her run. In six short days, she was due to report to The Farm for nine months of intensive instruction. Her long-awaited career was about to begin. Yet a growing reluctance had set in during the past month, forcing her to question her plans.

She had done everything in her power to forget Lucas. She'd intentionally not entered Lucas's contact information into her old cell phone when it turned up in Larry Martin's office. She'd then mailed the android Fitz had given her back to him. The furniture she'd had delivered to Lucas was meant to pay him back for all the money he'd spent on her, ensuring that guilt wasn't the reason he came to mind so often.

One thing she couldn't seem to give back or even take off was the ring he'd given her. She told herself he'd wanted her to keep it. But it didn't help that every time she looked down at her left hand, she thought of him and the wonderful—sometimes terrifying—time they'd spent together.

She might have gotten over him by now if he didn't constantly appear in her dreams. Night after night, he showed up in the nick of time, sometimes saving her from some aggressive locals in a foreign country who'd found out she was a spy. Sometimes he brought children with him—*their* children, she later realized—and they all had to escape a hostile country together. Waking up after dreams like those, Charlotte was left feeling lonely and adrift.

She had recently sought help from the same counselor who'd helped her cope with her parents' death three years earlier. First, they discussed her godfather's betrayal and how that affected her trust. When she'd confessed her waning enthusiasm about joining the CIA, Dr. Guhl had expressed shock.

"This is news," he had commented in his sing-song voice. "What do you suppose is causing your reluctance?"

Lucas had sprung immediately to mind, but she hadn't mentioned him. "I have no idea."

Dr. Guhl had suggested that, having coming to peace with her parents' passing, she was open to more options and free to forge her own destiny.

The word "options" had stuck with Charlotte, making her ponder what she could do with her future if she didn't join the CIA. Then on Christmas morning, she had opened a present from none other than Special Agent Casey Fitzgerald, who'd sent her a gray FBI T-shirt and an application form for the FBI. On a sticky note, he had written, *21 months of training gets you a job in Norfolk working with me.*

That option had lodged in her head ever since, making her realize she needed to make a decision fast. Usually a hard run helped Charlotte think more clearly, but it wasn't helping the way she'd hoped it would.

Blowing warm air on her frigid fingers, she sought divine help. "What should I do, God?"

Then, rounding the corner of Duke Street and South Royal, she came to a dead stop. Lucas's truck was in front of her townhouse, and he was in it, pulling away from the curb.

No! Wait! Apparently, he'd knocked at the door and assumed she'd already moved out.

"Lucas!" Chasing after his truck with her arms flailing, it hit Charlotte like a sledgehammer over her hard head—she was meant for Lucas all along. God had been trying to tell her that, but she'd been so busy seeing a mirage of her future, she hadn't seen what was right in front of her.

The flaring of his brake lights pulled a sob of relief from her. As he peered over his shoulder and carefully backed up, she tried to compose herself, then wondered what on earth to say.

Reversing into the space he'd just occupied, Lucas cut the engine and slowly stepped out.

Charlotte had forgotten his visual impact on her. He wore an unbuttoned wool coat, a blue button up and jeans. His hair was longer and his cheeks wind-chapped as if he'd spent a great deal of time outdoors. A day's growth of beard darkened the lower half of his face.

She wanted to throw herself at him, but dignity and the awkwardness that came from time apart held her impulse in check.

"I saw the FOR SALE sign, and I thought you'd left," he said. The rasp in his voice betrayed strong emotions.

With a shake of her head, Charlotte realized she never *ever* wanted to leave him. If only she'd realized that months ago! "You want to come in?" she asked.

"Sure."

Fetching the key from under a loose brick where she'd hidden it, she unbolted the door and ushered him into the warmth. He stepped inside, swept a look at the empty living room, then focused on her.

"You look like you're freezing," he commented.

"I am." She had to sniff against her runny nose. Longing for a hug to warm her up, she assured herself she'd get one in due time. Hopefully soon.

"There are still chairs in the kitchen," she said, leading the way to the back of the townhouse.

"Your house looks like mine used to," he commented. "Thanks for the furniture, by the way."

"Did you keep any?" she asked over her shoulder.

"All of it. It looks really good, in fact. You should see it."

Oh, she intended to. "You want something to drink?" Charlotte opened the fridge to see what she could offer him. "La Croix okay?"

"Sure."

She pulled out two chilled cans of the sparkling water and handed him one. He waited for her to sit before lowering himself into the chair right next to her.

"I read that Larry Martin survived his gunshot wound and is getting sent to some cushy federal prison in North Carolina, where he'll be joining Commander Dwyer," he said on a sarcastic note. Maybe they'll be roommates. Oh, no, they won't because everyone gets their own room."

Popping open his can, Lucas looked for her reaction.

Charlotte sighed. "Well, they still have to face God for their actions in the next life, so…"

Can you forgive him?" Lucas asked her frankly.

She frowned. "It's hard. I mean, he was always good to me, which makes it easier, but then I think about my parents, and I have to ask for grace to keep from hating him. But, yeah. I think I can."

"That's good," he said.

"So, how is everybody?" she asked on a brighter note. "Saul and Jaguar?"

"Saul is on a super-secret mission working with Black Squadron. I think he'll be gone for a year. Jaguar," Lucas added with a smile, "is our new XO and our acting commander while we wait for Dwyer's replacement."

"That's great. Then he's back on active duty. What about Master Chief?"

"Rivera surprised us by getting married."

"No way. To Whom?"

"A ballet teacher named Nina. They're perfect for each other."

"That's sweet, and how've you been?" Charlotte finally dared to ask. Growing warm in her thermal shirt, she concealed her nervousness by pulling it off while Lucas formulated his answer.

When she looked at him again, he was staring at the FBI logo on the T-shirt she was wearing underneath. "A Christmas gift from Fitz," she said.

He cocked his head. "I figured. I got the same one."

She had to smile at that. "Mine came with a job application. He wants me to join the FBI and work with him."

Lucas's eyes widened. Before he could ask, she added, "I'm going to do it."

Stunned, with hope emerging on his face, Lucas stared at her. "You're not going to join the CIA?"

Querying her decision one last time, she felt nothing but absolute conviction.

"Nope." Reaching for Lucas's hand, she was pleased when he not only let her take it, but clasped hers in both of his. "I almost made the biggest mistake of my life by walking away from you," she admitted in a suddenly husky voice. "I was about to contact you, and then, by divine intervention perhaps, here you are. Please tell me you haven't changed your mind."

"Oh, thank God." His eyes melted shut then opened again, bright with tears. "No. You asked me how I've been doing? I've been freaking miserable without you."

"I'm so sorry," she whispered. "I was so fixated on an old dream, I didn't realize you were my new one. We are meant to be together. I haven't stopped thinking of you for five minutes at a time."

He laughed with irony and shook his head. "Same," he said simply.

Charlotte sat up straighter, and then she stood. "I probably need a shower, but I also really need a hug."

With a slow grin, Lucas pushed to his feet. Wrapping his powerful arms around her, he drew her fiercely against him, nuzzled his cheek against hers, and rasped into her ear, "I love you so much, Charlotte."

Relishing the familiar feel of Lucas's arms encircling her, the scent of his sports soap and fabric softener, she thought to herself, *This is home.*

"I love you, too, Lucas. I've dreamed of you constantly—you and our unborn children."

He lowered his chin to eye her in astonishment. "Children?"

"Yep. I'm going to have your kids one day."

"Hmm. You've got your career to think about first, young lady.

Special Agent Charlotte Patterson," he added, hugging her more closely. "I like that. Has a nice ring to it."

"I'll have to do twenty-one months of training at Quantico first. But I think I get my weekends off."

"That beats the heck out of an overseas assignment in some unstable foreign country."

"Yes, it does," she agreed. Lifting a hand to stroke the side of his dear face, she let a tear that was trembling on her lower lashes slide down her cold cheek.

"Oh, Lucas. Thank you for giving me one more chance. I'm sorry it took me so long to come to my senses."

"Totally worth it," he assured her.

Rising onto her tiptoes, she pressed a fervent kiss to his warm, beautiful lips. "This is where I belong, where I've always belonged. Right here, in the United States of America with you."

"Then you'll marry me?" he asked with a searching look.

Charlotte looked at the ceiling, then back at him. "Is that a proposal?"

"Almost. I'd like to do it more formally sometime."

She shrugged. "Makes no difference to me. I'm already wearing your ring." She wiggled her fingers in front of his face.

"You never took it off," he observed.

Charlotte admired the pretty band with its Celtic knot. "No." She looked up at him wryly. "You would think that was a pretty clear sign where my heart lies."

"Where does your heart lie, Charlotte?" he asked, clearly wanting to hear her say it.

She put a hand over the center of his chest, feeling the strong, steady beat of his heart. "Right here," she said, "with you."

THE LOST IS FOUND

ACTS OF VALOR, BOOK THREE

The sound of Ethan's voice cracking through the air like a whip brought Rachel's head up from the design magazine she had stolen up to her bedroom. Given that her brother's voice was coming through her ceiling, he had to be up in her son's attic bedroom, no doubt lecturing Liam *again*. He must have caught Rachel's eleven-year-old doing something other than homework. The words that reached her ears confirmed it.

"I'm not sending you to private school so you can turn out like your mother."

Ethan's condescending allusion to Rachel scarcely fazed her anymore. Not only had she grown accustomed to her brother's snubs, but she had come to think she deserved his scorn. At twenty-nine, she had yet to pursue an occupation apart from stay-at-home mom. She had married Blake, her sweetheart, right out of high school. When Liam went off to kindergarten, she had enrolled in community college to study interior design, but she'd never transferred to a four-year school, let alone graduated.

To a point, Ethan's assessment of her was correct. She certainly wouldn't still be living with him more than two years after Blake's death if she'd been a go-getter like her older brother, would she?

Tucking a strand of ash-blond hair behind her ear to better listen, Rachel listened for Liam's reply.

"No, please. Don't!"

The horrified cry prompted Rachel to stuff the magazine under her pillow. She rushed out of her room and up the narrow staircase leading to the floored attic, an enormous space that stretched across the length of Ethan's brownstone. Liam had chosen to sleep up there, suffering the heat that rose to the third story during summer months, in return for the view out the narrow windows.

As she raced up the creaking treads, Ethan's words reached her ears.

"There. Now you won't be distracted from your homework. You'll never be a lawyer if you keep taking in every hurt animal you come across."

"I don't want to be a lawyer!"

Rachel had never heard her son's voice raised in hysteria before. Like her, he was meek and placid. She crested the stairs to find him with his fists balled, his face white and tight with rage.

Her gaze cut to Ethan as he took a threatening step toward his nephew. "You'll change your mind," he said with a certainty that sent a chill up Rachel's spine.

A vision of Liam dressed in the uniform of a Navy lawyer and wearing the same smirk that rode his uncle's lips flashed across her mind's eye. *Never!*

Ethan stepped back, nearly bumping his head on an exposed rafter beam and giving Rachel her first glimpse of the bird cage Liam had set before the window. The door hung open, and the cardinal Liam had been nursing back to health lay in a scarlet heap of feathers on the floor.

Realizing it was dead—that her brother had killed it—Rachel felt something inside her snap. Indignation rose in her, empowering her to hold Ethan's belligerent gaze as she marched toward her son and put her arms around him. Liam's rigid frame quaked. Nearly as tall as she was, he did not hug her back.

"You should go now," she told Ethan in a voice she scarcely recognized.

His expression registered amazement at her tone. But then, taking in the two of them allied in defiance against him, he broke eye contact and looked over at the cage.

Considering it a moment, he said in a voice devoid of remorse, "I'm sorry, Liam. I overreacted. Take a thirty-minute break outside, and then you'll be ready to study. All right?" He went to ruffle his nephew's hair, but Liam shrank from him.

"Just go," Rachel commanded.

Ethan's eyes narrowed at her uncharacteristic temerity. She could see the usual belittling words forming in his mouth, but because Liam was watching, he bit them back. He could not repress the dismissive *humph* that rasped in his throat, however, as he spun on the soles of his polished shoes and stalked toward the stairs.

She waited for the door at the base of the steps to shut before she released her son. Liam sank onto the bed as if his quaking knees couldn't support him. His gaze fell to the bird with its broken neck, and his face crumpled.

"I was going to let him go tomorrow." Tears of lament rose in the dark blue eyes he'd inherited from his father.

Rachel sat down next to him. To her dismay, he shifted away, reminding her forcibly of Blake as he fought for poise, dashing the tears from his eyes.

"I'm so sorry," Rachel blurted as guilt ambushed her.

Liam leveled a glare at her. "Why do we live here?" he whispered on a furious note. "I hate this house. I hate Uncle Ethan!"

Astonishment kept her momentarily mute. "I thought you liked him," she said, finally.

Her son's face twisted with incredulity. "Like him? How could anyone like him?"

Rachel blinked, reshuffling her assumptions and her reasons for putting up with their living arrangement. She had thought she was providing Liam with a father figure. Ethan had always taken such pride in his nephew. When Blake's parachute failed to deploy, and their whole world had imploded, Ethan had been their rock, stepping in as executor of Blake's estate. When it was all Rachel could do to draw her next breath, he had handled every necessary detail. Then, one year after her husband's death, when the Navy forced them out of base housing, Ethan had offered them a roof over their heads. They could live with him in his big, empty house.

At first, she had been grateful not to have to house hunt, to act as if she was back to normal when the truth was she could barely get out of bed in the mornings. Though Ethan had scorned her in her youth, in his defense, she *had* been ten years younger and adopted, to boot. The adult Ethan had seemed much more agreeable and willing to lend a hand. Most importantly, he had doted on his nephew, seeing promise in him, as he'd inherited his father's quick mind.

Liam's pointed question sobered Rachel to reality. *Have I been blind all this time?* Apparently, she had been. Her son, forced to attend a rigorous private school and to apply himself like a scholar when he would rather be outdoors communing with nature, was as mistreated as she was.

"Oh, Liam," she whispered. Fear gripped her as she envisioned what she secretly desired—freedom for both of them. She had fantasized from time to time about picking up and leaving. There were roadblocks *everywhere*. "It won't be easy to leave. We'll have to save up money."

"What about Dad's life insurance?"

She swallowed down the guilt that rose in her. "Your uncle invested it all into your college fund." As executor of Blake's estate, he'd had every right.

"What about the social security money?"

She was astonished Liam even knew about that. Currently, it went into a bank account co-owned by her brother, who'd set it up that way so he could deduct their rent and food.

"We still have that," she hedged, intending to open her own account immediately and get the deposits sent there.

"I don't understand why he thinks he's in charge of me."

Shame seared her. If grief hadn't put her in a depression so deep she'd needed to be hospitalized, Ethan would never have assumed so much control. "I'm sorry," she repeated. "I'll take care of everything," she promised. "We'll find our own place." Saying it aloud made it real.

Liam went still a moment, visibly picturing the future. He looked at her suddenly, his eyes wide with fear. "What if he won't let us leave?"

The question filled Rachel with inexplicable panic. "He'll have to. He doesn't own us."

Or did he? Her thoughts went to the paper he'd made her sign when she was hospitalized. It was a legal form meant to give him temporary custody, he'd explained, so he could take Liam to the doctor, for instance, while Rachel was indisposed. That paper hadn't made him Liam's legal guardian till he was eighteen, or had it?

"Listen," she added, wanting to encourage herself as much as her son. "God's going to help us. He helped me get strong again. He'll help us find our own place."

She'd been introduced to the Word of God for the first time while in treatment. The realization that Blake lived on in the afterlife had allowed her to put the pieces of her shattered heart back together—at least so it beat again. She had been assured God still had plans for her —plans to prosper her. She had rallied from despair to live out her intended purpose—and this was so not it.

"I'm going to pray about it," she insisted. "God will show us the way out."

Liam heaved a long sigh. "How long is that going to take?"

His despairing tone plucked at her heartstrings. Had her son lost total faith in her? He still believed in his father, though, whose memory he revered. In Liam's eyes, Blake could do anything. "Your dad's going to watch out for us," she comforted. "He's an angel in God's Army now. He'll show us the way."

Liam met her gaze and nodded. Hope chased off his bleak expression. "Yeah," he agreed."

Rachel glanced past him to the cage hanging open. That open door was a sign, wasn't it? The time had come for them to break free.

Dear God, help us. Fear paralyzed her as her gaze went to the dead bird lying at their feet. If they didn't leave soon, they might end up broken, just like the cardinal.

Available in Paperback and eBook from Your Favorite Bookstore or Online Retailer

ALSO BY REBECCA HARTT

The Acts of Valor Series
Returning to Eden
Every Secret Thing
The Lost is Found

ABOUT THE AUTHOR

Rebecca Hartt is the *nom de plume* for an award-winning, best-selling author who, in a different era of her life, wrote strictly romantic suspense. Now Rebecca chooses to showcase the role that faith plays in the lives of Navy SEALs, penning military romantic suspense that is both realistic and heartwarming.

As a child, Rebecca lived all over the world. She has been a military dependent for most of her life, first as a daughter, then as a wife, and knows first-hand the dedication and sacrifice required by those who serve. Living near the military community of Virginia Beach, Rebecca is constantly reminded of the peril and uncertainty faced by US Navy SEALs, many of whom testify to a personal and profound connection with their Creator. Their loved ones, too, rely on God for strength and comfort. These men of courage and women of faith are the subjects of Rebecca Hartt's enthusiastically received *Acts of Valor* series.

RebeccaHartt.com

Sign up for the Rebecca Hartt Newsletter Here

https://rebeccahartt.com/contact